Death
before
Dinner

Death

before

Dinner

An Otter Tail County Mystery

Gerald Anderson

MIDNIGHT INK
WOODBURY, MINNESOTA

First Edition
First Printing, 2007

Book design by Donna Burch
Cover design by Gavin Dayton Duffy
Cover photograph © 2006 SuperStock
Editing by Connie Hill

Midnight Ink, an imprint of Llewellyn Publications

Library of Congress Cataloging-in-Publication Data
  Death before dinner : an Otter Tail County Mystery / Gerald Anderson. —
  1st ed.
    p. cm.
  ISBN: 13: 978-0-7387-0874-4 (trade pbk.)
  ISBN: 10: 0-7387-0874-7 (trade pbk.)
    1. College presidents—Crimes against—Fiction. 2. Minnesota—Fiction.
  I. Title

PS3601/M536D43   2007
813'.6—dc22   2006052134

Midnight Ink
Llewellyn Publications
2143 Wooddale Drive, Dept. 0-7387-0874-7
Woodbury, MN 55125-2989, U.S.A.
www.midnightinkbooks.com

Printed in the United States of America

for Barbara

PROLOGUE

DR. GEORGE GHERKIN FURTIVELY glanced at the kitchen door to make sure he was alone. He grabbed two ice cubes from the bucket, silently slid them into the glass and reached into the top shelf of the cupboard to find his treasured bottle of Laphroaig, a ten-year-old Scotch. Now that was a fit drink for a university president! As he poured himself a generous three fingers, he smirked at the memory of the last time he'd had a faculty dinner party. He had placed Scotch in an elegant decanter on the sideboard, specifically to tempt his underpaid assistant professors. As counted upon, it was well received, to the point that one of his earnest English teachers had undertaken to deliver a discourse on the merits of fine Scotch. When he had asked Gherkin as to the label, Gherkin mysteriously let on that it was a private label of an unusual blend. "What a sap," he chuckled to himself at the memory. "It was a bottle of the cheapest booze I could find, mixed with a third of a bottle of awful vodka that I was planning to pour down the sink, and a cup of water to fill the decanter. Ah, but this single-malt Laphroaig!"

"The higher education business can provide well," he mused as he looked around his kitchen. He loved his Cuisinart appliances of enamel and chrome, his Calphalon cookware, his soapstone countertops, his birch cabinets of Scandinavian sleekness and efficiency, and the stainless steel double sinks. He moved to his Jenn-Air range and prepared two large frying pans with butter and olive oil. "Synchronizing this dinner could be tricky," he thought. "Perhaps I should have simply baked a rib roast. But what would have been the challenge to that?" He returned to the counter to put the finishing touches on his latest culinary masterpiece. The dainty, skillfully made portions of chicken Kiev nestled on a glass platter. They had been chilling most of the afternoon, giving the bread-crumb coating time to properly adhere to the tender breasts that enclosed the butter and chives. Gherkin sat on a stool and tenderly fingered the tiny paper frills that would adorn each protruding wing end, then bent over to neatly arrange, in order of frying time, the individual servings.

He noted the door opening and a person entering, but found the prospect of a conversation too boring to contemplate and responded with only a curt nod and returned to his final preparations. He could not know that these would indeed be his final preparations.

The person who entered the room was a murderer. The "perpetrator," as the person would soon be known in the terminology of law enforcement, had not considered being a murderer until that moment. But the mind of the perpetrator was an angry one. "How dare he?" the murderer thought. "Look at that fat, bald head, gleaming so much it is reflected off the refrigerator door! We must discuss this right now!"

The mind of the murderer became clouded. Gherkin didn't even turn around, and seemed impervious to the presence of another human being. He tediously turned over each chicken breast, probing for the slightest flaw in the coating technique. The hand of the murderer, certainly not the mind, found a heavy and very expensive Wüsthof meat cleaver laying on the counter. The hand tightly held the handle while the mind waited for Gherkin to display one ounce of acknowledgment that another soul was present in his mini-universe. The hand was impatient.

A few seconds later, the mind was aware that Dr. George Gherkin had a large meat cleaver stuck in the top of his head and his face had acquired an even coating of bread crumbs. The *entree* had become "chicken breasts in red sauce." The mind seemed to clear, and thoughts of anger were replaced with wonder. There had been no real sound, other than a rather satisfying thud. What blood there was had collected neatly in the pan, but there was not that much blood, when one considered it, almost as if the thick blade of the cleaver was acting as a cork. The mind observed the murderous hand. "Huh, no blood there at all. That's funny, you'd think there would be. How still he looks. Peaceful for the first time in his life, perhaps. All in all, his head looks like one of those stones that curlers slide along the ice, and the cleaver makes a perfect handle. I wonder if it would slide on the ice better if it had a layer of blood under it, or if that would slow it down. I suppose I should wipe that handle of the cleaver, I mean, that's what murderers do, isn't it? How did it come to this? My God, what should I do now? I suppose I should tell somebody. I didn't really mean to do this. But if anybody really deserved it . . . I mean, who could really blame me?"

The mind began to focus, and to appreciate the magnitude of what the hand had done. And from some distant memory came the words of Kurtz in *The Heart of Darkness*. "The horror! The horror!" was the benediction whispered over the warm corpse of George Gherkin.

ONE

MURDER IS AS COMMON as jay-walking in much of urban America, but in Otter Tail County, in west central Minnesota, neither occur. Unpleasant things, by custom and inclination, are just not done. In fact, being in possession of an overdue library book is openly frowned upon. And when it comes right down to it, there are few things more unpleasant than murder with a meat cleaver. To be sure, in the last hundred years there had been the occasional act of manslaughter, and maybe a shotgun blast now and then, but that sort of thing was usually done by people who really didn't belong in the community anyhow. But this murder, well, it was beyond unpleasant; it was, in fact, quite nasty.

Nastiness is out of place in Otter Tail County. There are 1,048 lakes there, all of them lovely, fresh, clear, and filled with fish and fishermen. It's a place where the prairie meets the lake district, where a wheat field is on one shore and a deciduous forest is on the other. Small towns are found in unexpected places and serve the needs of intimate family lake resorts that are almost too numerous to mention.

The jewel in the crown of Otter Tail County is Fergus Falls, home of a giant cooperative called, appropriately enough, Otter Tail Power Company, and of a giant state hospital, which held as many as twenty-five hundred mental patients in the mid-1950s, before society found alternative methods to institutionalization. Say "Fergus Falls" to the rest of Minnesota and you get an "Oh, yeah, all that electricity," or "Oh, yeah, they had to send one of the Carlson boys there once. Never saw him again." What many people don't know is that this is one of the loveliest small cities to be found in rural America. About thirteen thousand people live there, settled in comfortable homes nestled around Lake Alice, with its ubiquitous Canada geese, or around Grotto Lake or by Lake Charles or Opperman Lake, or even Hoot Lake. On summer days you can see these people on the carefully manicured fairways of the Pebble Lake Golf Course. Under normal circumstances, the last thing on their mind is murder. This would change.

Not all of the people in Fergus Falls are Norwegians, even if it does seem that way. To be sure, there is the annual Scandinavian Heritage Festival, now called the Summerfest, which is held every June, and there are Norwegian arts and crafts and foods and street dances. Other nationalities are represented too, but the musical accent that one hears in the street or in Perkins restaurant carries the sound of the fjords. Nevertheless, it's an All-American town, with fireworks in DeLagoon Park every Fourth of July and a Harvest Festival to crown the summer. Murders aren't supposed to happen in such an Eden, one of the reasons the Otter Tail County sheriff liked his job.

———

It was a quarter to twelve on a warm and humid Friday morning at the end of August. Sheriff Palmer Knutson had spent the morning working out traffic arrangements and personnel assignments for the Harvest Festival. Knutson anticipated an easy day as he sat down in the dappled shade of an elm tree on the top step of the stairs leading down to the west end of the river walk. It was a secluded place, hardly visible from street level, and amazingly quiet. He had to admit that putting in the river walk was the most useful thing that the Downtown Revitalization Task Force had ever done. "Oh, those poor saps who have to be cops in New York City, or Minneapolis, for that matter," he mused. "I can walk down from my office and amble along the river without getting shot in the head. . . . I wonder what's keeping Ellie?"

It had been a busy week for the Knutson family. On Sunday, the sheriff and his wife Elaine had taken their younger daughter off to Concordia College in Moorhead for freshman orientation. "Little Amy," Palmer sighed, not for the first time. "A college student!"

He had expected to handle that particular life milestone a little better than he had. After all, his other daughter, Maj, had graduated from Gustavus Adolphus College in St. Peter, and that was farther away. But the house seemed so empty that even the last chick in the nest, seventeen-year-old Trygve, missed being picked on by his sisters. Palmer reached down, plucked a piece of quack grass, stuck the end of it in his mouth, and contemplated getting old.

Sheriff Knutson didn't look old; in fact, he looked to be about fifty-eight. This observation would have cheered him little, however, since he was exactly that age. The color of his hair had always been rather difficult for anyone to describe—it had always been either a light brown or a dark blonde—but before long, he ruefully noted every morning as he looked in the mirror, people could be relieved of any uncertainty by calling it gray. He used to wear contact lenses over his light-blue eyes, back in the days when his handsome face was an asset on his campaign posters. Now, he worried less about his looks and less about getting elected, and he had reluctantly accepted the necessity of bifocals. Ellie had trusted him to select a pair of frames that would sit easily on his thin nose and make him look handsome. He disappointed her again. He thought she would like his brownish-gray, almost circular frames. Ellie said he looked like an owl.

Palmer had taken unusual pains to look presentable on this morning, and had shocked the office staff by showing up in a tie and a jacket. It was not simply that it was the weekend of the Harvest Festival and that more voters could be greeted on the street. No, today he had a special date with his wife. As a celebration of the end of summer and getting the girls off to college they were going to take a nice walk along the Otter Tail River, commune with nature, and go to the Viking Café for their noon smorgasbord. To some people, Swedish meatballs and lefse might seem a little "heavy" for lunch on a hot summer day, but Palmer had been looking forward to it for a week. Nevertheless, as he mentally pictured the varieties of comestibles soon to grace his plate, he unconsciously calculated the calories. He looked down sadly at the unattractive way gravity pulled his tie off of the mound that was his stomach to reveal the last two buttons of his shirt, which unsuccessfully strained to keep the seam straight. "Oh, well," he rationalized to himself, "it's not something we do every day."

———

"Sorry to keep you. Been here long?" Palmer looked up to see the green eyes of his short, somewhat plump wife beaming down at him.

"No, not really," he replied, hurriedly getting up and dusting off the seat of his pants. "Just loafing. Getting kind of hot, isn't it?"

"Yah. Wanna call off the walk?"

"No, not at all. Besides, it should be cooler down by the river. What kept you?"

"Oh, that old Henry Hartvig. He makes me so mad! I can never meet him without getting one of his right-wing sermons. I'm just walking down the sidewalk minding my own business and he comes up and says, 'Comrade Knutson'—he always calls me that—he thinks he is so clever—and he always yells it so everyone else can hear how clever he is. And then he goes into this long spiel about how, as the wife of a sheriff, I must be non-political and the Democrats in Minnesota are all Communists and how my husband should have better control over me. That's the one that really gets me! In one sentence he insults my political beliefs, my sex, and my family." Ellie fumed, her frizzled brown curls bobbing up and down as she descended the steps to the river.

"So, what did you tell him this time?" Palmer asked, with a measure of dread mixed with anticipation.

"Well, I thought about just reaching up and giving him a kiss on the cheek and saying 'God loves you,' but then I thought that would open the door for him to lecture me on my morality and about being on the board of Planned Parenthood and killing babies. So I just whispered low. He bent down to hear what I was saying and I looked around conspiratorially and said, 'Come the revolution, Henry, you'll be the first one we shoot.'"

"You didn't!"

"Sure I did. Why not? Were you counting on his vote in the next election?"

The sheriff sighed and said, "No, I guess not, at least I haven't really needed him in the past. What did he say to that?"

"Ha! For once he was too stunned to say anything. You know, he's never forgiven me for that protest march to the post office."

Palmer took Ellie's hand as they walked along the river. "He still remembers that? That was thirty years ago!"

"He's like an elephant. I hear he still has a picture of Nixon hanging in his home."

"Well, I know I'll never forget that day, but I have a better reason to remember it," the sheriff tenderly whispered, and kissed Ellie in the general neighborhood of her ear.

"You know," Ellie said, disengaging herself from her suddenly amorous husband, "I was helping Amy pack to go off to college, and she asked me again to tell her how we met. I thought that was sweet."

"So what did you tell her?"

"I guess I spent most of the time describing you. How handsome you looked in that cop's uniform. Tall, athletic, the army veteran, the big man on campus."

"Did you tell her how you looked?"

"I might have; but how would you have described me?" Ellie asked coyly.

"I would have said that you had this beautiful straight, long brown hair that flew in your mouth every time you shouted a slogan. That you had on a pair of jeans with a flag covering your cute rear end and they were so tight that I could read the date of the dime that was in your pocket. I have to admit that I could not have filed a decent report on the incident because," the sheriff lapsed into a soft croon, "'I only had eyes for you.'"

"How sweet, even if I don't entirely believe it. Do you remember how that old postmaster, Matthew Johnson, looked when I presented him with that anti-war petition?"

"Yah," Palmer laughed, "I don't think I have ever, in my whole life, seen anyone look so completely bewildered."

"But the post office was the most important United States government unit in town! Where else could we have gone? And he accepted it, didn't he? That was the most important thing. Do you think he really did forward it to Washington?"

"You know, I ran into him once about ten years ago, long after he retired and shortly before he died. And I asked him if he remembered that. He said it was the most exciting thing that had ever happened to him—apparently he didn't have any disgruntled postal workers shooting up the place—and that yah, he had actually forwarded the petition to the Postmaster General of the United

States. He also said he never got a reply or even an acknowledgment that it had been sent."

"Nevertheless, we did change the world that day."

"Maybe you did. I know you certainly changed my world. Did you tell Amy why I didn't arrest you?"

"Of course. I told her that you were a sensitive person with a commitment to social justice and opposed to the killing in Vietnam. I told her that you removed me from the scene of the confrontation, took me to the drugstore for a Coke, and before the day was over we were in love."

"You didn't really tell her that, did you?"

"Sort of. I mean, I said that I really liked you and that it seemed like every time after that, when there was any potential campus unrest, I was always on a committee with you and then I knew that I wanted to be with you for other reasons. But really, you know, I think I did fall in love with you that day. Did you fall in love with me that day?"

"Um, er, I was obviously attracted to you, but whether or not I actually fell in love at that moment, I don't know. Maybe."

"Oh, Palmer," Ellie sighed extravagantly. "You're so romantic. You should be glad I didn't tell her the real reason why you didn't arrest me."

"Which was?"

"That you were just a part-time cop and weren't really sure if you had the authority to arrest anyone. Are you hungry?"

"Yah, come to think of it, I am. And I'm looking forward to sitting in an air-conditioned room for a while. I don't really have that much to do for the rest of the day."

As they began to make their way toward the Viking Café, Ellie asked, "Got anything special planned for this weekend?"

"Nope. And I'm really looking forward to it. I might work on the bathroom tiles, maybe do some reading, and there's a Vikings pre-season game on tomorrow night. A lot of people come to town for the Harvest Festival, but it's always peaceful and we have enough personnel to handle it. It's going to be a great weekend."

TWO

It had not been a good summer for Sherwin Williams, and driving his old Volvo did not calm him down at all. Williams was a painter, and to his artistic and imaginative mind he was the undiscovered Vincent Van Gogh of America. This should have been the summer of his discovery. He had planned to visit the Netherlands and shuttle between the museums of Amsterdam and the Kroller-Muller Museum in Otterlo, letting inspiration wash over him like waves from a Turner seascape. Certain that studying in the Netherlands was his destiny, he had told virtually everyone he knew that he would be awarded a Fulbright grant. But now, a supercilious sneer unconsciously spread over his face as he remembered the day he received the letter from the Fulbright commission. He had waved it around the faculty post office and had ostentatiously taken it back to his office where, surrounded by some of his students, he had read the bad news. Not only had he been rejected, but the director had taken the unusual step of including a personal letter. It seemed that, although he had written a proposal that lauded the magnificence of Van Gogh, it would be impossible for him to receive a grant to study in Arles since that city was not in the Netherlands but was, of course, several hundred miles away in southern France. What galled Williams the most about the letter was the patronizing manner in which the director had thanked him for the application, and suggested that some year, instead of sending in "a spoof application that really did brighten up the day for all of us here in the office," he should send in a real application. Williams was unconsciously grinding his teeth again. "Why should artists be expected to know geography? Europe is Europe. Why should anybody be so picky?"

To go to Europe and finance the study out of his own pocket was not only fiscally impossible, but it was also a matter of principle. Williams felt strongly that governments must fund their artists! By staying home in Fergus Falls he was making a political statement. He reasoned that if Van Gogh had painted sunflowers and Monet had painted water lilies, there must be another subject for which the art world was desperately but unconsciously waiting. Williams had glommed onto the idea of the prairie wild rose— so lush, so delicate, so pink, so capable of being presented in any style from Oriental to Post-Impressionist. At sunrise and sunset, at noon on a sunny day and at midmorning in the mist, in most of the ditches and meadows of western Minnesota, Williams tried all the styles. Yet, with three finished (but unframed) canvases and forty-three unfinished canvases, he had yet to define the Williams style.

Although he spent every day making sarcastic comments about his students, his department head, his colleagues, his college, and his community, Williams was deeply grateful for his job at Fergus Falls State University. The teaching salary kept him in acrylic paint, and while the art world had yet to accept him as an "artist," the academic world had, however reluctantly, accepted him as "assistant professor." He always took consolation in the certain knowledge that he was an excellent teacher of painting and the "fundamentals of art." Unfortunately, it was an opinion that was not universally shared. It was true that some of the classroom evaluations from his students could be interpreted as less than positive, something his philistine department chair, Wallace Duncan, was always at pains to bring up. But that was simply a matter of reading between the lines. Some of his students were "barn smells" fresh off the farm and could never understand anything but stick men or pictures of Elvis on velvet. Who really cared what they thought? Besides, one had to "evaluate" student evaluations. What they really indicated, he maintained, was that he was a challenging teacher, one who could unleash their anger and turn it into creativity.

Williams had been counting on the "Dutch Experience" to lay the groundwork to get him out of Fergus Falls. He had been there for twelve years and was still an untenured assistant professor. It was a terrible injustice, he thought, one for which everyone but himself was to blame. The guidelines of the American Association of University Professors were clear on this point. If after six years one was not offered tenure at the end of his seventh year of full-time employment, the institution could no longer continue to employ said person. The art department had done everything they could to get rid of him and the students had started that mean petition, but thanks to good old President Gherkin he had kept his job. And how had Gherkin done it? By the simple expedient of putting him on eleven-twelfths time for his sixth year, thus circumventing the regulations and allowing him to start all over again as a "new" full-time employee in his seventh year. For another six years he had devoted his creativity to Fergus Falls State University and Dr. George Gherkin, teaching overloads and serving on every tedious presidential task force and stupid make-work, waste-of-time, screwball project there was. Therefore, at the end of his second six-year period of servitude he expected to be rewarded at last.

Williams looked down at the gas gauge and in a spasm of self-pity wondered if he would ever have enough money to fill the tank again. It was all Gherkin's fault. He felt a sickening knot in his stomach as he thought of his twelve-year professional relationship with the president of Fergus Falls State University. He pictured with loathing and disgust his recent meeting with Gherkin. As usual, Gherkin had greeted him with a boisterous bonhomie to which Williams always responded like a handicapped mouse.

Williams inwardly winced as he remembered how he had interpreted Gherkin's words to be those of genuine affection. He had been sure that the president was as pleased as he was that he had now served his double apprenticeship and could get a promotion and the security of tenure. "Promotion!" "Associate Professor!" The words had a melodious ring. No longer would he have to go to conferences where he would have to fib to his graduate school contemporaries about his real rank. An "Associate Professor" rank would mean that he was at last, well, an "associate" instead of the demeaning "assistant" professor. An "assistant professor" conveyed the image of one who carried the slide projector for the real professor and changed the batteries on his laser pointer. It would also mean more pay. Money to start a college fund for his son! Money to get rid of this old Volvo with the cracked plastic dashboard! Money to buy decent frames for his new "Wild Roses" series of paintings!

He went in to see the president with the expectation that they would talk contract, and he was not disappointed. As he drove along the highway and with mean intent tried to run down a striped gopher, Williams pictured himself sitting in Gherkin's office with what Williams decided in retrospect must have been a sappy, happy, loopy, stupid, naive grin. And he heard Gherkin say: "Sherwin, I'm glad you came in. I've got great news for you."

Williams was considering whether or not he wanted an automatic transmission in his new Volvo when Gherkin added, "I think I've found a way to keep you on."

A slight doubt passed over his somewhat ovine face, but assuming that Gherkin was into playful ribbing, the kind that hurt more than a root canal, Williams replied, "Well, that's good, at least."

"No, no. I mean it," Gherkin continued. "As I'm sure you know, tenure is out of the question."

"Out of the question?" Williams gulped.

"Of course. We can't give you tenure with the kind of recommendations I have in your file. I'm sure you can understand that. But I like you, Sherwin, I always have, and I think that if I put you on an eleven-twelfths teaching load next year, you can go back to full-time the year after that and it will be almost as good as tenure. I want to keep you, Sherwin, and I'll do everything I can for you."

Such was the sudden shift from fantasy to reality that Williams found himself thanking Gherkin for his concern and for his twelve-year stint as his personal advocate. He did finally mention, however, that he had been looking forward to the extra money.

But Gherkin was quick to reassure him. "The money? Oh, Sherwin, of course. I forgot to tell you. You won't lose a thing being cut back to eleven-twelfths. I've arranged for you to spend a little time with the admissions office—only about four hours a week, you know, make a few calls to high school seniors who are prospective art majors—that sort of thing. You'll love it! And you'll be making just as much next year as you are this year. No, no! Don't thank me. You've earned it! Oh, and by the way, I think we can even find a way to maintain your family medical policy at one hundred percent. It will take some doing, of course, but I think I can finagle it."

A belated thought occurred to the painter. In his usual negative and hang-dog style he asked, "I don't suppose it would ever be possible to be promoted to associate professor, I mean, without the tenure or without full-time employment? I mean, you know, just for the title?"

"No, I'm sorry, Sherwin. But, you know, that would be against policy."

"Policy? You mean the state board has a policy on all this?"

"Well, technically, that's somewhat flexible. That's why I've instituted my own policy. I'm sorry. No tenure—no promotion."

"But why?" Williams asked feebly.

"I've just explained, Sherwin. It's policy." As he rose from his chair in an obvious signal of dismissal he continued, "But I can't tell you how happy I am that I was able to work out a way to keep you with us for a while longer. I understand just how difficult it would be for you to get another job at this stage in your career, and I'm just glad to be of help to you. And say, this year we'd like to have you and your lovely wife out to the lake for our little 'back-to-school' get-together. I'll have Sally Ann call you with the details."

Yesterday, though, the scales had fallen from Sherwin's eyes. He had been brooding about his department's lack of support, blaming all of his troubles on that overbearing, undertalented fool who passed himself off as a department head. Communication had never been Williams' strong point, but he decided the present situation could go on no longer and it was time to beard the lion in his den. In his imagination he pictured just that, grabbing Professor Duncan by his beard and demanding satisfaction. The meeting, however, had not gone as expected. Duncan cut him off before he had time to utter a dozen words and said, "Look, I happen to think you're a bad artist and a lousy teacher, but over the last few years you've paid your dues and haven't done any real harm to our students. The whole department supported your promotion and tenure and I made a personal appeal to Gherkin, just like I did six years ago. I've put up with your whining and back-stabbing for about as long as is humanly possible and if it were not for your fine wife I wouldn't even agree to hire you part-time. Take it up with 'the Great One'!"

So it was Gherkin all along! Gherkin had kept him at the lowest possible salary! Gherkin had exploited his talent! Gherkin had turned him into a disgusting sycophant! Well, Gherkin had a surprise coming. He wasn't going to be Gherkin's lap dog anymore.

The scorned artist ruminated silently as he drove his nineteen-year-old beige Volvo through the western Minnesota countryside to President Gherkin's ostentatious lake home. Williams was a tall, thin, almost gaunt man with a wispy, graying mustache that matched his wispy, graying, and rapidly disappearing hair. He was always careful to affect the look of an artist, and tonight was no exception. For this formal dinner he had chosen a khaki cotton sport coat worn with a lavender shirt, open at the neck, and charcoal gray Dockers. On his feet he wore his usual Swedish clogs, but this time, in honor of the occasion, he wore socks.

In the years B.G. (Before Gherkin), the president had always lived in a modest home next to the campus. Gherkin, believing that a very public life required a very private residence, had built a modern eyesore on the shore of Wall Lake. (One year after it was built, the county had been persuaded to purchase a new snowplow to insure communications between the president and his university.) Driving through the countryside, Williams pretended to be listening to "All Things Considered" on Minnesota Public Radio, the radio station that he considered to be one of the most compelling arguments for living in such a wretched climate. This spared him the need to talk to Mae. He surreptitiously cast a bird-like glance at his wife, knowing that within two minutes she would be complaining once again about how there was no air conditioning in the Volvo and wouldn't it be nice if there were.

He had been surprised that Duncan's comment about his "fine wife" should have pleased him so much. He had grown "used to" Mae over the past ten years, and now life without her would be unthinkable. Such had not always been the case. Mae had been one of his students in his early years at FFSU, an impressionable young thing who was star-struck in the presence of a real artist. She had also put out not-so-subtle hints that she was available. On hearing the unwelcome news that she was pregnant, Williams considered following Gauguin's path to Tahiti, but realized, with some shock, that he actually loved the girl. In a state of romantic bliss and wearing the only tie he owned, he had proudly watched her being led to the altar of the Ulen Lutheran Church on the arm of her sourpussed old man. The soloist sang, the flower girl fidgeted, and the ringbearer made faces. Williams had loved it all. At last, following a homily that the artist would have sneered at had it been said before two other people, the minister said, "Do you, Mavis Brekke, take this man . . ." Mavis! My God! He was actually marrying a woman named Mavis! In all the days and nights with Mae that bit of knowledge had been withheld. At that moment the rest of his life seemed to be inexorably defined. He had to admit that he loved her more every year, and little Vincent was, after all, the nine-year-old apple of his eye. Still, there were times when he wished she wasn't such a "Mavis."

———

"It sure is hot in this car," said Mae, "and humid! We really should have air conditioning, you know. My hair is just going to be limp as a dishrag by the time we get there. I wonder how much it would cost to have air conditioning put in, or maybe you can't just put it into such an old car. Did you ever look into that?"

Her husband gave her a look of semi-comprehension, and Mae perceived that he was engrossed in a radio discussion on the rights of the indigenous peoples of Belize. It was just as well, for Mae was engaged in one of her favorite pastimes, reflecting about how good life was. In truth, it was just this optimism that made Mae so much more socially welcome than her husband. Sherwin had once told her that if Voltaire were alive he would have written a play exclusively about her and the "best of all possible worlds." Mae had smiled and thanked her husband, who always said the nicest things to her.

For Mae, evenings like this were among the most satisfactory rewards of being a faculty wife. She loved to rub elbows with those people who used to be her professors and to speak with them on an equal basis. Moreover, she knew that she was accepted. She had been so thrilled when Sherwin began to pay attention to her, perhaps a little too thrilled, she now admitted. But everything had worked out all right. She continued to take classes after Vincent was born and graduated with honors. To augment Sherwin's meager salary as assistant professor, she took a job in the registrar's office. Now, seven years later, she held the title of Assistant Registrar, and she could cite credit hours in semesters and quarters and handle transfer applications from the most bizarre of the private colleges. It had gotten to the point where the faculty advisors routinely told students, "I think this is all right, but you'd better check it with Mrs. Williams." Not bad for a farm girl, she thought, and she relished her ten-year high school class reunion, when she had the opportunity to show off her husband to her Ulen-Hitterdal high school classmates and to mention her title of Assistant Registrar.

Mental telepathy occasionally occurs between married couples. As she lowered the car window to let more air flow over her face, she remembered their wedding. She had planned everything just right, with the help of her three best friends from high school. Everything was pink and white and silver. She had prepared for everything but the vows. She was stunned when the minister turned to Sherwin and said, "Do you, Theodore, take this woman . . . ?" "Theodore!" All of their time together he had claimed his name was "Sherwin." Of course, Mae had not brought it up then, but Sherwin seemed so upset to learn that her full name was Mavis that she knew it was only a matter of time before they would have a discussion about names and marital honesty and candidness. Mae insisted that she had never intentionally misled him about her name, but Sherwin, for his part, did confess that he had tried to hide his first name ever since his first day in college. Sherwin's father had been a die-hard Red Sox fan, and had been proud to name his son after the Splendid Splinter, Ted Williams. In college, however, he had taken to signing his name T. Williams, and in graduate school, looking for a name that would sound a little more esoteric, he had hit upon Sherwin. It was under that name that he had applied for his job at FFSU. As he put it to Mae, "They only sold Glidden paints in my hometown. How was I to know?" But Mae had fallen in love with Sherwin, and Sherwin he remained.

Yes, thought Mae, things had worked out all right for them, and at last they were invited to share "the Great One's" famous chicken Kiev. As she thought about Gherkin, however, a dark scowl replaced the normally sunny countenance of Mae Williams. It was a look that did not become her. She had a flawless complexion and her perfect white teeth gleamed in a smile that could be blinding. Over the past ten years she had experimented with her dark hair, moving from long to curly to puffy until she finally discovered, quite by accident, the becoming short shag that she now wore. It was a little out of style, perhaps, but it was easy to care for and Sherwin said he liked it because it looked so "pert." Besides, it seemed to match her warm personality and her trim athletic figure. A composite of these assets would have made any other woman a nauseating specimen, but for some undefinable reason, they made Mae all the more delightful.

She blinked furiously as a speck of dust got under the contacts that covered her somewhat bulging blue eyes. The tears came from irritation, but they could just as well have come from anguish as she thought of Gherkin. Gherkin had helped her to get her job, she did admit that, but it hardly excused the way he treated her. He had a filthy mouth and a filthy mind and seemed to contrive situations where they would be alone together. He had also done his best to encourage office gossip that some sort of special relationship existed between them. She hadn't realized how vicious he could be until Sally Ann Pennwright, Gherkin's personal secretary, had asked her to cover the office while she had a dental appointment. Perhaps she shouldn't have been listening, but it was the noon hour and she had decided to spend her time with an apple and the latest Barbara Cartland romance. She could clearly hear Gherkin's voice from his office as he talked on the telephone.

"Yeah, well, I'm sure trying. She's a cute little thing. . . . No, not yet, but I'm keeping her no-talent artist husband around just so I can keep her near me."

Mavis heard a cruel, lascivious laugh and then "Give me a year. No, wait, she's warming up to me already. Give me six months. . . .

Yeah, sure I'll bet a steak dinner on it. . . . Well, you'll just have to take my word for it, won't you?" As the old Volvo brought them in sight of the lake, Mae's resentment turned to idle plottings of revenge against the despicable George Gherkin, who had, in fact, planned his last "back-to-school" dinner party.

THREE

SALLY ANN PENNWRIGHT EASED her sensible white Ford Fiesta out of the long driveway of what used to be the presidential house, a late Victorian home on the shore of Lake Alice, right in the heart of Fergus Falls. Her attendance at these annual dinner parties was traditional. In fact, she was the only guest who had been at every one since President Gherkin had started the annual affair some fifteen years earlier. Things had been different then.

Sally Ann had grown up in the moonlight and magnolia tradition of Dixie. She met George Gherkin when he was an aspiring dean at a junior college in Tennessee. She had just finished a master's degree in business, but was unemployed, and when Gherkin offered her a job as presidential private secretary, she considered it to be a good way to keep working until a real job opened up. She had fallen like a blind roofer and was soon much more than his secretary.

When Gherkin was offered the job as president of Fergus Falls State College (before it had attained university status) he asked

Sally Ann to come with him. She agreed for two reasons. The first was that Gherkin had offered her a job as vice-president. Although such a position did not then exist at the college, he promised to create one at the earliest opportunity.

At the time she had been a stunning Southern belle, with wavy ash-blonde hair and the kind of figure that made Southern gentlemen forget they were gentlemen. As a teenager, she was terribly nearsighted and had horrible teeth, but contact lenses and her father's dental talent had corrected those faults. She had a tiny cleft in her chin that gave character to an already beautiful face. Had she not had a feminine revulsion against beauty contests, she could have been in the Miss Tennessee pageant. Now she was twenty years older and in the past few days she was also considerably wiser.

For the beautiful Miss Pennwright, turning forty had been traumatic and depressing, but not nearly as traumatic and depressing as when Gherkin created national search committees to fill each of the two vice-presidencies that were created at the university. She applied each time, of course, but after being locked into a job as presidential private secretary, the opportunities to expand her experience and her education had been few and far between. Gherkin, her advocate and paladin, had come to her each time to explain that while he had done the best he could for her, the search committee had decided to choose someone else. Each time he proceeded to roundly condemn the new state-mandated guidelines that prohibited him from hiring the one he really wanted.

The second reason that she accepted Gherkin's invitation to join him at Fergus Falls, two wasted decades ago, was the health of Dolly Gherkin, who was to be the new "first lady" of Fergus Falls

State College. According to George, his wife's condition was inoperable and he had hinted strongly that within a year there would be a vacancy in the "first lady" position. Several years later, after Dolly received a gold medal from the governor for promoting healthy living by organizing marathon bicycle trips, Sally Ann used her position as insurance coordinator to get a look at Mrs. Gherkin's medical file. Dolly Gherkin was probably the healthiest fifty-year-old woman on the face of the planet. Confronted with this fact, Gherkin admitted that he had exaggerated his wife's illness (she did, after all, catch a cold every spring) but maintained that he had done it only because his life would have been empty without Sally Ann. No one ever accused her of being stupid, however, and Sally Ann ended the romantic side of their relationship that very night.

That was ten years ago, but it was Sally Ann's first real taste of power. She remembered the scene as if it were yesterday. At first, she was determined to make George choose, and was ready to spout the trite "It's either her or me!" But when the showdown came, as she looked at the perspiration gathering on his balding head and the terrified look that darted out from his expensive gold-framed glasses, she suddenly saw the situation in a new light. Why should she hope he would choose her? It wasn't him she wanted anymore, it was the power he could give her.

And Gherkin, after all, radiated power. He had a massive chest and kept himself in marvelous physical condition. At a convocation, in a boardroom, or in a private conversation, there was never any doubt about who was in charge. But that night, when she stood up to him, she knew she had a power of her own.

He had been his old confident self, putting his massive arm around her and assuming she would melt from his attention. That night, he tried his "honesty" approach.

"Of course, Darling, I may have merely been the victim of wishful thinking when I told you Dolly was ill. But I wanted you to come with me so much, and I just couldn't take the chance that you wouldn't. Perhaps it was somewhat of a white lie, but it was all worth it, wasn't it? Haven't we had a marvelous time these last ten years?"

Sally Ann remembered the triumph she had felt when she looked straight into his beady, overconfident eyes and said, "What marvelous time? Ten years of sneaking around? Ten years of being the subject of jokes and rumors? Ten years of feeling guilty while you publicly proclaimed your love for another woman and paraded as a virtuous family man? What a marvelous time!"

George tried to cajole her, oiling his way around the subject by wistfully saying how much they could accomplish together when she was vice-president in an adjoining office. "Surely you wouldn't give that up!" he had confidently told her, drawing her closer to him.

Perhaps it was that insufferable overconfidence that pushed her to the limit. In any event, Sally Ann remembered, with pleasure, her response. She had let herself be encircled by George's muscular arms and his perfectly manicured hands. George assumed he had won just one more little lover's spat and visibly relaxed. It was then Sally Ann declared her independence. In a calm, controlled voice she said:

"George, Sweetheart, if you ever touch me again I will have you arrested. But I'm not leaving you, George; not until I decide I'm ready to go. After all, I have a nice house to live in, don't I? I have a nice job, don't I? And I think I may be getting a raise soon, don't you think?

"Now, Georgie-Porgie, you have a nice house to live in, don't you? You have a nice job, too, don't you? As I see it, the only way you are going to keep the things you want is to let me have the things I want because, George, I have the sudden urge to tell the world of our love. Let's think about that. What would it mean to both of us? I lose my job at Fergus Falls State University. I go to another town and start again, educated and experienced and in the prime of my life. Now George, if I were to make public our eternal love, including a few rather indiscreet letters you've sent me when you've been off on one of your conferences, you would probably lose your family and your job, which means you would lose that home by the lake. It would also mean that a new administration may do a little closer supervision of some of the appropriations that have been made in the last ten years. I'm not sure you would like that, would you, George?" "But as I say, George, I'm not going to leave you. No, I think it will be to my benefit to stay around. And George, it will definitely be to your benefit to keep me."

As she drove toward yet another dinner party at the presidential home, Sally Ann smiled at the memory. Within the week, a legal document was drawn up, and Gherkin allowed her to rent the former presidential house with a twenty-year lease at below-market rates. Gherkin had also, almost officially, reiterated his promises about a vice-presidency.

Sally Ann's thoughts abruptly returned to last Tuesday, and her pretty face twisted into a cruel sneer. Dr. Westgaard, the chair of the physics department, had timidly brought in the minutes of the search committee that had been formed for the second vice-presidency. "I've had these notes in my files for over two years now," he said, "and I don't know what to do with them. I thought I'd just throw them away, but in these days of affirmative action and everything, I thought I should check first. Does the university need to keep them?" Sally Ann had unenthusiastically told him to leave the files on the desk and that she would take care of them. Later that day, as she was placed on hold during a routine call to the State University Board, she began to leaf through the minutes of the search committee. Much to her shock, she discovered that she had been the unanimous choice of the committee, but that their selection had been vetoed by President Gherkin.

Her eyes narrowed as she mentally rehearsed the showdown that was inevitable. She had tasted power, but power had to be maintained or it was no longer power. Gherkin would pay! Oblivious to the lush Minnesota farmland that was passing by her sensible Ford much too rapidly, she found herself exhilarated by the thought that this would be her last Gherkin dinner party.

FOUR

Dr. Isabel Corazon was the newest vice-president of Fergus Falls State University. She was short, and the more cruel of the FFSU students might have referred to her figure as "dumpy." Outside of a fascination with expensive shoes, she was not overly concerned about her clothing. She wore her dark hair severely swept back, a style that allowed her to display her global collection of earrings, and she covered her potentially attractive dark eyes under enormous and faintly tinted glasses. Her hands, always in motion as she talked, were festooned with rings—some cheap, some expensive, but all of them gaudy.

Dr. Corazon had been a dean of humanities in a small Texas state college when she first met George Gherkin at an "Objectives for Higher Education" conference in Corpus Christi. He had made no pretense of being interested in the conference, pointing out that a university-paid trip that allowed him to play green golf on the Gulf in January was his main reason for attending. This honesty rather appealed to her, amid all the pretentious academics who protested that they would have attended the wonderful conference even if the site were a snowbound hotel in Grand Forks, North Dakota.

"Yes, George could be charming," she admitted to herself as she drove her Mazda 626 along State Highway 210. It had turned out to be a fun conference and when Gherkin called two months later to inform her of the search for an academic vice-president, she was eager to apply. But Isabel Corazon was first and foremost an academic and knew that a vice-presidency at one college could turn into a presidency at another. Although she had taken a small cut in pay to accept the job at FFSU, Gherkin promised her that she would be overseeing the design and construction of a new humanities building with facilities for music, art, and theater, as well as new "classrooms of tomorrow." This could be her monument—the stepping stone to a presidency, national recognition, and, who knew, even a cabinet position.

For two years it was her consuming passion. With regular input from Gherkin she designed not only a new humanities center, but a whole new curriculum for humanities education in state universities. She published her plans in professional journals and always made a point to include her potential crowning glory, her designs for the building that would be the scene of "Humanities Education in the Twenty-First Century." She put together an impressive package of data that included line graphs, bar graphs, pie graphs, trends in college applications, employment prospects, and construction estimates, all packaged in a slick and attractive brochure produced on her state-of-the-art iMac computer.

It seemed as though the Mazda was driving itself as it penetrated its bucolic surroundings, for Dr. Corazon's mind was on the immediate past. For two years she had allowed herself to dream big dreams. For two years she had thanked her lucky stars for George Gherkin, who had rescued her from an institution staffed by misfits and academic vagabonds to a place where she could build her personal scholastic ivory tower. With every dream approved by the president himself, there seemed no limit to what she could accomplish. Each new idea was enthusiastically endorsed by a man who seemed dedicated to pioneering new directions in higher education. Tonight, though, she was seeing the president's cooperation and support in a new light. "After all," she complained out loud, "how many ideas were actually implemented and how much new money was actually spent? Nothing! Nil! *Nada!*"

Just three days earlier, Dr. Corazon had found the broken rung on the ladder of academic success. On that day she selected her power suit, gathered her presentation materials, and went to the parking lot to meet Gherkin for the appointed drive to Saint Paul. It was time for the big meeting with the state board, the showdown, the "big enchilada," as Gherkin had called it—an expression which now seemed a cruel and demeaning reference to her ethnic background, but which at the time had elicited no particular response from Isabel. Imagine her surprise, then, that when Gherkin showed up to collect her, she found that Francis Olson, the football coach, was already seated next to him in the university station wagon. As she loaded her over-stuffed attaché case in the back seat, she noticed Olson's slim manila folder on the dashboard, but attached no particular significance to it.

"How could I have been so blind?" she bleated, to the unhearing voice of the newscaster on Minnesota Public Radio. "I should have realized something was up when George didn't badger me to accept a cozy dinner at an out-of-the-way café as he usually does whenever he has the chance. Twins game! Ha! George and the football coach at a Twins game! I should have known his new-found interest in baseball was phony!"

Indeed she should have, for it seemed Gherkin was more interested in the Hubert Humphrey Metrodome than he was in any sort of athletic competition. At the meeting the next morning, Gherkin introduced her to the State University Board and Isabel gathered up her presentation materials. She was set to offer her best modest and self-deprecating smile to the board as she imagined George's fulsome introduction with a complete list of her accomplishments and praise for her innovation. Ha! How humiliating it had all been! To be sure, George introduced her, but with a hearty repetition of her title in a manner that called more attention to his wisdom in hiring her than to her accomplishments in the position. Then, as she put her hands on the table to boost herself into a more powerful stance for her presentation, Gherkin cut her off and called on Francis Olson. The football coach modestly accepted the board's accolades on yet another fine season and then unfurled a hastily-drawn plan for an indoor stadium tentatively called the "Fergus Falls Mini-Dome."

All eyes turned to the ex-quarterback and successful coach, and nobody saw Isabel's jaw drop to the table or noticed that smoke was almost visibly escaping from her ears. Olson, in his inarticulate way, mumbled about the financial gains that a domed stadium would bring to the athletic department. He slyly hinted that the excess revenue generated by the project would go to funding the nonrevenue-producing sports for women and made it appear that this was, perhaps, the most important reason for proceeding with construction as soon as possible. Olson even went so far as to assure them that there would be no gender bias tolerated in his athletic department. The board enthusiastically applauded and Gherkin assured them that, as indicated by the presence of Dr. Corazon, the whole university would be behind the project. Corazon, mentally picturing the walls of her humanities center tumbling down, had muttered, "Over my, or somebody else's, dead body!"

When she finally got Gherkin alone, he was the picture of innocence. "Why did you think this meeting would involve your humanities center?" he had asked with bland surprise.

"The last straw!" Isabel Corazon muttered to herself, squeezing the steering wheel of the Mazda until her knuckles turned white. In fact, those were the words she used in response to Gherkin that day.

"That's the last straw! For two years I have been pushing educational reforms under your nose. You sniffed them like hot apple pie and said they were great! I ran every graph and plan under your shiny red schnoz for your approval because I thought we were in this together. It was you who asked me to come along to this meeting! It was you who said I should be prepared to say a few words to the board! Naturally I assumed it was an opportunity to present my proposals for the humanities center. You know I can never support a loony idea like a domed stadium for a small college! Why did you need me to humiliate myself? I presumed that you respected all that I had been doing the last two years."

"Yes, well, Isabel," Gherkin had replied. "That's what we aren't supposed to do in academia, isn't it? Presume? I appreciate all the work you have done on the humanities program. There are always some alumni that need to be shown we are concentrating on academics. But it really doesn't bring in the bucks, does it? Now, be honest. Did I ever say we were coming down here to show the board a plan for a humanities center? I just thought we would have a better chance to get our suggestion for a new stadium approved if I could show them that an academic was at our side. You played your role nicely, by the way. With your presence and your silence, everyone assumed you were four-square behind the stadium. Besides, who knows? When the stadium is up, we can take another look at the humanities proposal."

After such a double cross, it may have seemed unlikely that she would have accepted Gherkin's invitation to tonight's dinner, but she already knew that Lance Sterling, the president of the alumni association, would be there. He was a possible ally, someone who had his own problems with Gherkin. She wondered if it would be advisable for her to bring up the importance of a humanities building to him, or whether it might be better to wait until such time as Gherkin would not be around. The thought occurred to her that if he were not around on a permanent basis it would be better for all concerned. As she began to picture the post-Gherkin era, with herself in an important interim position, she rolled down her window and let the breeze billow the yards of awning material that she called her summer dress. It did not cool her off.

FIVE

Francis Olson knew that rain was in the forecast, but he had washed his new Chevy pickup and, for what he considered to be a formal occasion, had even gone so far as to take the rifle out of the gun rack. He should have been on top of the world, or at least, his world. Football practice had already started and the season was looking good. He sadistically loved those weeks when he was running two-a-days, those times when he could demand calisthenics until the freshmen vomited in the morning, make them study the playbook in the early afternoon, and bring them back out during the hottest and most humid part of the day to run laps and wind-sprints and vomit some more. There were always a few wimps and a few quitters, but better to get them weeded out sooner than later. Besides, those he really worked to recruit were always kept on. With the incentives and "jobs" that he found for them, they could hardly afford to go anywhere else. And this was going to be another great team, no doubt about it. Furthermore, in a couple of years, with that domed stadium in place, FFSU would have the best athletic facilities of any small university in the country. And with that, of course, would come even more impressive recruits.

But Olson was not happy. Two weeks before fall practice could begin, a heart attack claimed the life of the coach of a Big Eight university. For three years he had been courting the attention of the alumni of that school, making subtle hints about how he could transform their losing ways into winning ones by applying the system he developed for the Fergus Falls Flying Falcons. Suddenly there was a vacancy, and he had confidently expected to be offered the job. It could be his big chance, maybe even a ticket back to the pros.

In fact, he received his first nibble barely three hours after the old coach died, when the president of the alumni association had called him and tastelessly proclaimed "Francis, I got some great news for you!" The job seemed to be his. The emergency search committee did mention, however, that they would have to seek permission from Fergus Falls State University before they could officially talk to him about it, since he was under contract. Olson assured them that it would be no problem, that he and Gherkin were "thick as hair on a dog's back." Now, as he observed Sally Ann Pennwright's Ford on the highway ahead of him, he remembered how he had swaggered into the office to give Gherkin the good news. Gherkin had smiled, patted him on the back, and said, "I'm sure everyone will be gratified to hear that our own 'Fabulous Francis' is in such demand. Let's just see what your contract with the old Flying Falcons says, should we?"

Olson was probably FFSU's most famous alumnus, and un-doubtedly its most recognized faculty member. He still retained the handsome features that had enabled him to become a television pitch man for everything from after-shave to snow tires. He kept his six-foot-four-inch body in remarkable condition and he had yet to lose a blonde hair from his Nordic head. Women found him attractive, but for only a limited period, as his previous wives were only too ready to testify. As a student he had taken the Flying Falcons to the national championship game for small colleges and, although his team lost, he gained the attention of the pro scouts. He played pro football for eleven years, most of them with the Philadelphia Eagles. When his knee finally gave out he was depressed to discover that the Eagles didn't particularly care what happened to him and that he was not really prepared for anything but playing pro football. Without the degree that he always meant to complete at good old FFSU, his job prospects looked dim. It was at this point that Gherkin stepped in. He simply doctored the transcripts and "discovered" that Olson had taken a couple of "independent studies" for which he had never received credit. Granting him a degree was now possible, and so was employment. Gherkin soon had the prestige of having an ex-National Football League quarterback as his football coach. It had been a mutually beneficial relationship ever since the day Gherkin watched Olson sign the twenty-three-page contract.

Of course, Olson never read the contract, but over the years he was aware of the fact that benefits that usually came to winning football coaches, such as local endorsements, were never paid to him but were instead diverted into Gherkin's own special discretionary fund. When Olson protested, Gherkin pointed out that the contract that he had signed was very clear on that point. Still, Olson was in awe of "the Great One," and remained thankful for all that Gherkin had bestowed upon him. Only now did he realize that the contract forbade him to accept another job in college or professional coaching until a period of two years from the date of his last employment at FFSU. Moreover, he had never joined the teaching union, because Gherkin insisted that he had a better contract than he could ever get if it were subject to any kind of outside scrutiny. Although this was probably true at the time, Olson now recalled one of the few things he had learned from his student days when he had taken the United States history survey course—the term "indentured servant." That's what he was, an "indentured servant"—forever paying off his master. Still, it was a personal contract, and if something were ever to happen to Gherkin, it could probably be nullified. Oblivious to the nauseating country music song about the neglected wife of a truck driver that was blaring out from his radio, he turned his thoughts on the most direct way of nullifying that contract.

Olson's somewhat neglected passenger was Dr. Harold Winston. It had not been Olson's idea to take him to Gherkin's dinner party, but the ever-thoughtful Sally Ann Pennwright had telephoned requesting that, as Winston did not own a car and the other guests drove small cars, it would be most convenient if Francis could offer him a ride. Olson's truck was a reasonable mode of conveyance, for Dr. Winston was a huge man. As he looked over at the mound of flesh next to him, it was hard for Olson to hide his disgust. Although he was slightly under six feet tall, Winston was a scale-abusing three hundred pounds, none of which was muscle. He had sparse gray hair smoothed over a balding head and thick, horn-rimmed glasses that seemed to be embedded in his pasty face. Although it was ninety-two degrees, he wore his usual black wool suit coat, liberally sprinkled with dandruff and offset with a hideous wide tie. His beard, although probably clean, had a grisly piebald appearance that suggested all manner of disgusting debris concealed in its tangles.

The two men, in fact, could hardly have been more different. Winston was the longtime member of the history department who had, in fact, acquainted Olson with his meager knowledge of indentured servitude. Winston was against everything Olson stood for. He was a dedicated foe of the athletic department and prided himself on his lack of football knowledge, a pair of words which he considered to be an oxymoron. As a means of waging his personal war against all things of an athletic nature, Winston managed to get himself placed on the university athletic committee. Here he was a constant grain of sand in Olson's personal oyster. Yet, curiously, over the years a stalemate had occurred that produced a grudging mutual respect. Perhaps they could never be real friends, but Winston had discovered, to his absolute amazement, that Olson was the only person in Fergus Falls who could defeat him in chess. Winston did not appreciate Olson's constant football analogies, and was quite certain that the queen on the chessboard did not "have to think like a quarterback," but since they also shared a preference for drinking copious amounts of beer directly out of quart bottles while they were playing chess, a measure of tranquillity had settled in between them.

"So, anyway, there should be some free beer out there, don't you think?" Olson ventured. "I mean, you don't just schedule something on a hot day and not serve beer, do you?"

"Do you mind?" Winston asked, as he snapped off the radio and enjoyed the blissful silence for a full two seconds before replying. "It has never been my pleasure to be invited to one of Gherkin's soirees, but I've heard that the liquid refreshment is a highlight of the evening second only to the chicken Kiev. It may not always be one's choice of company, but the food's good and the beer's good and two out of three's not bad." As Olson automatically reached forward to turn the radio back on, Winston protectively put his hand over the dial. "No, please, I can't take it. It's giving me an 'achy-breaky' head. How can you stand to listen to that stuff, anyway? For better or worse, you are listed as a faculty member of a university. Have you no sense of propriety? That kind of music is like a declaration of war against man's attempt at intellectual betterment."

"Ah, lighten up, Harry. A little stompin' music never hurt anybody. What kind of music do you want? Some of that long-hair stuff on that public station? You're out of luck. I just got AM on my dial."

Winston had stiffened up at being called "Harry," but decided for the tranquility of the moment to let it pass. "Let's just leave it off. We don't have much farther to go, and it is rather pleasant driving through the countryside. I don't get a chance to do this very often, you know."

"Yeah, I've always wondered about that. How come you don't have a car like everybody else?"

"It's simply a matter of economics and priorities. I calculated how much I would spend on a car—initial outlay, fuel, insurance, maintenance, and so forth—and I decided that for my needs I could rely on public transportation and conserve my money for something I really wanted to spend it on, like books, music, and good food. Besides, I have discovered that I am really not a very good driver."

"But a man without a car, I mean, that's weird!"

"Weird? This from a man who spends his days teaching other men the proper ways to maim and hurt people? This from a man in his forties who measures his contribution to the universe in terms of how many inches of real estate he can wrest from an opposing group of men once every Saturday for eleven weeks out of the year?"

Olson was just about to lose his temper when he looked over to see that Winston was smiling and realized that he was merely the subject of good-natured ribbing. At which point Winston added, "I must admit, though, however weird it may seem to me, you are awfully good at it."

"Well, I take that as a compliment, coming from such an expert judge, and as usual I will send you a complimentary season ticket. Perhaps this year you may actually use it."

"Perhaps I would, if I didn't have to spend the whole time bundled up on a cold bench. That's such an uncivilized thing to do."

"He hasn't heard about the domed stadium proposal yet," thought Olson with inward glee, "and this is no time to tell him. I don't want to be around when that fly hits the ointment. In fact, I don't want to be around here at all." To Winston he merely replied, "Just give us a chance and we'll make you as comfortable as we can. It is the best game in the world, you know."

"The best game in the world? How can you say such an outrageous thing?"

"It's true! Look, what other game combines the elements of strength, speed, and agility that you find in your modern football? I mean, you get these guys who weigh two hundred and fifty pounds and you think they are clumsy oafs filling up space. They're not. They're fine athletes. I got a kid on my team who must be close to three hundred pounds. He plays on the golf team in the spring. He was all-state in basketball. And he has one other element that you need these days, he's smart. He made the dean's list last quarter."

"So now you're telling me that football players need to be intelligent?"

"You bet I am! Look at your other sports. A baseball player hits a ball with a stick. He has his route all planned out for him and the bases are numbered just to make it easier for him to find his way around. What's intellectual about that? Either he hits it or he don't, and either the fielder catches it or he don't. And basketball? Hey, there's a real mental challenge! Find a guy who is a foot taller than anyone else and have him stand under the basket. I would venture a guess that you would only have to explain to him what to do with the ball one time before he cottoned on to what was expected of him. And hockey? Huh! A bunch of guys skating around looking for an excuse to get into a fight, a game where your ultimate accomplishments are measured by the number of teeth you retain. And, oh yeah, soccer. A bunch of sissies running around in short pants, kicking the ball around for no apparent reason until, purely by the law of averages, it ends up in a goal, which gives them all an excuse to run together to hug each other.

"Now you take football, on the other hand, where you have a team of specialists. Each person on that team has to do his job every play or the play isn't going to work. On offense, each player has a man to block or a route to run. Even if the person isn't involved in the play he has to carry out fakes. On defense, each person has to take responsibility for his man or—and this is more complicated, but I've always thought more pertinent to life—to his zone. Think about it. It's a parallel for Western Civilization. Each man must defend his zone for the ultimate good of all. It's wonderful. You, who teach history, can certainly appreciate the metaphor. Look at the crucial battles of Western Civilization. Gettysburg! The defeat of the Spanish Armada! When the Greeks defeated the Romans at the Battle of Salamis!"

"Persians."

"What?"

"At Salamis, the Greeks defeated the Persians, not the Romans."

"Whatever. But you see what I mean. Careful planning, meticulous execution, trust that the person next to you will do his job. Just like Napoleon planned the battle of Waterloo!"

"You may recall that Napoleon lost that battle. But I see your point. Napoleon's plan was not that bad, it was just the execution. But that's the way it always is in battle. No battle has ever gone the way it was drawn up on the blackboard."

"Aha! You see, in football it does! Or at least, it does sometimes. You don't just put a ball in the middle of the field and run around until the ball falls in the net like in soccer."

"You must realize that soccer, which the rest of the world calls 'football,' is played by millions more people than our football. It is truly the 'world sport.'"

"Yeah, and 80 percent of the world goes to bed hungry every night, too. Probably the same ones who spend their time playing soccer. So what? What's the number one nation in the world? The U.S.A.! And what country plays the best football? The U.S.A.! Are you trying to tell me that's just a coincidence?"

Winston let loose with a deep chuckle that began to shake the several chins hidden beneath his beard. Eventually it broke through with a full and harsh guffaw. "You're right! So what! To tell you the truth, I've always thought soccer was a dumb sport, too. Chess, now, well, that's something different."

"Absolutely! Hard to drink beer when you're kicking a ball around, isn't it?" replied Olson, and got the giggles as he pictured a soccer player running down the field with a quart of beer in his hand.

"Good. Truce for this evening then? I want one man in my corner as far as Gherkin is concerned. I'll eat the man's food and drink the man's beer, but if he thinks he is inviting me out to dine in order to enlist me in one of his schemes, he's dumber than one of your scholar-athletes. Er, no offense."

Winston's dislike for Gherkin had ripened over the years and had advanced from a mild distaste for the man's style to a mature and robust loathing. He was at FFSU when it was still a state college, long before Gherkin had arrived. In the course of his career he had produced more books and articles than the rest of the history department combined. A bachelor by choice and inclination, he shared a house with the university librarian, a happy coincidence, since his personal library was the largest in western Minnesota. But for all of his publications and teaching awards, there was one achievement that had been denied to him. He had never been selected to chair his own department.

After a moment of silence, as Olson realized that he may have found someone of a kindred spirit in the hatred of the president, he asked, "Something happen between you and George lately?"

"You might say that."

"I thought now that you were going to be chairman you might, you know, start leaning more toward the administration."

"Who told you I would be chair of the history department?"

"Well you are, aren't you? Whatzizname retired. Who else would they have?"

"Who indeed?" Winston exploded. He twisted his massive body around so violently that he got tangled in the safety harness, which had already been stretched to its maximum. The violence of his language, ostensibly directed against the inert safety straps, shocked even Olson, the veteran of years spent in professional football locker rooms. Olson was awed into silent admiration. At last, having disconnected the entire apparatus, Winston continued.

"Sorry. I guess I was just thinking about Gherkin. He thought we should modernize our department, see. I mean, we had a nice stable of scholars and some decent, if not spectacular teachers. But we didn't have a bona fide 'social historian,' you know, the kind who can talk on and on about the life of some poor yahoo who lived and died and nobody cared for him so he didn't make it into the history books. Well, your social historians are trying to rectify that by taking these fellows, who never did anything of note in their lives, and giving them credit in the history books for never doing anything. Most of them spent their lives eating and sleeping and grunting, sort of like how your football players manage to graduate. Sorry, no offense. But anyway, they are now busy telling us how the average people in a given age lived, and I suppose that's good. Dull, tedious, and boring, of course, but it is 'new ground to be plowed' and that's always a consideration for bringing in the grants. Well, Gherkin decided we needed one of them on our staff, and he found one. Then he discovered that the person he found was a computer whiz. Well, say no more, say no more. Gherkin just had to have him. We've already got one computer whiz on our staff. He sits there all day staring at that screen doing and redoing his syllabus. Gherkin sees that syllabus and suddenly we are told that every one of us should have a syllabus like that. I mean, the guy never reads anymore, he just sits at that computer rearranging things. But Gherkin, well, he thinks the man is the wave of the future. And, I don't know, maybe he is. But so, anyway, when Gherkin hears this social historian is a computer whiz to boot, well, he just has to hire him. Hearing Gherkin pant in his ear, our new professor says he will come only if he is made chairman and Gherkin says, 'Isn't that a coincidence! Our chair just retired. You can be our new chair if you'd like.'"

"You really wanted that chairmanship, didn't you?"

"I think I must have. I didn't realize how much I wanted it until Gherkin gave it to someone else. I would have gotten a little release time to do research and got paid a little more, but it wasn't that. After a life given to this institution I guess I wanted a little honor, thin as it may be. I've only got a few more years until retirement, and I thought I deserved that."

"Harold, I'm really sorry to hear that. And if it is any comfort to you, the whole university admires the work you have done and will be appalled by this news. That Gherkin has no sense of honor. What a pig!"

"You know, Francis, I may not admire your sport, but I certainly do appreciate your judgment of men!"

SIX

LANCE STERLING WAS GOING to be late for the dinner. He intended to be late, as a thumb in George Gherkin's eye. He regretted that in doing so he might upset Dolly, that saint of a woman who was married to "the Grate One," as Sterling called him. He sat in the driveway of his elaborately trimmed Tudor house on Vernon Avenue and lovingly fiddled with the CD stereo in his aging silver Sterling sedan. He could afford to drive a Jaguar, but he loved little symbols. He had somehow developed a golden touch in the real-estate business and was clearly the wealthiest man in Fergus Falls. It was a reflection on his character that he enjoyed embellishing his first initial into the British Pounds-Sterling symbol. He took a reassuring glance into his rear-view mirror and saw a distinguished businessman, hair graying slightly at the temples and receding only in the right places. He was dressed in a lightweight gray suit that he had purchased during his last trip to London, in Savile Row, of course. It did a marvelous job of hiding a less-than-attractive waist-line. And yet, however expensive the suit and haircut were, Sterling unintentionally gave the impression of being a smarmy, shiny-pants hustler.

If it were up to him, he would have rudely turned down the invitation, but Dolly had called Ruth, his wife, and Ruth always loved such affairs. No, as far as he was concerned, the less he had to do with George Gherkin the better he felt about life. As he waited for his wife, he clumsily tried to get his favorite CD into the dashboard stereo. He loved all Broadway musicals, the cornier the better, but his all-time favorite was *The Sound of Music*. In his private moments, he pictured himself on stage with Julie Andrews, praising the purity of edelweiss.

This evening, however, it was a measure of his mood that he could not even be heartened by "Climb Every Mountain." Instead, he relived his grievances against the FFSU president. Hadn't he been president of the alumni association for twelve years? In that time, hadn't he raised more money for the school than all of his predecessors combined? Besides, a significant proportion of that money had been his own. And why? Because Gherkin had always promised him that ticket to immortality, a business building named the "Sterling Center for the Study of International Business." Sure, the building had been built—with Sterling money purchasing virtually every brick—but when it came time to dedicate the building, it had suddenly been named after the governor. It was a transparent political ploy and everybody knew it, with the possible exception of the governor, who acted as though he deserved the honor. Still, building names had been changed before, and they could be changed again, but not under a Gherkin administration. That, too, perhaps, could be arranged.

At last Ruth Sterling joined her husband for the drive to what Lance called the "FFSU Presidential Compound." She was a happy person who loved fine clothes and the opportunities to wear them. She ordered her own fabrics from Milan and had her own dressmaker to construct all of her apparel. This was fortunate for her, in that clothes off the rack could never be found to complement her figure. Mrs. Sterling had been born without a waist, as most humans are, but unlike other members of her species, she had not developed one with the passing of the years. Nature refused to take its usual course, and after the birth of her four children she accepted her shape. She was neither fat nor slim, but only her dressmaker could give her a figure. She was carefully coifed, manicured, and tanned, and Lance always liked to say "she's the real sterling in the house." Although her husband had his differences with "that dreadful Gherkin," she was looking forward to an evening in the company of educated people free of rancor of any kind.

Ruth was into charities. She was the perennial chair of the Fergus Falls United Way and the acknowledged tsarina of social programs at the Fergus Falls Presbyterian Church. As she settled into the elegant-but-clammy leather seats of the Sterling, she immediately pulled down the visor to contemplate her image in the mirror. Although she was generally pleased, she passed a small brush through her henna-colored hair and, like a cat washing its whiskers, she licked her forefinger and smoothed the eyebrows that gracefully arched over her kind, somewhat bovine, brown eyes.

Mrs. Sterling felt strongly that those on whom providence smiled should take responsibility for those upon whom it frowned. For months she had been trying to convince Dr. Gherkin to serve as an honorary co-chairman for the Heart Fund, but instead of accepting it as an honor, he had ridiculed the whole project. Furthermore, he had done so publicly and Ruth had felt humiliated. What a dreadful man! How could Dolly stand him?

As she primly straightened her skirt and reached for her seat belt, her husband sarcastically asked, "Do you think we can go now?"

Taking the question literally, Ruth replied, "Yes, I think so. I think I have everything."

"If you had everything, we could just as well have gone directly out to the lake from Gherkin's place. But oh, no, we have to come back into town so you can change for our weekend at our other house. It just doesn't make sense, darling."

"You men! I can hardly wear this kind of dress to our cabin, can I? I want to look nice in case Nicole brings her boyfriend—fiancé maybe?—out to the lake home this weekend. These are two separate occasions and I'd just feel better if we could come back into town. Besides, it might storm tonight and I always feel safer when we are in town."

This short conversation included references to the two passions in Ruth's life that could almost, but not quite, equal her passion for charity work. She took pride in their lake home, an architectural gem that had once been featured in *Minnesota Monthly*. She also kept a lasting interest, and a tight rein, on her children, even though all but the youngest had married and left home. Lance took pride in the fact that he named them, but she raised them, and continued to do so, much to the alternating amusement or annoyance of her daughters-in-law. Lance named his two sons Frank and Mark, and his first daughter Penny. Extending the financial theme for his last daughter had been a challenge—with Ruth rejecting such suggestions as Peso, Yen, and Ruble—and putting her foot down when it came to her husband's favorite, 'Shilling Sterling'. Ruth had been relieved when Lance thought of 'Nicole,' and congratulated him on his cleverness.

Lance Sterling was also fond of the lake home, and found himself spending less and less of his time in town. It meant two lawns to mow, two houses to furnish, two roofs to repair, and two properties on which to pay taxes, but he defended this on the grounds that it was a nice place for the family to get together. Nevertheless, he regretted his failure to raise his sons to a level of responsibility where they would take care of a few of the maintenance chores. Lance, though, was a man of action, and if someone else wouldn't do things, he would do them himself.

"Sweetheart," Ruth cooed, oblivious to her husband's impatience, "do me a favor, will you? If at all possible, will you see to it that I don't get stuck sitting next to George tonight?"

Lance eased the car out of his driveway, enjoying the responsive handling and privately wanting to turn up the volume on the stereo. "I tell you what, Ruth. You stick with me and you'll be as far away from George as you can get. I don't like the man, and I don't trust him."

"I don't either! Why do you suppose we were invited, anyway?"

"When you've been in business as long as I have, you come to realize that you don't have to like your business associates, or even trust them as far as that goes, but you've got to remain ready to do business."

"I thought after that fiasco where you were supposed to get your name on that building you would not want to cooperate with him again. You know the old saying, 'fool me once, shame on you;

fool me twice, shame on me; fool me three times, . . .' What was supposed to happen when you were fooled three times?"

"Nothing, Dear." Sterling patiently explained to his wife. "The whole point is that you are not supposed to get fooled more than once, let alone three times."

"Whatever. But anyway, are you sure you won't get fooled again?"

"Look, the business center had to be built. It's going to be a major asset for the university. As president of the alumni association I can still take a great deal of pride in the fact that I spearheaded the drive that resulted in the construction of such a wonderful building. It truly is an accomplishment that will live on long after I'm gone. Sure, I would have liked the honor, but I can take pleasure in the thought that the building is there largely because of my dedication."

"That's very noble, dear, but I don't believe a word of it. You'd rather have your name on a bus shelter than anonymously donate a cathedral. You would be more than happy to torpedo Gherkin once and for all and then smear his name for all time. Admit it! You know you would."

"Perhaps, but only when I'm done with him. In business, you have to have an eye to the long-term benefits of a relationship. I figure Gherkin owes me, and I intend to collect."

"Collect? From that deadbeat? For twenty years I've seen people falling all over him. 'Let me do this for you. Let me do that for you.' And what does he do for anyone besides George Gherkin? Nothing! He's incapable of doing anything for anybody but himself. Look at poor Dolly! A saint! She raised those kids by herself, you know, and considering what she had to work with, she did a great job. The best thing you can say about them is that not one of them turned out like their father.

"And it's not so much that he gives nothing back to his community. There are a lot of people who don't live up to that responsibility, especially the ones who have the most to give. But what gets me about George is the way he enjoys being a slacker. When I finally got in to see him last Monday about the Heart Fund, he was just revolting! He had dodged me for weeks and so I waited for him at the conclusion of a faculty meeting. I mean, I didn't think he could say no in front of all those people. So here I had him cornered, and he just smiled and said, 'No.' I said, 'What do you mean, no?' And he said, 'No' again and smiled. And I said, 'You mean you won't even be an honorary co-chairman for the Heart Fund?' And he said, 'Got it in one, Ruthie. Don't slam the door on your way out.' Can you imagine the cheek of the man? I was never so embarrassed in my life!"

"Yes, well, that's George. Do you think I felt comfortable having a picture of the *Sterling Center for the Study of International Business* on my wall for two years, only to have it named on a political whim? Oh yes, I felt like a real horse's patoot standing there as the governor came up to have his hand shaken. But, you know, the easiest thing in the world would be to play his game. I could have denounced him and dramatically resigned from the Alumni Association and issued a public call for his resignation. There is certainly no lack of charges I could have made. But like I said, that would be playing by his rules. I didn't do all of this work for the university to come up empty-handed. And there's one more deal in the works that could make it all worthwhile."

"Oh, Lance, you mean that conference center idea of yours?"

"Now Ruth, one can't say for sure, but I think I lined up a few things today, and if George can give the go-ahead, it may be worth all the sucking up to him we have had to endure."

"I don't see how it can ever be worth that! Besides, couldn't the same project be put together with a new president?"

"What are you getting at, Ruth?"

"After the way he spoke to me, I would prefer to get rid of George by any means possible and trust our luck to a new man."

"You may be right, and we may soon know for sure. I intend to feel him out tonight if I get a chance."

SEVEN

THE LAST VEHICLE ON its way to the Gherkin dinner party was a silver compact Cadillac driven by Abigail Armbruster, the mayor of Fergus Falls. Armbruster was the widow of Arnold "Armbuster" Armbruster, probably the most incompetent mayor ever to serve a Minnesota city. As a political wife, she had kept in the background and made a few important friends. When her husband was "called home," she had agreed to serve out the remainder of his term. Given a taste of power, she discovered she liked it. More importantly, she revealed a real talent for government that no one, especially herself, had ever suspected. She studied government and, equally important as far as she was concerned, parliamentary procedure. In her first meeting as mayor, she had asked that a resolution be passed stating that all official meetings would be run strictly by *Robert's Rules of Order*. The rest of the city council had voiced no objection because each had wanted to avoid revealing that the *Rules* had never been used before. She knew the rules, they didn't; and soon she had power to go with her title. She learned on the job, and she learned a lot. After her term as acting mayor was over, she ran for the job on her own and received a larger margin of votes than her husband had ever received.

She had done wonders for the town. At first she sought small industries, but in the past few years small industries had been seeking her. Her conservatively planned industrial park, ridiculed by many as being over-ambitious, was already in need of expansion. Nor had she ignored the social services. The parks were a source of pride for the entire city, and tourists regularly took photographs of themselves next to the concrete otter by Grotto Lake. The transformation of Abigail had been even more noticeable than the transformation of the town. Her Macy's credit card started to wear out as her mousy frocks were replaced by designer suits and she now had her frosted brown hair cut at a salon instead of by her next-door neighbor. She had recently turned sixty, but publicly joked that she didn't look a day over fifty-nine. Wire-rimmed aviator glasses made her brown eyes look bigger, gave her a look of calculation and cunning, and helped to erase the bland expression that she'd habitually worn when her husband was still above ground. She was scrupulously honest but, since gaining office, she had learned to turn her knowledge and experience into personal gain.

One of the most important sources for her civic pride was Fergus Falls State University. She reveled in the football championships, sponsored "Welcome Back Students Day" every September, and did her best to avoid any "town and gown" controversies. But then there was Gherkin! Seeing the potential for the growth of Fergus Falls long before anyone else, Armbruster acquired a strip of commercially zoned land between Interstate 94 and the Fergus

Falls State University golf course. Last month Wal-Mart offered to purchase the land from her if they could also acquire a fifteen-foot strip from the University. Armbruster had assured them that it would be no problem. But there was, and his name was Gherkin. That he had his price was certain. Whether she could pay it, or would pay it, was another matter.

Abigail Armbruster's escort was another of the leading citizens of Fergus Falls. Walter Wahl was a sixty-four-year-old widower who provided her with undemanding companionship. Wahl was not a dynamic person and his own departed wife had once commented that he had "all the animation of damp Post Toasties." Although he wore a pacemaker in his chest, he was in reasonably good health. No one ever accused Wahl of being handsome, for he had a rather prominent, almost bulbous, nose, and a mostly bald head with a gray-haired fringe. His face seemed to hang out of his head like an under-inflated pink balloon, yet—for undefined reasons—he was pleasant looking. As usual, he was impeccably and correctly dressed for the occasion, wearing gray slacks with a blue linen double-breasted blazer and a striped tie. He had made his fortune in the construction business, and was known to all as "Brick."

Brick Wahl had not been eager to accept the invitation to Gherkin's house. Ever since he started his construction business he had been the lowest bidder on every project at Fergus Falls State University. He was willing to take a much lower percentage of profit on any building at "his" university. Even though he himself had never attended the institution, he was one of the university's most active promoters. He prided himself on finding summer jobs for FFSU students, even those lazy, goofing-off athletes that Francis

Olson palmed off on him. Therefore, when bids were invited for the construction of the business center, Brick had assumed that he would once again have a project on campus. His open face, totally incapable of deceit, had registered shock when Gherkin announced that an out-of-town builder was awarded the contract. That was mild, however, compared to the disgust Brick's face had registered when Gherkin publicly admitted that although the contract submitted by Wahl was "slightly less" than the winning proposal, he had decided to award the contract to another builder to "increase diversity on campus and avoid the perception of inbreeding that is so common to small universities." In other words, Gherkin had found a thicker envelope passed under the table. As Brick rode along in silence to Gherkin's cottage, he reflected upon how, in some of the urban areas he had heard about, construction companies or unions knew how to take care of people like Gherkin. There were rumors swirling about that bids would be invited for the construction of a new football stadium to be called the "Mini-Dome." Perhaps he could have a quick word with Gherkin tonight. Perhaps he could make him an offer he couldn't refuse. "Too bad he doesn't have a horse," thought Brick Wahl, smiling in secret pleasure as he pictured himself imitating "the Godfather."

His reverie was ended when Mrs. Armbruster said, "So, have you heard about Gherkin's latest scheme?"

"What do you mean, his latest scheme?"

"I mean, about the new stadium."

"Yes, I had heard something about that. Do you think he's serious?"

The mayor cackled with undisguised glee and said, "You bet your chubby Norwegian hind-end he is. We had a long conversation about it a couple of weeks ago. It is still hush-hush, of course, so don't quote me on anything, but he and Francis Olson were down in the cities a few days ago and charmed the pants off the state board, and I expect it will be announced any day now. It's going to be big, Brick. Real big!"

"Can the university afford such a thing? Can such a thing pay for itself?"

"Of course not. Stadiums like that never can. But paying for themselves is the last thing anyone really expects stadiums to do, especially if it has a dome. I mean, you can't tell the people that. You got to come up with all sorts of rosy projections that totally ignore such things as how you heat and maintain the place and conveniently forget to include the cost of lockers and scoreboards. But that's for the public to discover. Sooner or later the state gets stuck with extra payments and the city will probably have to rescue the project."

"Then I take it you're against it?" asked the conscientious contractor, who took pride in paying his bills on time and operating according to a strict budget.

"Of course not! It's going to be a big thing for this town."

"But you just said it would lose money. I mean, even if it is only the taxpayers' money, I, being a taxpayer, resent such a cavalier attitude. I'm all for it if it can be proved to be financially feasible, but even though I should like to bid on the project, I do not wish to see our university saddled with a white elephant."

"Brick, you've got to see the big picture. It's about more than just putting up a building and paying for it. It's not like the other buildings you've put up on campus."

"No? What's the difference?"

"Look. You build a huge building like that. How many people does it put to work? We're talking builders, electricians, plumbers, architects, landscapers, road builders for the access streets—I mean, the boost to the town from construction alone would be fantastic. Then, once it's built, there would be scores of people hired to clean the floors, provide security, and sell tickets. One of the things I've learned over the past few years is the multiplier effect. When a dollar is spent in the community, it doesn't just sit in someone's till. The construction man buys a sack of potatoes. The grocery man uses that money to buy a pair of socks. The clothing store man uses that money to buy some gas. The filling station operator uses that money to take his wife to the movies. And so you go. All because something was in town to provide the construction man with a little money in his jeans."

"Yes, well," the contractor uncomfortably began, "I admit there might be something in what you say, but once the thing is built, won't it become a sewer that will suck in all the money in the community and make us poorer than we were before?"

"That, of course, is a chance you have to take. I admit that such things have happened in less blessed communities. But the thing is, Brick, sometimes you gotta take a chance. Now think of it. The dome isn't just for football, although that in itself will bring in a lot of money. Picture concerts! All over the western part of the state people will come to town to attend concerts. Rock concerts, country music jamborees, maybe even a religious crusade or two. Now, who benefits from that? Restaurants, motels, gas stations! This means that restaurant owners, motel owners, and gas station owners have more to spend in the grocery store, the clothing store, and the movie house. And that's just the beginning. We can have tractor pulls, the circus, and maybe even get the Minnesota Timberwolves to play an exhibition game or two."

"I don't know, Abigail. It still sounds risky to me."

"That's the trouble with you, Brick. You lack 'the vision thing,' as President Bush the First used to call it."

"Don't mention that name to me. I hold George Bush directly responsible for the dismantling of the 'Reagan Revolution.' If he had only kept true to Mr. Reagan, our nation's problems would have been solved a long time ago."

"You really believe that, don't you! Well, you go right ahead. I suppose there are worse things to believe in. As they say, that was then, this is now. And what we do now is going to hold the key to the future of Fergus Falls. Sure, the mini-dome may fail in the short run, but twenty years from now they're going to praise our vision. See if they don't."

"If I'm around to see anything twenty years from now, I'm going to have to praise someone else," Brick lugubriously replied.

"Lighten up, Brick. They might be praising us sooner than that. What would you say if I told you that a major retail development might spring up along the interstate? The kind of project that just might be looking for a local contractor?"

"I might be interested, as long as it isn't a Wal-Mart or something like that."

"What's wrong with a Wal-Mart?"

"Nothing, if you like all your local businesses being sucked dry. It happens all over, you know."

"'There you go again,' if I may quote your hero. You are such a Gloomy Gus. Remember what I told you about that multiplier effect? Everybody benefits from a growing economy. Anyway, if you go building the mini-dome, I suppose you will be too busy to build a mere shopping center."

"What makes you so sure my company will get the bid for the mini-dome? We've never tackled anything that big before."

"But could you do it?"

"Of course we could do it."

"Then Brick, with your method of bidding, I think it's in the bag."

Brick turned to Abigail and detected a look of conspiracy. "How much does she really know?" he wondered. After a few moments of silence, Brick said, "Abigail, just supposing I did get the contract for the mini-dome. I mean, just supposing. That would be the crowning project of my career and I think I would like to retire afterward. Now, I've been alone since, well, a long time, and, ah, you know, we do get on well together, and maybe we could . . . ."

"Ah. Here's Gherkin's place. We'll talk about things like that some other time. What do you say we put aside business for tonight, shall we, and just enjoy the evening?"

Brick knew that he wouldn't be putting business aside, and the thought occurred to him that if Abigail did, it would be the first time since she became mayor.

EIGHT

DOLLY GHERKIN HELD THE screen door open with her foot as she rolled the drinks cart out onto the patio. The ice in her own tumbler of gin and tonic rattled as she wheeled the cart across the smooth bricks into the shade of the elaborate awning. Her glass was now only one-third full, and the other two-thirds had helped to relax her in the midst of her hostess preparations. Dolly had never acquired the regal aura that seemed to surround the wives of the other university presidents with whom she was often forced to associate at social functions. The students at FFSU had nick-named her "Jolly Dolly," and it was perhaps not inappropriate. Probably the most beloved person to be associated with the university, she volunteered her time to virtually every student fund-raiser and amateur review. At times she had even taken a shift as a nurse, her original calling, in the student health service.

No one, perhaps not even George in his courting days, had ever called her beautiful, but she had the inherent prettiness that comes with a genuine smile. A peek at her driver's license would have revealed that she was sixty-one years old, but on varying days she could pass for anything from forty-five to seventy. Tonight, to be sure, she appeared to be more at the latter end of this range. Her hair was a light brown and she made no attempt to hide the relentless creep of gray. She wore enormous red and gold glasses that made her large face look smaller than it was. It was a kind face, although somewhat in need of a depilatory. She had a plump, rather busty figure that was hidden by the white sari that her eldest son, a missionary and Bible translator, had sent from India.

From the patio she could see the first car coming along the gravel driveway. The sound of *I Pagliacci* could be heard coming from the kitchen speakers, accompanied by the voice of her husband singing along with all of the male parts. George had always done that, but lately, or so it seemed to Dolly, he had gotten worse. She downed the last drop of her gin and tonic, sucked on the lime, and went to greet her first guests.

"Not again," groaned Sherwin Williams as he brought his Volvo to the front of the presidential house. "We're the first ones here. As usual! I don't know why you were in such a rush to go. Maybe I could have finished 'Prairie Roses in Brass Bowl.'"

"What's the difference?" retorted Mae. "I enjoy talking to Dolly. I'm sure George will have locked himself in his kitchen until supper's ready so we don't have to put up with him. Besides, this gives you a shot at more hors d'oeuvres and more free booze. As I recall, you were able to take full advantage of that the last time we were invited out."

"Yeah, well, I'll probably need it. Anyway, it's not supper, it's dinner. Supper was what you had on the farm when the chores were done."

"You don't have to be snotty to me, Sherwin, and remember to be polite to Dolly. She probably doesn't like George any more than you do. Personally, I don't understand how she has put up with him all these years. He's constantly demeaning her appearance, her house cleaning, and her general intelligence. Besides, with the possible exception of his famous chicken Kiev, I wouldn't doubt that she's even a better cook than he is."

Williams carelessly parked the Volvo so that it partially blocked the front sidewalk and looked up at the Gherkin "cottage." Gherkin could not have found a more incongruous architectural style for his house. Set amid the harsh climate of Scandinavian Minnesota was a huge Spanish/Italian pastel-colored villa. The left side of the house, as one looked toward the lake, contained three bedrooms and a large bathroom built over a three-car garage. This wing of the house was always rather conspicuously closed off whenever there was company, and tonight was no exception. The main entry was in the middle of the right wing of the house. A short entryway with coat closets on either side gave way to a narrow hall. To the left was a spacious guest bathroom and to the right was a formal dining room. Passing through the dining room one came to a vast living room with large glass sliding doors that gave a spectacular view of the lake and access to the patio where Dolly had recently parked the drinks cart. Another door, now closed, was directly across the hall from the main entrance.

This door opened to the kitchen. It was Gherkin's pride and joy, and guests were allowed to inspect it only after a meal. Gherkin had thought it arty to hang copper pots from the ceiling and, much to Dolly's surprise, he had actually started using them. There was a small breakfast nook with windows overlooking the patio and providing a panorama of the lake, and there was a door that opened directly onto the patio. The kitchen was equipped far more elaborately than the food service at FFSU. Indeed, there were those who claimed that some of the equipment was originally destined for the food service and had somehow never made it to its government-mandated and budgeted home. It was here that Gherkin produced his masterpieces of epicurean delight, and he always claimed that he was never more at peace than he was amidst his knives, cleavers, and chopping block, practicing his artistry and singing along to his favorite operas. But like a master who preferred to work in secrecy, he would allow no one to observe his creations before their time. Therefore, whenever George was at work, the blinds were drawn and the door was locked. Indeed, the only evidence of his presence before the meal was elegantly presented was an occasional kitchen noise, continual opera music from the kitchen speakers, and George's perpetual sing-along.

Dolly met Sherwin and Mae at the front door and led them through the dining room. The table was already set for dinner for twelve, with modern Danish silver and English Spode china. Reflected in the simple, but expensive, Swedish crystal, like a series of curved translucent mirrors, was a large centerpiece of cut gladioli. Noting with pleasure Mae's appreciation of the table, Dolly took them directly through to the cavernous living room, deftly fielding Sherwin's usual compliments on the beamed ceiling. George's voice soared over—and mistreated—another aria as Dolly ushered her guests through the sliding glass patio doors, quickly closing them again so as "not to let out the air conditioning."

"Not to let out the air conditioning? That makes no sense," thought Sherwin. "I wonder if she has started on the booze without me."

The patio was surrounded by a low ledge covered with geranium pots. In the middle was a cedar picnic table, covered with a red and white tablecloth on which platters of hors d'oeuvres were placed. There were "Little Smokies" sausages neatly wrapped with bread; cut cauliflower and broccoli surrounding a bowl of sour cream dip; a huge wedge of Jarlsberg cheese amid a variety of crackers; a tray of chilled strawberries, fresh pineapple, and grapes; a plate of thinly sliced ham rolled around cream cheese and cut into pinwheels; and an enormous clear glass punch bowl filled with an attractive, creamy-red liquid. At the end of the table were several small glass punch cups, a stack of luncheon plates, and a neatly arranged fan of napkins embossed with the Fergus Falls State University logo.

"Please," Dolly said, "make yourself at home. I think I hear another car coming." If anyone could "flounce" in a sari, it would be Dolly. She proceeded to the living room, closed the door to "keep in the air conditioning," and left Sherwin and Mae to themselves.

"I know you want to dig in, Sherwin, but at least wait until a few more guests arrive," Mae admonished.

"Yes, yes, yes! I promise I won't embarrass you. But nobody is going to notice a missing strawberry," said Sherwin, popping the berry in his mouth and carefully disposing of the green top in a geranium pot. "You know, I don't particularly want to see Gherkin, but I think it's rude of him not to greet his guests. I suppose he thinks it adds to his mystique, but you notice how Dolly has to do all the work. Look how all the kitchen blinds are down, as if someone were really going to peek in and steal his chicken Kiev recipe. Ah, now who do you suppose this is?"

Dolly slid open the patio door and said, "Come on out on the patio, Sally Ann."

Sherwin inwardly groaned. If there was anyone he did not want to spend time with it was Gherkin's number one sycophant, Miss Pennwright. Nevertheless, he put on what he considered to be his ingratiating grin and said, "Well, Sally Ann, isn't this pleasant?"

"Hello, Sherwin. Hello, Mae. Yes, it is lovely this time of year. And Dolly, it looks like George has outdone himself with the appetizers, as usual. You're such a lucky woman to have a man around the house who can cook!"

"More than you'll ever have," thought Sherwin, but aloud he said, "Well, are you all ready for school to start?"

"Actually, no, I never am completely ready, you know, with all the projects I have to catch up on. What about you?"

Sherwin had never been good at recognizing empty social questions, and saw in such a query an opportunity for a little self-promotion. With the not-unreasonable supposition that a sure way to impress Gherkin was to impress Pennwright, he launched into an exaggerated summary of his artistic and pedagogical efforts. Old habits die hard, and even though at the moment he was more willing to impress Gherkin's head with a dent, he could not stop justifying his existence.

Sally Ann's eyes looked beyond him, and at the first possible moment she interrupted and asked, "And Mae, I suppose you will be busy next week at the Registrar's Office?"

Mae assured her that she would and soon retreated to the safe haven of conversations about enrollment trends, the weather, the area crops, and the flowers. Sherwin slyly filched two grapes and thought it could be a long evening.

Dolly, who had been skillfully keeping the conversation going, excused herself once again to receive more guests. In the ensuing silence, the muffled bellowing of George Gherkin could be heard from the kitchen. In a short time Dolly reappeared, leading Lance and Ruth Sterling to the patio. Ruth and Mae had not previously met, and Dolly introduced them in a manner designed to put them at their ease. Mae mentioned that she had heard that the Sterlings had recently returned from a trip to Scotland, and this gambit was all Ruth needed to launch into an effervescent commentary on the Highlands.

Lance and Sherwin, thrown together by their gender, uncomfortably tried to find common ground.

"How 'bout those Twins, huh?" tried Lance.

"Yeah, they're doing great, huh?"

"Great!" Lance exploded. "You call a five-game losing streak great? It's the pitching. It always comes down to the pitching! Lately, if the starters do well they don't get relief, and if the relief saves one game the starter the next game is lousy! I mean, where's the consistency? They gotta bring up someone from the minors before it's too late. If they let the White Sox get too far ahead, they can just as well start thinking of next year. What they really oughta do is . . ."

Sherwin let him ramble on, nodding at what he hoped were the appropriate places. He was not a baseball fan. Like all Minnesotans, he had heard names like Harmon Killebrew and Kirby Puckett, but he was relatively sure that they didn't play anymore. In fact, he wasn't even sure of the difference between the infield and the outfield. Indeed, it did look like a long evening.

His mood brightened when Dolly ushered to the patio two more guests. He had never had any meaningful conversation with Francis Olson, but Harold Winston was another matter. He had learned more art history in casual conversation with Winston than he ever had from his graduate school art history courses. Besides, he was a logical candidate to start in on the food. After the required pleasantries, this is precisely what he did. Sherwin grabbed a plate and followed him, thus constituting a line that encouraged the others.

Dolly, meanwhile, indicated a large Styrofoam cooler filled with imported beer. Winston immediately grabbed a Beck's and Sherwin helped himself to a St. Pauli Girl. Francis Olson rummaged through the selection and asked Dolly, "Got any Budweiser?"

Dolly voiced her regret and suggested that Olson might try a Dutch Amstel, to which he condescendingly agreed. The rest of the guests gathered around the drinks cart and proceeded to accept Dolly's potent gin and tonics, or refilled their cups with punch, which, they had been delighted to discover, was liberally spiked with tequila. The initial reserve began to melt away and, partly due to the absence of George, the assembly began to enjoy themselves.

At this point, eager to make room for the guests yet to come, Dolly suggested that perhaps some of the guests might like to take their food and drinks down to the lake. The lakeshore was only about a hundred feet from the patio. A large dock extended about twenty feet over the water and then made a right angle to protect a metallic gold and white Glastron speedboat, one of George's favorite toys. The elaborate dock, covered with blue outdoor carpeting, was always put in the lake around the first of May by FFSU football players who were paid out of "work-study" funds. At the end of the dock sat a round white plastic table and four matching chairs. An aluminum pole through the center of the table supported a yellow and blue sun umbrella. The late afternoon sun glared off the water, producing the type of scene one sees on "Explore Minnesota" travel posters, with several sailboats and a few water-skiers.

Lance Sterling, with his gin and tonic, and Francis Olson, with his beer, needed no further hint. As fishermen, they felt a need to satisfy themselves as to the dock's construction, the speedboat's accessories, and the horsepower of the motor. "All they need is one more good left-handed hitter," said Sterling, as they moseyed down to the dock. "Like I was telling that artist guy, Sherman Whatzhizname, it all comes down to hitting. I think the Twins pitchers can hold their own." A short time later Ruth Sterling and Sally Ann Pennwright joined them and the foursome entered into a remarkably unrelated pair of conversations.

The patio was therefore less crowded when Isabel Corazon entered, saying, "I heard voices out here so I just followed my ears. Oh, Dolly, you have set such a beautiful table! I heard George singing along to his opera as I came through the house. I rapped on the kitchen door, but I suppose he didn't hear me. Ah, that punch looks good."

Dolly, who had been trying to interrupt to voice her apologies for not greeting her at the door, was finally able to do so as Isabel took a deep gulp from her punch glass. "I guess with the noise of the conversation and with George's singing I just didn't hear the bell. I'm so glad you felt at home enough to come on through. Help yourself to hors d'oeuvres. I think I hear someone else at the door."

Isabel loaded up her plate with vegetables and dip, topped off her punch glass, and was soon engaged in conversation with Harold Winston about her new pet project, a humanities forum. In a moment Dolly returned with Abigail Armbruster and Brick Wahl. Introductions were made where appropriate and the newcomers were provided with their preferred libations.

Dolly flitted among the guests, playing the perfect hostess. Winston was supplied with another Beck's and Williams hurriedly downed the last of his beer to try a bottle of English ale. When Dolly suggested that some of her guests might want to sit in the air-conditioned living room, Winston, who never cared for the great outdoors or standing up while drinking beer, readily agreed and Corazon and Williams joined him. Dolly, meanwhile, catered to the needs of the contented people on the dock.

Over the course of the next half hour, guests would change places from the living room to the patio to the dock, stopping by the drinks table for "a little more ice" and by the picnic table for "just one more of those." Even Harold Winston found his way down to the dock, and amused himself throwing bits of crackers into the water to see if a fish would find them. Most often they did.

Brick, Sally Ann, and Mae were in the living room when the tape of *I Pagliacci* finally ended, with George's voice accompanying it to the very end. Dolly, who had just come in, sighed with relief and said, "Let's just put on something that George can't sing along with, shall we?" She proceeded to the stereo system with the double tape deck and fiddled with the tapes and dials. "MPR has such lovely classical music on Friday nights. Why don't I just leave the radio on?" Playing the attentive host, she also switched the system from the remote kitchen speakers to the main living room speakers. "That ought to shut George up!" she added with a guilty giggle. The sounds of an Erik Satie etude filled the room. As Dolly rushed out to attend to her other guests, Brick muttered a hope shared by many when he said, "I hope it won't be too long before we can sit down to that chicken Kiev I've heard so much about."

NINE

HAROLD WINSTON THOUGHT THAT the evening was already a success. He had left an empty bottle of Beck's on the patio, on the dock, on the patio again, and soon would discreetly leave one on the low table in front of the couch. It was pleasant down by the lake, and he intended to return there after his necessary trip to the bathroom, but it had suddenly looked like a long trip, and when Isabel Corazon cornered him and grilled him as to his views on trade policies and international affairs, he sank his enormous posterior into the nearest couch. It proved hard to get up again.

It wasn't that he was hungry; his prodigious consumption of snacks had taken the edge off his appetite. Nevertheless, he had been looking forward to the chicken Kiev, and it seemed to him that it was already well past mealtime. He had paused on his way back from the bathroom and considered knocking on the kitchen door to find out how George was doing, but that was just not done. Funny, though, how he had not even heard a sound from George since the opera ended. He leaned forward and borrowed a cracker from Isabel's plate.

As the senior faculty member present, Winston was holding court. "The thing is, you see, Reaganomics was never about economic policy at all. It was only political. No economic policy would ever be constructed to transform us from the largest creditor nation to the largest debtor nation in the world in a few short years. We recovered a bit during the nineties, but now it's gotten much worse. We'll be paying for that the rest of our lives, of course, but the impact will also be felt in our foreign policy."

Brick Wahl stiffened. He felt deep in his heart that Reagan had saved the nation, in spite of statistics dished out by smarty-pants academics. On the other hand, he knew better than to get into an argument with an erudite professor. He could take comfort in his own bankbook. If things were so bad, why did his net worth grow so spectacularly during those years? He had contracted for projects all over the state. He had put up most of the recent buildings on the FFSU campus, and even if things had fallen off lately, mainly due to that double-crossing Gherkin, he would rebound very nicely, thank you. What did Winston know about meeting a payroll? At least Gherkin, to give him his due, knew how business operated. Apparently Wahl had just been outbid on his under-the-table kickback to Gherkin. Wahl wouldn't make that same mistake twice. Nor would Gherkin!

Isabel was working hard. She nodded with complete understanding at everything Winston said, just as she had bit her tongue and sided with Francis Olson on his complaints about NCAA regulations and had shown support for Sherwin Williams when he railed about the lack of federal support for the arts and his meaningless comparisons about Dutch funding for the arts compared with the U.S. policy. She had thus touched bases with the social sciences division, the humanities division, and the athletic department. She would present such a united front of the faculty behind her reorganization and building plans that, when a new president would be inaugurated for FFSU, she could implement them immediately. She would have to try to position herself near Lance Sterling during the meal. It wouldn't hurt to have alumni backing as well.

Out on the patio the drinks cart rattled from time to time and the punch was getting low. Dolly nervously kept looking at her watch, wondering aloud when George would be ready. Abigail Armbruster, adopting what she thought would be an interesting and germane topic for academics, had launched into a presentation about how the Fergus Falls city library and the FFSU library were being connected by computers that she had acquired through persistent begging from Dell. Sherwin Williams, who had been ensnared in the conversation while on a mission to unobtrusively pilfer just one more bottle of expensive beer, hypocritically voiced his profound appreciation. He had planned to go back to the dock, or at least make one more trip to the bathroom, but now he became resigned to waiting until dinner was called. "What's keeping 'the Great One' anyway?" he wondered. The same thought occurred to Sally Ann Pennwright, who was used to these dinners and could predict with uncanny accuracy the moment when George would emerge with his supercilious smirk and announce, with fake modesty, that dinner was served. He was long overdue.

Down on the dock, the temperature had dropped. A high semi-circle of clouds hid the late afternoon sun. The wind had disappeared and the lake was almost completely calm, with only the barest ripple lapping against the shore. It was unusually silent—the only sound came from the other side of the lake as a speedboat pulled a foul-mouthed teenager on water skis. Francis Olson, Mae Williams, and Lance and Ruth Sterling had also grown silent. Simply put, Mae and Ruth had run out of things to say to each other, the forecast and the chances of severe thunderstorms having long since been debated. Olson had long ago despaired of Sterling's genuine lack of real knowledge about any sport but bowling, and was brooding over his lost chance for big-time coaching. Sterling himself had finally wound down on his favorite subject about what the Vikings needed to do to get to the Super Bowl and was in the midst of a brown study about the market for lakeshore property in light of the Minnesota tax policy on lake homes.

At last Sterling opened his mouth, drew in air, and expelled it in a wheezy "Nooooooo. I don't know about the rest of you, but I'm getting a little hungry. What do you suppose George is doing in there?"

As if conditioned by a prior rehearsal, all eyes turned toward the house. Olson finally observed, "He must be cooking in the dark. The lights are already on in the rest of the house, but he hasn't even bothered to turn on the lights in the kitchen."

"Maybe it just means he is ready to serve," offered the ever optimistic Mae. "Let's go on up."

The four guests unhurriedly gathered up their plates and napkins and walked up to the house. Sherwin and Sally Ann were grateful for the interruption. Sherwin went to greet his wife while Sally Ann exchanged views with the Sterlings as to the probability of a thunderstorm. Olson walked directly to the patio door and innocently announced, "I think I'll take a, er, go to the bathroom before supper." The rest of the guests followed him into the house in a parade that made Olson wonder if they were going to follow him to the bathroom as well.

There were now more people than could be comfortably seated in the living room. Sherwin plopped himself down on the sofa next to Winston while Mae lounged on the arm. The entry of the rest of the group had put an end to Winston's dire proclamations on the decline of the West, only partly plagiarized from Spengler. The resulting silence coincided with the end of the classical music program on Minnesota Public Radio and the announcement of the upcoming Minnesota Orchestra Friday evening concert. Winston tugged at his beard, now encrusted with the debris from countless hors d'oeuvres, and wistfully willed the gathering to be silent so he could hear the music. Curiously, they were. And in the ensuing calm, ten people stared at the floor or glanced uncomfortably at Dolly.

The air conditioner continued to distribute cold air into the room, but something else was present. It was a coldness of apprehension and unease. The forbidding dark clouds produced an unnaturally early night and, in the distance, flickering lightning lit up the western sky.

Dolly had been uneasy for some time, casting expectant looks at the kitchen door and anxious glances at her guests. "I can't imagine what is taking George so long. He's never made anyone wait this long before. I wonder if there is something wrong. I know how he hates to be bothered, but I'll just see if he can tell us how much longer it will be." The Minnesota Orchestra began to play "Pictures at an Exhibition"—a Sherwin Williams favorite.

With that, Dolly went to the dining room and timidly knocked at the kitchen door. "George? How are you doing, George? Do you need any help in there? George?" Dolly rapped louder, a look of concern gathering on her face. "George? Let me in, George!" She put her ear to the door. "George? Are you all right?"

Abigail Armbruster and Brick Wahl had tentatively followed Dolly into the dining room. They gathered around Brick as he hammered on the door with his fist and bellowed, "George! Open up in there!" His pounding resounded through the house and when he stopped, the silence was oppressive.

Abigail, trying to stifle a feeling of panic, turned to Dolly and said, "Do you have another key to the kitchen?"

Dolly suddenly looked pale. "Do you have another key to the kitchen?" Abigail repeated.

"Oh. Oh, yes. I have a key to the kitchen patio door. On my key-ring. Where did I . . . oh yes . . . here." Dolly went to the hall closet and from a hook on the back of the door removed a key-ring that featured car keys, house keys, and a chartreuse plastic trout that became a flashlight when its belly was squeezed. She fumbled for the keys and went back out through the patio, most of her guests trailing along. Harold Winston even considered getting up from the sofa. Nervously, Dolly inserted keys until she found the right one and unlocked the door. "It won't open," said the exasperated Dolly. "He must have the bolt turned. George! George! Let us in!"

"Let's break it down!" yelled Francis Olson.

Dolly and the rest of the guests just looked at him. People didn't really do that kind of thing, or even suggest it. Nevertheless, once he had made the suggestion, everyone looked to Olson to do something. Realizing the ball was now in his court, Olson half-heartedly threw his body against the door. This activity produced nothing but a sore shoulder and the perception that he was not only a man of action but also a man of ineptitude.

"For heaven's sake," interrupted the ever practical Mae. "Can't you just open a window?"

"I'm afraid not," said Dolly, growing increasingly more nervous. "George feels strongly about air conditioning and insulation. He has the kitchen windows shut tightly during the summer so as not to let the air conditioning out."

"Then break the kitchen window," suggested Sally Ann Pennwright, a note of hysteria creeping into her voice. Lance Sterling ran over to the drinks cart and proceeded to wrap a small towel around his fist. He was about to smash the window when Winston, who had finally heaved his body into an upright position and followed the action to the patio, grabbed his hand.

"For God's sake, get hold of yourself! Don't go breaking windows and shattering glass all over the place. If you insist on breaking in on George's privacy, let's just force the interior door. It's far easier and will cause much less damage."

Winston's voice of reason prevailed and the whole party followed him into the dining room and waited expectantly before the kitchen door. He nodded at the football coach and said, "Well, Olson. Don't just stand there. Do your thing."

Remembering his pathetic attempt at the other door, and noticing that all eyes were on him, Olson launched his muscular frame against the door. It gave so easily that he lost his balance and plunged face forward onto the kitchen floor. He put out his hand to brace his fall and it slid out from under him. He cursed under his breath as he quickly got up to notice that everyone was stupidly looking beyond his shoulder.

Winston clumsily fumbled along the right side of the kitchen wall and found the light switch. The kitchen was bathed in a glaring light and revealed George Gherkin slumped over the kitchen counter. To his left, the ingredients for pureed potatoes with truffles were neatly arranged. To his right was a large bowl of butter lettuce and arugula, a pile of alfalfa sprouts, a stack of thinly sliced onions, pine nuts, and a row of artichoke hearts, removed from a jar of oil and already starting to dry out. In the center, like a garish *pièce de résistance*, was the head of George Gherkin. A needlessly large meat cleaver had parted his scalp and remained embedded in his skull. Blood dripped neatly into a Corning Ware dish.

Dolly Gherkin emitted a low, inhuman moan and Sally Ann Pennwright deftly embraced her and led her back to the dining room. Olson moved robotically back to the kitchen door and with his dry hand tried to shoo away the guests and close the door. His voice cracked as he said, "Call 911. Get a doctor. And call Palmer Knutson."

TEN

It was not the usual habit of Sheriff Palmer Knutson to be in his office on a Friday night. After his leisurely lunch with Ellie, he had chewed three Rolaids and spent the rest of the afternoon finishing up some paperwork. He left at four o'clock to go home and sit in his screened porch and do the Minneapolis *Star Tribune* crossword puzzle, all the while nursing a small but, to his mind, well-deserved gin and tonic. All in all, a nice ending to a pleasant day.

Ellie, giving due consideration to her husband's noon-time gluttony, brought out a nice taco salad for supper. Trygve was at a friend's house, and Palmer, figuring that he had done his share of intimate conversing with the wife for one day, leaned over to the portable black-and-white television that he kept on the porch, mainly for baseball games. The evening news featured a weather bulletin warning that most of western Minnesota was under a tornado watch. Palmer leaned back and spoke to the weatherman.

"Oh, groan, groan, and more groan. I don't want to go back to the office tonight."

"Why should you?" said Ellie, interrupting the one-way conversation. "Do you think you can protect the residents of Otter Tail County from a tornado?"

"No, but every time there is something like this, everybody calls the Sheriff's Office. If they sight anything that remotely looks like a funnel cloud, they call us. I don't know why. One time somebody called and reported a funnel cloud just above their neighbor's house and then, just as we were going to issue an alarm, she called back and said that it was a mistake; that one of the hooks on the drapes had come loose and what she really saw was just a piece of cloth hanging down where it shouldn't be."

"So, you think you have to be there for that?"

"Well, no, but if a tornado really did strike it would be nice if the people could rely on their sheriff, don't you think?"

"I suppose so," Ellie conceded, and then, as she gathered up the dishes, leaned over and kissed him on the top of his head. "You really are a good sheriff, you know."

By a quarter to seven, as Knutson drove up to the Law Enforcement Center, there were reports of severe weather in eastern North Dakota. Alone in his office, he sat back in his swivel leather chair, propping his feet on his desk while carelessly reading through the reports of his warrant officers. This held little interest for him, and besides, his mind was really more on the Minnesota Twins. He leaned forward to fiddle with the dials of his desktop radio. As usual, it was tuned to Minnesota Public Radio, and although some pleasant and familiar theme from Erik Satie was being played, Palmer was in the mood for baseball. It was a crucial series with the Detroit Tigers, and the Twins were already down by two runs. Unfortunately, the game was broadcast on an AM station, and static from the approaching storm was already starting to interfere with the broadcast.

Palmer Knutson had made the sheriff's office into his own realm. His new black steel desk with the wood-grained formica top was generally kept clean except for a brass name plate, a gift pen set, and a telephone. A half swivel of the chair away was the real work station with an iMac computer that Palmer was doing his best to understand, but which he secretly hated. To the left of his desk was the United States flag, and to the right was the flag of the state of Minnesota. On the wall behind the desk, between the two large windows, were two maps: one of Minnesota, and the other a detailed map of Otter Tail County. On the right wall was a large wolf skin, complete with the head, backed with a dark green felt, and on the other side there hung a framed map of Norway. On either side of the office door were antique oak credenzas covered with white Hardanger lace, evidence of the handiwork talent of his late Norwegian mother and a sort of memorial to her. It was an impressive office, for Palmer was never blind to the political realities of serving as an elective county official.

Palmer had not looked like a sheriff when he was first elected. Some thought his reddish-blonde hair was too long and that his mustache "made him look like a hippie." But that was a long time ago, and now everybody in Otter Tail County thought he looked like a sheriff, even though he had never completely outgrown the freckles that could still be found on either side of his thin nose. The mustache had disappeared when it started to turn gray. His hairline had receded a bit but, with judicious combing, no one really noticed—or so he thought.

He had grown up in rural Otter Tail County, near Underwood, in a home where hard work and Christian love were both taught in abundance. His grandparents on both sides of the family had emigrated from Norway in the 1890s and by the time Palmer and his siblings were born, the line between what was Norwegian and what was American had become blurred. His parents had always spoken Norwegian to each other in the home, especially when they did not want the children to know what they were talking about—as Palmer put it, "they always spoke Norwegian at Christmas time!"—but they spoke English to the children. Still, Palmer had picked up a lot of Norsk, and only when he went into the army was he aware of the fact that not all of his words were English. English or Norwegian, however, all words were rendered in the musical rhythm of the Norwegian accent.

There was never enough money for Palmer to go to college when he graduated from Underwood High School. There was a tradition of respect for higher education in his family, however, since his oldest brother Rolf had graduated from Concordia College in Moorhead. Rolf had attended college on borrowed money and scholarships, had gone straight into the seminary, and was now pastor of the First Norwegian Lutheran Church of Fergus Falls. Although Palmer had been a rather good student in high school, he had never considered college because that was for ministers and he had just never "gotten the call." Instead, he felt a call to get away from home, and right after graduation he had enlisted in the army to become a paratrooper. After basic training at Fort Leonard Wood, he completed his required number of jumps before "fear and common sense" prevailed and he was able to transfer into the military police. It was in this capacity that he had served in Germany, enjoying a chance to travel and experience a foreign culture. He completed his hitch and got out just in time to avoid the Vietnam quagmire. With GI benefits and nothing else to do, he decided to go back home and enroll in Fergus Falls State College.

The next four years were turbulent ones for America, but they were good ones for Palmer Knutson. In college he had majored in political science and minored in sociology, an academic path that was as close as one came to a "criminal justice" program in those days. Because of his background in the military, he was able to land a weekend and summer job with the Fergus Falls Police Department which, together with his GI benefits, enabled him to pay his tuition and live in relative comfort. Fergus Falls State College had not been immune to campus disturbances during the 1960s, and Palmer was frequently called upon to keep order between protesters and the administration. Like many college students he had eventually taken an anti-war position, yet, because he was a veteran and because of his excellent record with the police department, he was trusted to do his job. The result was that whenever disorder threatened, he was called upon as a mediator as much as a law enforcer. His fellow students trusted him and although there were some grumblings from some of his police colleagues, his police chief realized his value and supported him. The college students saw him as the best kind of anti-military vet, the faculty praised him for his grades, and the townsfolk thought he was the only thing that stood between them and having another Berkeley on their hands. The football coach, who had a high regard for the way the military built men, even wanted him to come out for the team. He hadn't, although every fall he still daydreamed about what might have been, and saw himself cradling a pass in the Flying Falcons' end zone.

Upon graduation, old Sheriff Fjelde offered him a job as deputy and with his marriage to Ellie and little Maj on the way, it seemed like a logical choice. The voters of Fergus Falls had come to view him as a certain successor to the post. On Fjelde's retirement, the rest of the county seemed to agree and he was elected by a comfortable margin. He liked his job, and, if pressed, even he would have to admit that he was good at it.

Palmer wore his full uniform only on special occasions, and his "Smoky Bear" hat only for funerals. He also had an aversion to wearing a gun. He kept a .38 revolver in a locked desk drawer, but hadn't fired it in over three years, the last time he had gone down to the pistol range with a new recruit. He knew he was supposed to practice more often, but he had never pointed a gun at anyone, even in the army, and he didn't intend to start. Besides, he hated the thick belt with its loop for handcuffs and the big clip for the portable radio. He thought it made him look fat. Tonight he was wearing his tan uniform trousers and a navy blue golf shirt, but he always kept, in the outer office, a brown nylon jacket with the Otter Tail County sheriff's badge printed on the back just in case he had to look more official.

He had been slimmer, he had to admit, as he ruefully observed how the golf shirt really didn't flatter his figure. As he started to contemplate doing sit-ups "some day," his mind wandered to the game on the radio. Two on, one out, and the clean-up hitter coming up to bat. He was so engrossed he didn't hear Orly Peterson come into the reception area.

Orly was one of twenty-six deputies employed by Otter Tail County. Although the permanent population of the county might not have warranted such a large force, thousands of people owned lake homes in the county and summer always brought problems that usually ranged from beer-soaked college students to a fish-hook in a child's ear. Orly had recently been promoted to detective and in an eager-beaver manner that made Palmer tired, he kept poking through old files to find something to detect. Orly had graduated with the new criminal justice major from Fergus Falls State University and, although Knutson took an instant disliking to him, he recognized that he was clearly the best candidate for the job. Over the last few months he had learned to tolerate him and was even, against his better instincts, starting to like him.

Orly knocked on the door and, in the manner that always irritated Palmer, pushed it open at the same time. "Hey, I noticed your light on. What are you doing here this time of night, Palmer?" Before he had been promoted to detective, it had always been "Sheriff Knutson." Palmer had noticed the abrupt change, but had decided he liked it.

"Well, you know, there's that tornado watch out and since it's a home game and the Twins aren't on TV anyhow I figured I might just as well come in and see if the grateful citizens need me. What're you doing?"

"Been out in the lake country. Shortly after you left this afternoon a call came in from North Turtle Lake. Seems some guy ran his new boat into a fishing pontoon. You shoulda seen it. A Larson All American 170 with a 4.3-liter V-6 engine. He just about cut the pontoon in two. He was drunk as a lord, of course. I took him in and hooked him up to the Breathalyzer 5000 and with the reading I got off that thing I could have arrested him six times over!"

Palmer nodded grimly. The passion that Orly had for boats was exceeded only by his passion for the Breathalyzer 5000. Orly had asked why it was called "the 5000" and, for want of any knowledge whatsoever, Palmer had told him that it was because it cost five thousand dollars. Orly accepted this and now treated the device, which measured the percentage of alcohol in one's system, with the same awe and reverence that he paid to his computer.

Orly always looked like he had just stepped from the pages of a uniform catalog. His spotless, pressed tan uniform featured dark-brown epaulets and brown pocket flaps with his deputy badge carefully centered on his left pocket. The points of his collar, adorned with gold-plated O.T.C.S.D. initials, neatly framed a perfectly knotted brown tie kept in place by a five-pointed star tie clasp. He worked out regularly and this gave his six-foot frame an athletic appearance. He had closely cropped brown hair, and brown eyes that were hidden at every opportunity by his treasured official Los Angeles Police Department sunglasses. He also wore his gun, a nine-millimeter 92F Beretta, on every occasion except water-skiing. Most deputies, when they reached the detective level, preferred to be plainclothesmen, but Palmer allowed him to continue to wear his uniform, even though he suspected that Orly did so mainly because he thought it appealed to women.

"So what did you do with him?" asked Palmer.

"I put him in de-tox and am charging him with operating a boat while intoxicated and with reckless endangerment. He's a former General Mills executive from Minneapolis and has never been in trouble before. He told me a dozen times how much he regrets his actions, although I suspect he regrets the fact that his boat is at the bottom of the lake even more. I'll give him a couple of hours to think about it and take him home."

"Other than that it's been quiet?"

"Yup," acknowledged Orly, "been real quiet."

In rapid succession three noises broke the silence. The first was a low rumble of thunder announcing the approaching storm. The second was the sound of the Westminster chimes from the clock in the outer office announcing that it was now eight o'clock. The third was the strident ringing of the telephone. Palmer answered it himself.

"Yah, Otter Tail County Sheriff's Office. This is Palmer Knutson. What can I do for you?"

Palmer had been listening to Orly with only one ear and a grin had started across his face as he heard the Twins tie the game. The grin rapidly disappeared.

"What? . . . Is he dead? . . . You sure? . . . Who is this? . . . When? . . . Uh-huh . . . Have you called a doctor? At his place on the lake, right? Yah. . . . Okay, we'll be right out. Keep the kitchen door closed. Don't touch anything and don't let anybody leave. . . . How's Dolly? . . . Make sure someone stays with her. What? . . . I don't care. I'm sure you could use a good belt. . . . Yah. Ten minutes tops. See ya."

Palmer turned to Orly, "Well, detective, this is what you've been waiting for. A chance to detect. George Gherkin has just been murdered."

Orly gaped at the sheriff. "Gherkin? President Gherkin? Are you sure?"

"Well, it's not the sort of thing people usually joke about, is it? Let's go!"

Knutson went directly to the outer office and took his jacket from its perpetual roost on the antique hat rack. As he pulled the door shut to lock behind him Orly asked, "Aren't you going to take your gun? This is a murder case."

"I doubt if anybody is lurking to gun down the sheriff. Besides, I see you have yours. You can do all the shooting. Let's take the Chevy."

———

Orly slid easily behind the wheel of the large white Chevrolet Impala with the emblem of the Otter Tail County Sheriff's Department painted on the door. In the darkened sky, brownish-gray mammary clouds heralded the coming of severe weather to the west, now lit up by almost constant lightning, and one could make out the low advance of the squall line. As they turned onto highway 210, Orly reached down to activate the siren.

"Don't do that!" admonished Knutson. "You'll scare half the people in the county into believing that a tornado is coming. From what I heard I don't think any amount of speed is going to help George Gherkin."

Nevertheless, the excitement and dread of seeing his first murder victim made it impossible for Orly to drive normally, and the large car tilted sideways as he turned off the highway onto the gravel road leading to Wall Lake. As Knutson pitched uncomfortably toward the center of the car, he muttered a condescending, "Easy, son."

It was still dead calm as they drove by the shore of the lake, the kind of foreboding silence that always comes before a major storm. As Knutson looked to the sky at times like these he always thought of the stories his grandfather had told him about the great Fergus Falls tornado in 1919 that took several lives and almost destroyed the town. If it happened once, it could always happen again and he wished he didn't have to be away from Ellie on nights like this.

———

Francis Olson, who had scrubbed his hands three times since his unfortunate discovery, met them at the door. "God, it's awful! You should see him in there, it's awful!"

"Calm down and get back in the house," Knutson admonished. "I want everybody to stay put for a while. Besides, with this storm coming I don't want anybody out on the road."

At this point Lance Sterling, with somewhat inappropriate concern, interrupted and said, "It looks like hail. Could I just run my car in under that elm tree?"

Knutson opened his mouth to tell Sterling to get back in the house but with one more quick look at the sky just shrugged and said, "Oh, I suppose, but do it quickly."

Olson led the sheriff and his deputy through the dining room into the living room, nervously passing by the kitchen door. The entire dinner party was there, with Sally Ann Pennwright patting Dolly's hand as they sat on the sofa. They all looked up at him with a mixture of relief, curiosity, and dread. In a way it was a relief to have the sheriff to take control of things, but at the same time, his presence somehow confirmed the reality of the murder.

In a voice into which Knutson unconsciously put all of his authority, he asked, "Are you all here? Is there anyone who was here this evening who is not in this room?"

Harold Winston was about to note that Sterling was not there when he came bursting through the door at the same time as the first of many loud thunder claps shook the house. Large drops of rain had created a piebald pattern on his expensive jacket. With a barely perceptible nod of his head Knutson commanded him to take a seat. From the potpourri of glassy eyes that looked up at the sheriff, it was apparent that more than one of the assembled party had taken the opportunity to calm their nerves by taking their turn at the drinks cart, which had now been brought inside.

"Let me start out by saying how sorry I am about your loss, Dolly, and I can promise you that we will do everything we can to make this procedure as unobtrusive as we possibly can. We all share your loss. Now, I understand that a doctor has been called?" Responding to the several nods, Knutson said, "Good. Now before he gets here . . ." At this point thunder shook the house, drowning out his words, and a sixty-mile-per-hour wind began to tear branches off the trees. "Before he gets here," he tried again, "Orly and I are going to examine the bod—er, the kitchen. It's not going to take us long, and when we're done we'd like a short statement from each of you. I think I can promise that you can all go home when the storm lets up. And maybe you ought to turn on the TV just in case there are any tornado warnings. Anyway, it might help take your minds off things."

Sherwin Williams got up and slid back the panel in the entertainment center to reveal a large and very expensive flat screen TV. Unfortunately, the program that came on was a flippant murder mystery. He quickly turned it to a situation comedy which he had always held up as "the dopiest show in the history of television." Everyone thought it was a fine choice.

Knutson and Peterson slowly pushed open the kitchen door. As they did so the electricity went out for a few seconds and the flashing lightning lit up the kitchen like a strobe light, revealing a hideous black-and-white portrait of murder. Orly thought it was the most unnerving few seconds of his life. The sudden return of the bright kitchen lights, however, brought no relief from the horror. Knutson walked over to the corpse and, without touching anything, examined the wound. "I think," he said blandly, "we can rule out suicide."

There would be nothing for them to do here for a while. The sheriff had long ago learned to appreciate an effective scene-of-the-crime team that could dust for fingerprints, take photographs, and collect other physical evidence. He would call the state Bureau of Criminal Apprehension in St. Paul and let them handle it. As he looked at the surprised, yet somehow serene, expression on the late educator's face, he noticed that standing straight in front of him, like a pale cheap tombstone, was a clear plastic recipe card-holder bearing the recipe for the now quite unservable chicken Kiev.

ELEVEN

IT WAS THE MORNING after the murder. Gray, low clouds moved rapidly across the sky, pushed by a cold northwest wind. It was the kind of Saturday despised in the lake country. Cottage owners had come up from the Twin Cities or down from Fargo-Moorhead with thoughts of one last summer weekend of water-skiing, only to be reduced to puttering around their tiny estates in jackets and sweatshirts. On the southern end of Wall Lake, Larry Anderson, the operator of Larry's Convenience Store, knew that it would be a bad weekend for bait and beer sales, but hoped that he might be able to rent some of the thirty-four titles from his ever-expanding video library. The scene around the Gherkin lake home was particularly depressing. Large tree branches, broken off by the previous night's storm, covered the lawn. The wind whipped the lake and produced frothy whitecaps that splashed on the underside of the dock and rocked Gherkin's boat with a violent rhythm. Palmer Knutson had started to drive his personal car more frequently since acquiring the black Acura Integra. He had longed for a Saab

Turbo for several years, but always felt that it would not be politically correct for an elected official to drive a foreign car. The last two elections had removed any real concerns about his re-electability, however, and when his cousin, the suburban car dealer, had called with an offer on a slightly used Integra, well, he just couldn't refuse. He loved the way it handled and he loved the sound system. He had an eclectic, some would say weird, collection of CDs in his glove compartment, but most of the time kept his radio on one of three stations, the ubiquitous Minnesota Public Radio, the classic rock station, or the country music station that broadcast the Twins and the Vikings. He had equipped his personal car, at his own expense, with a police radio and a cellular telephone. Therefore, although he could always be in immediate contact with his office, he could also create a pleasant isolation, driving through the Minnesota countryside with his windows rolled up, the air conditioning on, and The Who playing at a volume to shake the windows. As he pulled up before the Gherkin residence and parked his car next to the nondescript van of the Minnesota Bureau of Criminal Apprehension, he popped out the old "Who By Numbers" CD and tried to look "sheriffy" again.

It had been a trying morning. News of the murder had leaked out very rapidly, and a high-profile victim like Gherkin excited news bureaus throughout the state. There had been the necessary news conference, with cameras and reporters from the Fargo-Moorhead stations and all of the Twin Cities stations. Meat cleaver murders do not occur with regularity, and there was speculation that the story of the murder would be picked up by the networks, since Saturday was always a slow day for national news. Under the glare of the television lights, Knutson had tried his best to look in control of the situation, assuring the public that there was no reason to believe a Jack-the-butcher killer was stalking the citizens of Otter Tail County.

While last night had been real bad for George Gherkin, it had not been real good for anyone. Knutson and Peterson had kept Dolly and her guests huddled together in the living room to wait out the storm and for thirty-five minutes everyone stared uncomfortably at the television or looked out of the window at the storm. Gradually the perception dawned that it was almost certain that someone in the room was a murderer. Conversation had been short and strained. Knutson assured them that they would all be allowed to go home as soon as the storm subsided. At last, as the wind abated and the rain tapered off to a gentle shower, Lance Sterling, who had been congratulating himself on the wisdom of parking his car under the large tree, thought he and Ruth could reach it without getting too wet. As he was about to make his request to leave, the ambulance arrived and Knutson told him to get his car out of the way and go home. Sterling and his wife ran out to the car. Ruth had the good sense to wait in dry comfort, but Lance took the time to stand in the rain in front of his Sterling screaming obscenities at the heavy dead tree branch that had made a large dent in his hood. This undignified performance had, however, started a near stampede for the door as the sheriff warned them once again not to leave the area.

Sally Ann Pennwright had remained near Mrs. Gherkin ever since the discovery of the murder and insisted that Dolly should pack a small bag and stay at her home. After a minimum of resistance and with the encouragement of the sheriff, she had agreed to leave her late husband in the hands of the authorities.

With the house cleared, Knutson had ordered Peterson to take several photographs of the scene of the crime. Adhering to a strict procedure, in a manner that would have surprised those who did not know the professional side of the sheriff, the body was summarily inspected, placed on a gurney, and wheeled out to the ambulance. The sheriff decided to accompany the body to the county morgue, but considered it unwise to leave the scene of the crime unattended. Orly Peterson was not very enthusiastic about Knutson's order that he should stay and guard the premises overnight, and the sheriff had finally agreed to ask Harvey Holte, the aged deputy who did night duty in the lake area during the summer, to come over and keep him company.

Orly had spent a disagreeable night. Holte welcomed the opportunity to spend the night out of the rain on official duty, and promptly laid down on the couch in the living room and went to sleep. Orly knew that the body had been taken away, but there was still something spooky about spending the night in a house where a murder had just been committed. It didn't seem to bother old Harvey, but as Orly looked around the room and saw framed photographs of the late college president, there seemed to be something about those pictures that filled the house like a bad smell. Lingering lightning and distant thunder served to heighten the imagination that Orly tried to keep down. He was glad to see dawn come, but waited until Harvey was awake before they went into the kitchen together to brew some coffee. Orly tried to tell himself that he waited to go in together so that he could be sure that Harvey "didn't touch anything that could be evidence." When the BCA investigators and technicians came, Harvey, claiming the need to catch up on his sleep, blissfully went home. Orly introduced himself to the BCA men, showed them around, and left them to their work.

As Knutson came up the sidewalk, Orly intercepted him with a somewhat insubordinate "So, you finally made it out here. What's going on back in town?"

Palmer was not unduly offended by Peterson's tone and provided a rundown of the whereabouts of the guests, now bearing the title of "suspects." It was the first time that either of them had used the word in connection with the men and women who just hours earlier had been looking forward to dining on Gherkin's chicken Kiev. He also told Orly about the news conference, not to satisfy the deputy's curiosity, but to provide him with a general sketch of the line he should take with the press should he be questioned. Orly perked up when Palmer reported with disgust that the story might even make network news and thought that perhaps he should shave and go back to the office just in case the press needed any of his opinions or reactions.

Knutson could see that eager-beaver glint in his eyes, but he told his deputy, "I want you to go home. Catch up on your sleep. You've done your job here and I'll need you later. Just let me talk to the BCA guys for a minute and then I want you to tell me any thoughts you may have concerning the murder." This appeal, couched in a manner that let him know that the sheriff really did value his opinion, pacified Orly and he led Palmer into the house.

Palmer Knutson had a rather quiet pride in his knowledge of modern investigative methods. Yet, he knew his limitations. The Bureau of Criminal Apprehension team had equipment and expertise and, as a result of previous experience with them, he valued and trusted their work. In turn, they appreciated his respect and non-interference. As Palmer told them, "You guys can collect the facts, just give me an equal opportunity to interpret them." As a result, the relationship between Otter Tail County and St. Paul was the best in the state. As they entered the Gherkin kitchen, Palmer observed the familiar procedure of dusting for fingerprints and the pursuit of microscopic evidence. He stayed out of their way and amiably chatted about the weather and mutual acquaintances in St. Paul. They promised an oral report by six o'clock and a written report by Monday afternoon. Palmer helped himself to a cup of coffee and motioned Orly to join him in the living room.

When they were comfortably seated in the room, which only a few hours ago had held the entire dinner party and now seemed strangely larger, Knutson said, "So, what do you think?"

Orly responded, "You mean, who do I think did it?"

"Yah, that. And how, and when, and why. I think 'where' is rather definitely established."

"Well, you know, I was thinking about that last night, while I was listening to Harvey snore. Who? Well, we've got the ten guests, so I suppose we've got ten suspects."

"Eleven."

"What?"

"You didn't count Dolly."

"Dolly?"

"Rule number one, from Sherlock Holmes to Inspector Clouceau. Never overlook anyone."

"All right then," allowed Orly, "eleven. Is there anyone at this point that we can definitely omit?"

"I suppose there are some that I would consider unlikely to commit murder," admitted Palmer, "but no, I don't think at this point we can rule out anybody. The one thing everyone seemed quite certain about last night was that there was no one else who came to the house. Still, even that can't be ruled out."

"All right then, when?" Orly continued with growing intensity. "We can probably get a closer idea on this when we get a report from the medical examiner and when we take individual statements, but from what I gathered last night, everyone arrived somewhere between six o'clock and six-fifteen. They all agreed that they could hear Gherkin singing until about seven. The body was discovered shortly after eight. Ergo, the murder occurred between seven and eight o'clock."

"That seems logical. Go on. How?"

Orly hesitated for some time. Finally he said, "You ever read any John Dickson Carr? He was a mystery writer—in the thirties, forties, or fifties, I suppose—who was noted for locked room mysteries. He had this fat professor character, Dr. Fell, who always solved them and made them seem so painfully obvious in the last chapter. So help me, I think we've got a locked room mystery on our hands."

"That had occurred to me too. And yah, I've read some of those Dr. Fell books. They're mostly predicated on the theory that you take all possible explanations and eliminate the impossible and whatever is left, no matter how improbable, must be the truth. In fact, I think that goes right back to Sherlock Holmes. So what are the facts, Orly, as you see them?"

"Okay," the deputy began, gratified that the sheriff seemed to value his input. "The room, for reasons best known to the late Dr. Gherkin, is locked. It is locked from the inside. The key to the interior door, giving access from the dining room, was, in fact, found in his pocket. According to Mrs. Gherkin, no other key was known to exist and it was necessary to break down the door. Witnesses? Everybody who was present. The door to the patio was also locked. Not only locked, but bolted from the inside. The windows were also locked. Again, from the inside. This was observed not only by all present when they tried to open them, but I checked them this morning. No one had been near them since last night and the latch on each window was firmly in place. Chimney? In an electrically heated home? There is a fireplace, but that's in the living room. Besides, that's absurd. Hidden passages? In a 1980s Minnesota lake home? Also absurd. Besides, I checked. I also checked for trap doors and ceiling vents."

Knutson had been nodding his agreement with the systematic logic of his deputy. "So?"

"So? So? Sew buttons on your underwear!" blurted Orly, then wished he hadn't recalled his childhood rejoinder. "I'll tell you how it spooked me. Last night I started to wonder if it could have been an accident. I thought maybe he kept his knives all hung from a ceiling rack and one of them unfortunately slipped. It was the first thing I checked this morning. Needless to say, there is nothing on the ceiling that could hold a meat cleaver. Could he have been practicing to be one of those whatyoucall'em Japanese chefs that toss their knives around, hoping to impress his guests when he had the move perfected, only to have one slip and come down on his head? Could he have had a small electromagnet in his head that was activated by some enemy by remote control which caused the cleaver to fly into his skull? Or was it a ghost?" Orly, his lack of sleep combining with his frustration with the evidence, suddenly became aware that he was starting to rant. "I don't know. You're the sheriff. You tell me."

"Take it easy, Orly, we don't have to solve this case today. We'll think about it for a while. It's obviously not going to affect Gherkin one way or the other. I think, though, that once we know the method, we'll know the murderer. Proof, however, . . . well, we'll see what the BCA team finds out."

As if by common agreement, they both stood up. In an almost fatherly manner, the sheriff said, "Meanwhile, like I said, get some rest. Take the Chevy back into town and then go home. Do me a favor and don't share any of those theories with reporters, but don't stop thinking either. If anything occurs to you, call me up. If not, I'll call you tomorrow and we'll start going around taking statements from everyone who was here last night."

With that, Orly gratefully left the sheriff and was soon heard spinning his tires on the muddy driveway. As he drove away, the image of his secure little bed seemed positively alluring.

Palmer spent the next half hour counting steps from the dock to the patio and from the patio to the living room and from the living room to the bathroom. He carefully noted the time it took to go from the dock to the bathroom and back again, allowing for minimum time spent in the bathroom. He mulled over the flimsy lock on the interior kitchen door and even spent some time checking out Gherkin's tape deck and tape collection. It was actually with some difficulty that he found the *I Pagliacci* tape. "This is curious," he thought. "Why would Dolly have gone to the trouble of carefully putting it away in its allotted slot while she had guests?" With a shrug of resignation, he extracted the tape that was in the recording portion of the tape deck. It was unmarked. Out of curiosity he played a portion of it. "Ah, that's a composition by Erik Satie. I've always loved that piece." He had never heard of Satie before Blood Sweat and Tears had done something called "Variations on a Theme" on an album in the late sixties, and he had grown to appreciate *fin-de-siècle* French music to a degree that would have shocked his old army buddies and most of the voters of Otter Tail County. He left the music on as he perused and approved of Gherkin's music collection. With a final envious appreciation of the sound system, Palmer decided to take his own advice to Orly and went home to think about the case.

TWELVE

SHERIFF KNUTSON EASED HIS Integra into the driveway of his fifty-year-old, two-story wood and brick house. He inwardly groaned as he noticed more paint peeling from the eaves and realized that one more summer had gone by and he still hadn't gotten the house painted. With an exaggerated wheeze he managed to extricate himself from behind the wheel and slowly ambled to the front door. It was only then that he noticed the television van parked by the curb. Ellie was at the door to greet him. He immediately noticed that she was made up and dressed more formally than she was on most Saturdays.

"Hi, Ellie, have you had lunch yet?"

"Yes, but never mind that, we have company."

"Reporters?"

"Yes. They've been waiting here for over an hour. I made some coffee and some sandwiches from that ham that I was planning to use next week. There's someone from the St. Paul *Pioneer Press* and the Fargo *Forum* and from three television stations. They're very nice and I told them you would be home soon and wouldn't mind talking to them. You don't, do you? I mean, I could have sent them away, but they have a job to do, too, and they seemed so nice, I mean, not pushy at all, so I just told them to come in and wait. Is that all right?"

"Well, I suppose. But I did have a press conference only a couple of hours ago, and I haven't learned anything new, and I didn't have much to tell them in the first place." Privately, and all the while keeping a pleasant expression on his face, he thought, "Oh, Ellie, Ellie, Ellie. Why do you always have to be so nice?"

Entering the living room, Knutson interrupted a somewhat rancorous discussion on the future of cable television. He fielded the greetings of the press and pulled up the last remaining chair.

"All right, I know you guys have a job to do, but I did hold a press conference earlier and I want to make it short. I suppose you have to have some TV footage, but just tell me when that thing is on so I'm not caught picking my nose or something. As you know, there has been a homicide. And yes, it is the first homicide I have ever dealt with as sheriff of Otter Tail County. The victim, of course, was George Gherkin, president of Fergus Falls State University. I have just returned from the scene of the crime where the Bureau of Criminal Apprehension is collecting evidence. They have promised me a verbal report by this evening and lab reports by early next week. At this point I cannot speculate on the perpetrator or the motive behind the crime. But go ahead, ask your questions, and then, at the risk of being rude, scram."

The cameraman from WDAY of Fargo nodded and got into position. Ellie sidled up to Palmer so that there was no way of leaving her out of the picture. Nobody minded. The members of the fourth estate soon began to pepper the sheriff with questions.

"We've heard that the death was caused by a blow to the head with a meat cleaver. Is this right?"

"Yup."

"Was this an ordinary kitchen meat cleaver?"

"Yup. A little on the heavy side, maybe, but an ordinary meat cleaver. Gherkin did quite a bit of cooking, I guess. Apparently he used it all the time."

"Was the victim struck from behind?"

"Looked that way to me."

"Would it have been easy for the murderer to sneak up behind Gherkin without giving away his presence?"

"Possible, I suppose, but not likely."

"So the murderer was more than likely someone well known to the victim, perhaps someone he trusted?"

"How do I know if he trusted anybody? But, yah, more than likely it was someone known to Gherkin."

"So it was someone who was a guest at the Gherkin home?"

"Not necessarily. We can't rule out, at this time, the possibility that someone paid him a quick and rather deadly visit."

"How's Mrs. Gherkin taking it?"

"How would you expect her to take it? Actually, the last time I saw her she was bearing up pretty well. Sally Ann Pennwright took her back to her place and I haven't seen her since." No sooner were the words out of Palmer's mouth than he realized what he said.

"So Sally Ann Pennwright was at the President's home last night. Who is she?"

"She is, er, was, Gherkin's personal secretary."

"Who else was there last night?"

"Look, I'm not going to provide you with that information. The last thing I want is for you to track down innocent people whom you may deem to be suspected of a murder. I realize that this is a small town and that before long everyone will know who was there, but we haven't had a chance to talk to these people ourselves. Over the course of the next couple of days we will do so, and when we do I don't want to have to stumble over reporters. I promise you, when I have something to tell you I'll let you know. All right, one last question."

The reporter from the Fargo *Forum* beat the others to the punch. "Do you know the approximate time of death?"

"I haven't had an official report yet, but last night the doctor estimated that the time of death was between 5:30 and 7:30 p.m. We do have reason to believe that it took place after 7:00."

The *Pioneer Press* reporter tried for a quick follow-up. "And how many people were in the home at that time?"

"Several. And now, if you folks will excuse me. I have things to do."

The implication was obvious, and Knutson was able to shepherd them to the door with little trouble. Since they had enough footage to fill space on the six o'clock news, they decided not to be greedy. After a round of sincere thank-yous to Ellie, Palmer closed the door on the last of them, sighed, and put his arm around his wife.

"What do you have to do now?" she asked. "You said you had things to do."

"Yah, well, I wanted to sit down, have a little lunch, and read the paper and do the crossword puzzle."

"Do you think you would have time to do a little sanding in the bathroom this afternoon? I bought paint for the ceiling yesterday."

Once again Palmer did not let his face show his inward groan. The bathroom was rapidly becoming the bane of his existence. It had started out innocently enough. The pale green tub had become scratched beyond reclamation and Ellie had wanted a new one. But then, the sink and toilet had to match the tub. And the new tub was a different size than the old tub and a new floor covering had been called for. Then a new wall had to be built for a shower door, and a new light fixture was needed because the new wall made one half of the bathroom dark. All of this had meant that new wallpaper had to be installed to match the new floor covering, and new paint had to be applied to all other surfaces.

Well, maybe mindless sanding would help him concentrate on the case. There was something bothering him about the simple facts of the murder, something that didn't seem right, even as he had been talking to the television reporters, but he couldn't quite put his finger on it. He sat down in his faithful leather chair and reached for the last ham sandwich that had somehow survived the ravenous press. "Let's see, a three-letter word for 'table scrap.' That would be 'ort.'"

He had left orders at the office to call him only in case of an emergency and to let deputies handle the routine calls. He had left his answering machine on to screen the calls, and heard an almost constant request for news and gossip from members of the town and university community. Shortly after he went upstairs to begin sanding, however, Ellie came up and said, "The office is calling. They think it might be important."

Palmer went downstairs in a fog of spackle dust and talked to the deputy on duty. "Yah, what is it?"

"Sheriff? We just got a call from Hjalmar Lundberg. Know who he is? Well, anyway, he says you got to get out to his place right away. I really couldn't understand what it was all about, I think half of what he said was in Norwegian, but he said there was blood all over and yelled something about how you had to stop them before they did it again. Know where he lives?"

"Hjalmar Lundberg? Yah, he lives out around Underwood, not too far from where I grew up. He's kind of a screwball, but he's harmless enough. Are you sure you can't handle it?"

"All I know is that he asked for you, and what with the murder last night and everything, I thought I should tell you."

Knutson thought about going back to sanding the bathroom and said, "Yah, sure, I'll go out there."

The wind was dying somewhat and the sun was breaking through the clouds by the time he reached the Lundberg farm. He doubted that there could be any connection with the events of last night, but the farmhouse was only about four miles from the Gherkin lake home, so it could be important. He was surprised to see old Hjalmar out by his mailbox to intercept him. Hjalmar was an Otter Tail County rustic. He always wore bib overalls, and there was some speculation as to whether or not he owned more than one pair. The thought occurred to Knutson that Hjalmar had never been anything but an old man. He always chewed snoose and long ago had lost part of his lower lip to cancer. That had not stopped him from chewing, however, and now his randomly spaced lower teeth acted like a sieve for the juice that was always dripping off of his chin, which was always shaven, but never what one could call "clean shaven."

As Knutson got out of his car, Hjalmar took off his striped engineer's cap and waved it at his mailbox and, in the thickest Norwegian brogue in Minnesota, he said with disgust, "Yust look at dis! Dere's blood all over da place and I tink I know who done it, tew!"

The sheriff was instantly alert. "Blood? Where? Calm down, Hjalmar, and tell me what this is all about."

Hjalmar strode over to his mailbox and jerked it open. Inside, the corpse of a striped gopher, the ubiquitous symbol of the state, oozed blood. Appropriately, the flag on the mailbox had been raised. "It's dem damn Bakke kids. I know it's dem. Dey get a big kick out of driving around da country sticking dere guns out da vindow and blasting gophers and sticking dem in my mailbox. Dere's some kind of fedral law against dat, ain't dere?"

After the events of the last eighteen hours, Knutson was gratified that at least a part of his life was back to normal. With a scowl on his face he asked, "Any stamps on the gopher?"

"Huh? Stamps?"

"Well, if somebody is trying to mail a gopher without any stamps, I suppose that would be against the law. Who's it addressed to?"

"Huh? Ah, you're yust foolin' me aren't ya? Dis ain't funny, you know. You gotta stop dis kind of ting. Ve didn't elect you to yust sit around in town, you know."

Palmer thought about what was rapidly becoming the most sensational murder case in western Minnesota. There was something very comforting about Hjalmar's request. Here, at least, was a case he could handle. He reached into the mailbox, daintily picked up the late gopher by the tail, flipped it into the ditch and said, "You bet, Hjalmar, I'll look into it. By the way, did you have any company this morning?"

"Nei, da only vun here vas Carol, my niece, you know, Edna's daughter. And she brought along her kid, Larry."

"Uh, Hjalmar, what did, uh, Larry do when he was out here?"

"Vat did he do? I don't know. He yust borrowed da twenty-two to go out shooting at cans or rabbits or someting. Why you ask dat?"

"Well, it rained pretty hard last night, you know. There's only one set of tire tracks in the mud by your mailbox, and I suppose that's from Rus, the mailman. You did get your mail today, didn't you?"

"Yah, so?"

"Was there anything in the mailbox then?"

"Yust da noospaper!"

"Well, it's just that before I go arresting the Bakke boys I think maybe you should ask Larry if he has ever tried to mail a gopher, if you know what I mean."

"You mean you tink dat little . . . Yah, all right, I suppose maybe he did it, da little . . . vell, I suppose it ain't dat big a deal."

"Well, you let me know if you want to press charges, but I'm not sure you or I would want to face Edna if we put her grandson in jail. Meanwhile, I suppose I'd better get back to town."

Knutson crawled back into the Integra with a feeling of accomplishment. Case solved! If only all murder investigations could be concluded as quickly and surely as "the case of the unpostmarked rodent." As usual, it turned out to be the one least suspected. Now, wondered Knutson, who did he suspect least in the murder of George Gherkin?

THIRTEEN

SHERWIN AND MAE WILLIAMS didn't talk about the murder after the sheriff allowed them to leave the Gherkin home. Sherwin had been in a hurry to leave, and as he crawled into the Volvo he did not notice that the vinyl seat held a pool of rainwater that had poured in from the window he had carelessly left open. Sitting in a cold puddle was a fitting ending to the day. That bothered him, of course, but there was something more, something that he couldn't get out of his mind and would later keep him awake. He went to bed as soon as he returned from bringing the babysitter home, only to find Mae already asleep, or at least pretending to be asleep. As he tried to empty his mind, the image of Gherkin's head hosting a meat cleaver kept recurring. But instead of feeling horror at the memory, Sherwin felt only a feeling of satisfaction. He was ashamed of himself for that, but what was equally horrible was the unmistakable look of triumph that he had seen spreading across the face of his wife when she caught the briefest glimpse of the late president.

On Saturday, Sherwin had hoped to complete what he viewed as the final installment of his prairie rose series, a painting of rotting blossoms that heralded the end of the season. He thought, perhaps, that they could be viewed as a metaphor for life. But it was windy and cold and he didn't feel much like painting anyhow. He spent most of the day putting lattice stripping on some of his almost finished canvases.

Mae hadn't slept much the night after the murder either. She didn't want to talk about it. It bothered her that she felt no remorse for Gherkin, but there was something more. Where had her husband been while she waited for him on the patio? It had been an unimportant thing at the time, but they each had their own agenda for the evening, and they had to coordinate their actions. She thought perhaps Sherwin could tell her something about Dr. Corazon's latest book and maybe she and the vice-president could have a pleasant chat. After all, it wouldn't hurt to be on good terms with her in the event she got a sudden promotion. But Sherwin was nowhere to be seen, and when he did appear he had such a guilty look about him and he seemed to be avoiding her. Furthermore, after the discovery of Gherkin's body, as everyone had sat around waiting out the storm, and coming to the conclusion that they were sharing space with a murderer, that guilty look still seemed to distort her husband's face. And yet, she needed to trust him now more than ever.

Emotions on Saturday were raw and strained. Mae's mother called to talk about the murder, but it wasn't something Mae enjoyed talking about. When friends called to ask about it she cut them off with a rude comment about the sheriff's request that it not be discussed. Every time she did so, she wondered just how much Knutson knew. She was able to get through the day by taking Vincent to the shopping mall to buy his school clothes and a new box of crayons.

The Saturday evening pizza was shared without enthusiasm. Both Sherwin and Mae seemed to be overly concerned about whatever opinion little Vincent might have, individually realizing that it was a way of avoiding sharing opinions with each other. A sense of foreboding seemed to hang over them, and for the first time in their married lives it was intensified by a genuine sense of mistrust. They silently watched a rerun of an old movie on television and with exaggerated politeness had retired early. This night they did sleep.

In fact, they were both sound asleep at eight o'clock on Sunday morning when the telephone rang. The terrible, urgent ringing woke Sherwin from an unpleasant dream about Gherkin and Mae, who was rubbing her hands together and chanting, "Out, out, damned spot." He violently jerked the phone from the bedside stand. It was a voice he did not want to hear.

"Mr. Williams? This is Sheriff Knutson. I wondered if we could come out and see you this morning. There are a few questions I wanted to ask you about the other night. How does nine o'clock sound?"

"Ah, er, yeah, I suppose that would be okay." He anxiously glanced at his now wide-awake wife. "Did you want to talk to both of us?"

"Yah, if we could. I'll have Orly Peterson with me."

"All right, I'll tell Mae. We'll be looking for you."

The sheriff did not like to engage in any official duties on Sunday. On Sunday mornings he usually attended services at First

Norwegian Lutheran Church, one of several Lutheran churches in the overwhelmingly Scandinavian community. He sang in the choir, as did Ellie and whichever of his progeny happened to be available at the time. It was a natural thing for him to do, something he had been doing all his life. To be sure, he didn't always listen to the sermon and if pressed would admit that he really didn't believe everything he was supposed to believe, but it was a comforting part of his life. It gave rhythm to the week and to his existence. Still, a murder investigation was undoubtedly a good excuse to skip church. Palmer also avoided sheriff business on Sunday afternoons. In the fall, of course, he had to watch the Vikings every Sunday afternoon, but everybody did that, even lawbreakers, presumably, because there was never anything for a sheriff to do at that time. In summertime, though, he made it a point to go to the various church midsummer picnics and small-town festivals. The food was good and Palmer reasoned that it was meet and right for a public servant to be seen. The more people he knew in the county, the more effective law enforcement officer he could become, sort of the neighborhood cop on the beat writ large. Besides, it was great politics.

He had contacted Orly before he left home and instructed him to meet him at headquarters with a car. Warm weather was returning to the lake country and, in recognition of his official duties, Palmer wore a standard uniform short-sleeved shirt with a standard brown tie. He was not shocked to see Orly dressed exactly alike, with the addition of his LAPD sunglasses and his gun.

As the sheriff crawled into the passenger side of the white Chevy, Orly received him with a pleased grin.

"All right, who was it this time?" asked the Sheriff.

"What do you mean?" Orly asked innocently.

"When you give me that look, I know you enjoyed yourself last night. Who was she?"

"Well, since you asked, it was Allysha Holm. And don't think anything smutty. We just had a very nice time. I wanted to get out of town, a chance to drive and think about the case, you know. So we went all the way to Detroit Lakes. They were having a big dance at the pavilion. Good times. And no, I didn't wear any part of my uniform, and no, I didn't discuss the case with anyone. By the way," Orly offered, "I heard a pretty good Norwegian joke last night."

Knutson inwardly groaned. Normally he liked Norwegian jokes, but Peterson was a Swede. There was just that little hint of smugness when he talked about the latest "Ole and Lena" joke. Coming from a fellow Norwegian, Knutson would have loved it, but coming from Peterson, well, he still resented it. Of course, he could not let that show. "Yah, so you'd better tell it, then."

Peterson was already starting to giggle in anticipation of the punch line. "Well, you see, Ole, he decided he was going ice fishing. And he gets out his ice drill and he starts to make a hole in the ice and all of a sudden there's this big voice, I mean it just fills the air around him, and it says, 'There are no fish there, Ole.' Well, so Ole he picks up his tools and he moves down the ice about fifty feet and starts to make a new hole. So he's drilling away and drilling away and again he hears this booming voice, 'There are no fish there, Ole.' So Ole goes a few more yards away and starts working his third hole. Sure enough this voice booms out and echoes 'There are no fish there, Ole!' Well, Ole he just can't figure this out and finally asks, 'Is that you, God?' And the voice booms back, 'No, Ole, this is the ice rink manager.' Pretty good, huh?"

Palmer, who in spite of himself did laugh, had to admit it was another good one but was just as glad to change the subject with a "Turn here, the Williams house is the third one on the left."

Sherwin and Mae met them at the door. From a room off to the left they could hear the mayhem from a Sunday morning cartoon show and knew that little Vincent would not bother them. As they were led into the living room Mae offered them coffee and both accepted. There was tension in the room, and Knutson couldn't tell if he was the cause of it or if it was caused by something else. He tried to put them at ease by commenting on the art that was everywhere in the house. In truth, Knutson hated it, but one does not last as a county sheriff without learning to be diplomatic.

"Say, you really have some nice works here, Mr. Williams. Did you paint them all?"

Williams pretended to take an inventory of the art hanging on virtually every open wall space. "Yes," he finally said, "these are all mine. As painters we sometimes like to exchange works, but in this room, yes, these are all mine." In fact, Williams disliked going through the humiliation of trading art. He remembered being offered a small, unframed watercolor by a Moorhead State University art professor in exchange for one of his four-by-six-foot oil paintings.

Knutson peered closely at a painting that appeared to be a wilting prairie rose. He noticed that there was a little round sticker on the bottom of the frame with a price of $400 marked with a ballpoint pen. In fact, as he now noticed, every painting was marked with a price. Knutson could not know it, but the practice dated from the time Williams' department chair was ridiculing a colleague at another university. He had sarcastically said, "That man even prices the stuff in his own home." Sherwin Williams, missing the sarcasm, had thought it a swell idea.

Mae entered with four cups of coffee on a tray and nervously sat down next to her husband. She darted back to the kitchen and returned immediately with a plate of doughnuts which had been defrosted in the microwave oven. "I know that technically you're not policemen, but I did have these doughnuts in the freezer and I thought you might need a little something to go with your coffee." From anybody else the offer would have seemed snotty and impertinent. Coming from Mae, however, Knutson accepted it for what it was, a sincere offer of doughnuts for the law. She then asked the ultimate hostess question: "Would either of you care for cream or sugar?"

Knutson and Peterson both mumbled their disinclination and finally the sheriff got down to business. "We just want to talk to you today to see if there is anything you can tell us about the other night. Now, I know that if you had seen something important you would have told us right off. But sometimes one can observe something that has absolutely no importance at the time, but will be important in solving the crime."

Sherwin looked up, "What do you mean by that?"

"Well," the sheriff continued, "supposing you see someone coming from the kitchen and you think to yourself, 'I wonder what he was doing there?' Well, you don't think any more about it but maybe two days later you realize that it was about the time of the murder. So maybe you've seen the murderer or maybe you have told us about someone else who could have seen the murderer. Actually, er, ah, we have found it most helpful to interview people individually, so if you don't mind, er, which one of you would like to go first?"

Mae and Sherwin looked uneasily at each other. Finally, Mae said, "Why don't you go first, Sherwin. I'll just see how Vincent is doing." Mae left and went into the family room.

Knutson noticed how Sherwin's hand shook as he set his coffee cup down. Peterson had surreptitiously taken out a small Aiwa tape recorder and informed Williams that the interview would be recorded. He also took out his notepad and was ready with his pen. Williams glanced uneasily in the direction of the family room and said, "Yes, well, what can I tell you?"

Knutson sucked in a breath between his teeth and asked, "What time did you get to the Gherkin residence?"

"About six o'clock, I guess. 'All Things Considered' was just announcing a break."

"And who was there when you arrived?"

"Just George and Dolly."

"So you were the first to arrive," Orly interjected.

Knutson cast the deputy a withering glance and said, "I think he made that abundantly clear." Peterson had no doubts about who was going to conduct the interview.

"Did you at any time of the evening see Dr. Gherkin?" Knutson continued.

"No, actually, I never did. We could all hear him singing from the kitchen, and we knew enough to stay away. His insistence on isolation while he was in the midst of his culinary creativity was legendary. Woe to anyone who interrupted. Supposedly an English teacher once walked in on him and caught him adding a packet of onion soup mix to a recipe and he was terminated the next day. Of course, that was before we had the union we have now."

"Is that true?" Orly interrupted. "He could really fire someone for that?"

"Personally," Williams confided, "I rather doubt it, but the mere fact that I can repeat the story and other people at the university believe it rather says something, don't you think?"

"Now," resumed the sheriff, "during the whole time you waited for dinner, did anything strike you as unusual?"

"No, other than the fact that we seemed to have to wait longer than usual."

Orly again jumped into the interrogation. "So you have been to other dinners there?"

"No. I mean, I suppose, waiting longer than I thought we would," Williams admitted.

With a sidelong glance that silenced his deputy, Knutson continued, "Did anyone act nervous or jumpy or in any way out of the ordinary?"

"Well, as it was getting late, and the punch was getting low, Dolly kept looking toward the kitchen, wondering what George was doing, I suppose. And I think everyone was getting hungry and probably we were running out of things to say to one another. But, no, I can't say that I thought at the time that anyone was acting weird."

"And in the course of the evening did you leave the party or notice anyone else who seemed conspicuous by their absence?"

"Conspicuous by their absence? That's a nice choice of words. No, of course not."

"Think hard, Mr. Williams, this could be important."

After a pause, Sherwin said, "I suppose you are going to ask other people the same question. Well, I suppose I'd better tell you. I sneaked out for a cigarette."

"You sneaked out for a cigarette? You sneaked?"

"Yeah, well, I promised Mae I'd given it up and told my insurance company that I didn't smoke. But I bought a pack of Salems to ward off the mosquitoes when I was painting *au naturel*—outdoors, I mean—this summer, and I had them under the car seat. I was nervous from a chat with Corazon and figured I could use a smoke. Of course, nobody smokes anymore, and you're a social pariah if you do. So I went outside and was gone maybe ten minutes. You don't have to let Mae know, do you?"

"Probably not," Knutson sighed, silently amused by the image of an *au naturel* painter, "unless it turns out to be important. Did you see anyone enter or leave the house while you were out by the cars?"

"No, everyone had arrived by then. No one else came or left." As he stated this, Williams looked somewhat uneasy. He was never good at lying, although he thought he excelled at it, and he remembered clearly how, right after the music stopped, Mae came out of the house, looked furtively around, dashed to the car, and put her gloves, which he had told her would be unnecessary and look out of place, in the glove compartment of the car. In fact, the thought struck him that in all his life this was the first time he had seen anyone put gloves in the glove compartment. What a stupid place to hide them! The first place anyone would look! But no one had looked, for it would be ridiculous to think that Mae could have anything to do with murder. After a pause of twenty seconds,

Williams felt it necessary to add, "No, no, I was alone out there the whole time."

"Can you think of anyone, especially those present at the dinner party, who would have a motive to murder George Gherkin?"

"No, of course not. Still, he may not have been everyone's favorite. I mean, he had held Winston out of his chairmanship, even though he has clearly been the outstanding scholar of that department for years. Not the most attractive, perhaps, but he was the man everyone knew should be the chair. And then there's Lance Sterling. He thought he was going to get a piece of immortality in the form of a building named after him. Gherkin saw a chance to make a point with the governor and shattered his dream. Frankly, I thought it was hilarious, but Sterling was hardly pleased. Then there's Dr. Corazon. She's been measuring the president's office for new drapes. Brick Wahl didn't get his contract. The mayor stands to lose a bundle on the Wal-Mart deal—everybody knows about that. There's always been talk about Sally Ann Pennwright and Gherkin, maybe something went sour there. In fact, now that I think about it, about the only ones who didn't have anything against him, who were there, were Sterling's wife—what's her name, Ruth?—and she may have resented him just because her husband did—and Francis Olson. Hard to see Olson killing the goose that lays the golden egg. Olson gets anything he wants from Gherkin. Come to think of it, that's just the people who were there. When you think of all the people on campus who would have liked to have swung the cleaver, it's amazing it hadn't happened before now!"

"What about you, Mr. Williams?" the sheriff asked, and after a significant pause added, "And your wife?"

Sherwin choked, coughed, and got coffee on his shirt. He grabbed a napkin which Mae had thoughtfully placed on the table and dabbed at his clothes, using the time to gain his composure. Finally, he was able to look up and say in what he thought was a steady voice, "You just can't believe anything like that about Mae. Sure, Gherkin may have had dirty little designs on my wife, but she wouldn't do anything like that. She wouldn't and she couldn't. As for me, well, you'll probably find out anyway, but I had always viewed Gherkin as my sponsor and advocate. It turns out, as I have just learned, that he was the one who manipulated the system to abuse and exploit me for the last dozen years. I certainly didn't kill him, but for what he did to me and my family, by keeping us at an insulting pay level all these years when I could have used the money to study in Europe or to buy a decent car, years when I was kissing his rosy-red behind in gratitude, well, I guess I'd like to thank the hand that held the cleaver."

"That rather makes you a prime suspect, you know."

"Yeah, I suppose it does," allowed Williams, reddening. "But I didn't do it."

"One more thing," Palmer continued. "You mentioned Gherkin's 'dirty little designs' on your wife. What did you mean by that?"

"Oh, that was nothing. It was just that Mae overheard Gherkin imply to somebody that he kept her around for her looks and not because she could do her job. Just a mean, sexist thing he once said. Mae was pretty upset about it at the time."

"All right, Mr. Williams, I think that will be all for now. Will you go and ask your wife to come in and talk to us?"

Peterson leaned forward and turned off the tape recorder. As Williams got up to leave, he whispered, "You won't tell Mae about the cigarette, will you?"

Peterson tried to give him the old "we men have got to stick together" nod and, partially reassured, Williams left the room. In a few seconds Mae came in carrying the pot of coffee and asked, "Would either of you care for more doughnuts?" There being only a slight reduction from the original serving, Orly and Palmer declined.

"Please sit down, Mrs. Williams," said Peterson, in what he thought to be his most ingratiating manner. "This will be a taped interview, if you don't mind. I'll just keep the recorder here in front of us. Now then," he asked, glancing at Knutson as if for permission to speak, "we understand you were the first to arrive?"

"Yes, it must have been just six. That's the time we were invited for. I like to be on time."

"And what did you do upon arrival?" continued the deputy.

"Dolly met us at the door and showed us onto the patio. We chatted for a few minutes and then other guests started to arrive."

At this point, Knutson, who had been eating another doughnut just to make Mae satisfied that she was being a proper hostess, dabbed at his mouth and said, "And did you at any time during the course of the evening see George Gherkin?"

"Of course!"

"You mean you did? You actually saw him?" asked Peterson, unable to suppress his excitement.

"Well, I mean, we all did, didn't we? With the big knife in his head? It was terrible!"

"No, I mean, er, did you see him alive that night?"

"Oh. No. I don't think any of us did. Any of us guests, that is. I don't know if Dolly did or not. It would be kind of strange, wouldn't it, if you were giving a dinner party and didn't talk to your husband the whole time? As far as I know, though, I didn't even see her go into the kitchen."

Peterson, thinking it was safe to ask a question that Knutson had asked her husband, asked Mae, "Did you notice at any time that anybody was acting unusual, or weird, or suspicious?"

Mae wrinkled her nose as though she thought it to be a stupid question and replied, "What reason would I have had for looking for anybody acting suspiciously during a dinner party?"

"Well, that's just it," Orly proclaimed. "Did anybody act differently than you might expect they would at a dinner party?"

Mae shrugged and answered, "No, I can't say that I noticed anything different."

The sheriff leaned forward, looked Mae in the eye, and asked, "At any time did you notice anybody who left the house or was gone for a while?" Since Knutson already knew Williams had "sneaked out" for ten minutes, it was a good opportunity to test either Mae's veracity or her powers of observation. She did not disappoint.

Mae recalled the fury with which Sherwin had told her of Gherkin's duplicity. She also recalled those few frantic moments when she had looked for him, even to the extent of checking the parking area as she put away her gloves. Finally, she remembered the guilty look on Sherwin's face as he returned to the patio as mysteriously as he had vanished. But to the sheriff, she merely said, "No."

Knutson noticed that, for the first time in the interview, she had not looked him in the eyes. Mae was a very bad liar. He continued, "Can you think of anyone who may have wanted to murder Dr. Gherkin?"

"I've thought of that. And you know, I can't think of anyone that I know who could take a human life. Certainly nobody at the party seemed like a murderer. Still, the more I thought about it, Gherkin, you know, was not a very nice man. There were a lot of people he had really hurt; he kept stringing along that poor Miss Pennwright, for instance. And some of his business deals were not on the up and up, I've heard, and with Lance Sterling and Brick Wahl and Abigail Armbruster there, I mean, who knows? But murder? I can't believe it."

"What about your husband, Mrs. Williams? I understand he had reason to dislike Gherkin."

"Dislike, yes, but not enough to kill him. Even I disliked him."

"And why was that, Mae?" Palmer asked. "What had he done to you?"

"Oh, it was nothing. He just had this attitude that he was God's gift to women and that I should be grateful to him for my job and show my gratitude in demeaning ways. I refused to do so, and that's all there was to it."

At a nod from Knutson, Peterson reached forward and turned off the tape recorder. "Thank you, Mrs. Williams. I know this is not a pleasant topic and you have been very helpful. And thanks for the coffee and doughnuts. We have to go and interview some of the other people who were at the dinner party, but we may have to contact you again, so don't either of you leave the area without informing us."

"Of course, Sheriff. Just a minute, I'll see if Sherwin has anything to add. Sherwinnnnn," Mae bellowed in a surprisingly loud roar, "they're leaving now."

Williams came in and looked anxiously at Mae. "Well, see ya," he said, and somewhat unexpectedly thrust out his hand. Orly and Palmer obligingly shook it and went out to the car.

As the car pulled away, Peterson gave Knutson a knowing look and said, "I think he did it."

"Oh yeah, why do you say that?"

"He lied about going out for a cigarette. You could tell it. And he had motive. Means, I haven't figured out yet, but I think he's our man."

"What about Mrs. Williams? She lied, too."

"What do you mean 'she lied'?"

"She lied about how she felt about Gherkin. You could tell she hated him far more than she was willing to admit. She lied about not noticing if anyone left the house. Either she was lying to protect the fact that she was gone for a while, or she was lying to protect her husband."

"You surely can't suspect Mae Williams of committing murder!" Peterson was aghast.

"Why not?"

"Well, because this was obviously such a man's crime, for one thing."

"Orly, Orly, Orly. I thought your generation was supposed to be more free of sexual stereotypes."

"Well, we are. But I still say splitting a skull with a meat cleaver is a man's crime."

"Orly, I've got two words for you."

"Yes?"

"Lizzie Borden."

FOURTEEN

"So, where to now?" asked Orly Peterson, pointing the car in the general direction of the office.

"Oh, sorry, I thought I'd told you. Drive over to Lake Alice. We've got a 10:30 appointment to talk with Dolly Gherkin. She's still staying with Sally Ann Pennwright. In light of what we were just told about her relationship with Gherkin, that's rather bizarre, don't you think?"

"Yeah, well, you hear about things like that, like the wives of a bigamist who both become widows and discover they have more in common than their taste in husbands and shared bereavement. But you'd think that Dolly would want to scratch her eyes out. Maybe she didn't know about it."

"I don't know," the sheriff said hesitatingly. "She's pretty sharp. I wonder if that will come out. Obviously, this is going to be a case where we must not interview them together."

It had turned into a spectacular Sunday morning. As they drove by the large First Norwegian Lutheran Church, not far from

Sally Pennwright's home, the first service had just ended. Palmer's brother Rolf stood at the door, shaking hands with the worshippers who were in no particular hurry to go home. Rolf had assured him that he never took mental attendance at church, but Palmer could never shake the notion that if he didn't go to church his saintly big brother noticed it. It was already about eighty degrees and men in short sleeves and women in sundresses gathered in small clusters on the lawn. It was a scene from a Norman Rockwell painting, with the tall steeple reaching to the sky over a town at peace with itself. It was hard to believe that only hours before someone in this town had become a murderer.

Sally Ann Pennwright still looked pretty good, Knutson had to admit to himself, as she greeted them at the door of the carefully restored Victorian home. She ushered them into a parlor paneled with dark oak and furnished with an antique chintz sofa and a low coffee table. Knutson and Peterson sat next to each other and both politely accepted coffee from a white carafe.

"So, how's Dolly taking it?" the sheriff inquired.

"Pretty well, actually," answered Miss Pennwright, self-consciously straightening her skirt as she sat down. "The funeral is set for Wednesday. I think she would have liked to have had it earlier, but the whole state seems to want to be here for it—the governor, both senators, and the other state university presidents. I think, if you ask me, it has been good therapy for her, planning the funeral. She said she was willing to talk to you whenever you wanted her. She is on the phone talking to her son in India now. Meanwhile, what can I help you with?"

Orly pulled out his tape recorder and said, "As this is an official interview, I hope you understand that we prefer to record this. It's as much a protection for you, of course, as it is for us."

"Certainly. Anything I can tell you that will clear up this dreadful business will help us all. Go ahead."

"All right, now," began Knutson, "when did you get to the Gherkin residence?"

"It was shortly after six. Sherwin and Mae Williams had arrived just before I got there."

"As a long-time employee of the university and a Gherkin associate, you must have attended several of these gatherings before. I understand it was a traditional beginning of the academic year event?"

"Yes. In fact," she added wistfully, "I think I've been to all of them."

"Would you describe this gathering as being different from any of the previous ones?" Even as he said it, Knutson winced.

"At no previous one had the host been murdered. I'm sorry, I know what you meant. No, I could tell no difference. As usual, George holed up in the kitchen until he could present his *pièce de résistance*. He may have bellowed a little more consistently than usual, I don't know. Of course, we had never had to wait for much more than an hour before, and I thought that was strange at the time, but we know the reason for it now, don't we? The faces always changed, but the general pattern of drinks on the patio and general socializing before the meal was the same, as far as I could tell."

"At any time, did you leave the party?"

"Well, at one point it was necessary for me to use the bathroom, the main one just across from the kitchen. I had to—" she hesitated, blushed, and continued, "well, I suppose I was in there for about ten minutes."

"Did you notice anyone else leave the party?"

Sally Ann thought for a while before replying. "After a while, as more people arrived, one really didn't pay attention to everyone. If anyone did leave I suppose I would have assumed they also had gone to the bathroom. I did notice, come to think of it, that Sherwin Williams had gone in the direction of the bathroom shortly before I did, but he was nowhere to be seen when I got there. Other than that, if I were at the lake and someone else was in the living room I would hardly have a good idea if they had gone anywhere, would I?"

"Can you think of anyone, especially among those at the dinner, who would have a motive to kill Dr. Gherkin?"

Sally Ann Pennwright's beautiful eyes narrowed and no longer looked beautiful. She seemed on the verge of saying something else before, almost visibly biting her tongue, she said, "No, no, of course not. He may have disappointed some people from time to time, but a university president is paid to do that, isn't he?"

Knutson studied his shoes for several seconds before looking up and saying, "I have to ask you some personal questions. It's part of the job, but rest assured that your answers will remain confidential unless they have a direct bearing on the case. Just what was your relationship to the late George Gherkin?"

Pennwright took a deep breath and looked up at the stairs, reassuring herself that Dolly would not be coming down to hear this part of the interview. For the first time, her face betrayed a sense of emotion and pain. It lasted only for a moment, however, and she finally said, "I suppose you will have heard some rumors already. They're mostly true, I'm afraid. George, he, well, to use an old-fashioned term, he swept me off my feet. I was young, educated but with no job, and suddenly I was the second most important person in a college. I thought he cared for me, and I think he did, as much as George could ever care for anyone. It's easy to fool oneself when things look rosy on the surface. I pictured marrying George as soon as Dolly died, which he had led me to believe would be at any time. I had this picture of myself as the wife of the college president in a marriage in which we would run the college as a team. I had no doubt that I was indispensable in running the university. I still am, by the way. But I made the mistake of thinking I was indispensable to George. Anyway, the affair came to an end about eleven years ago. Since he is no longer around to press charges, I can admit to you that I essentially blackmailed him. I got to keep my house and my job at the price of keeping my mouth shut. I don't know, maybe it all worked out for the best. I got experience and a career out of it. Nothing is certain yet, but I think I will be offered a job as administrative dean at St. Cloud State. My only regret is that now, after all those years of seeing Dolly as an obstacle to be removed, I have a terrible guilt about what I did to her."

Gaining a sudden insight into the character of the late president, Knutson asked, "Did President Gherkin support your application to St. Cloud State?"

At this, Sally Ann seemed to lose her composure and tears began to well up in her eyes. Peterson thought she was breaking down and moved to comfort her. Ironically, however, she angrily reached for her purse and took out a small contact lens case. Muttering a curt, "Excuse me," she popped out her left lens and looked furiously at the deputy. After a few frantic blinks, she said, "No. In fact, although I realize I'm setting myself up as a prime suspect, he told me he would never let me go. So in that respect, I'm free at last, free at last, Great God Almighty, I'm free at last."

Knutson and Peterson, feeling unreasonably embarrassed, looked down at the floor. Finally the sheriff asked, "Since you knew the house, and the way Gherkin isolated himself when he was cooking, did you notice anything about Friday night's physical setting that was at all different?"

"No, I don't think so. Same booze, same tedious opera music, same chicken Kiev."

"Anything unusual about the social mix that night?"

"Other than the fact that they all disliked the host? No. Of course, that was no longer very unusual in itself."

"When the murder was discovered, was there, among the people you could observe, anyone who acted, well, differently than you might have expected?"

Pennwright appeared to consider the question carefully before replying, "Now that you mention it, I guess everyone had the proper reaction of horror and shock, with the possible exception of Ruth Sterling. She seemed to have a look of satisfaction and pride about her."

"Can you explain this further?"

"No, I really can't," she said curtly. "It's just that when she saw George doing his corpse act she simply grabbed on to her husband's arm, led him out to the drinks cart on the patio, and poured him at least a triple shot. I couldn't tell if it was for shock or for a triumphant toast."

At a nod from Knutson, Orly reached forward and shut off the tape recorder. The sheriff said, "We really do appreciate your candor and cooperation. We may have to talk to you again, and in the meantime, you and everyone else who was at the dinner remain suspects in a murder case. We ask that you do not leave the area without consulting us. Now, if Dolly is available, perhaps you could ask her to join us. We would, of course, like to interview her alone."

"Of course. I'll run up and see if she's available."

As soon as she left the room Peterson asked, "Well, what do you think? It would appear she had a motive."

Knutson, with an eye on the door, took the opportunity to adjust his shorts. He nodded as he said, "And she's not alone, it would seem. I don't know. She's a remarkable woman, the kind they used to call 'strong willed' but now call 'assertive.' I suppose she could have done it, what do you think?"

Orly blandly proclaimed, "It's hard to believe a beautiful woman like that could wield a meat cleaver."

"Oh, Orly, Orly, Orly," the sheriff moaned. "Not that man's crime stuff again! Or is it because she's pretty? Do you think Isabel Corazon would be more capable of murder because she's homelier?"

As this question echoed off the walls Dolly Gherkin tentatively peeked through the door of the parlor and asked, "You wanted to talk to me?"

"Yes, please," replied the obviously embarrassed sheriff. "And let me extend once again our condolences. How are you bearing up, and how is your family?"

Dolly ignored his red face and graciously replied, "As well as can be expected, thank you. You know, I never realized how busy one became with a death in the family. That's good, I suppose, in a way, because it keeps you active and not moping. In fact, I would appreciate it if we could get this interview out of the way because I've got so much to do."

Knutson urged her to sit down, poured her a cup of coffee, and after Mrs. Gherkin agreed to having the interview recorded, asked, "I understand that you have had these beginning-of-school dinners for some time now, is that right?"

"Yes, I think this was the eighteenth consecutive year we hosted one."

The sheriff leaned forward to ask, "Did you or did President Gherkin choose the guest list?"

"Well, to a certain extent, we both did. George would tell me who he wanted to invite and if we had some places left over I would suggest someone."

"On what basis did your husband choose whom to invite?"

Dolly sipped her coffee before she replied, "I suppose that varied from year to year. This might sound crass to you, but it depended on what George needed out of somebody. Some years it was to prepare the way for a certain administrative strategy where someone's crucial support was needed and sometimes it was just to soothe ruffled feathers from the previous year. Occasionally it was to honor somebody, especially among the newer faculty, who still thought it was a sign of recognition to be asked to dine with the president. Some years it would be all three at once and some years it clearly marked the beginning of one of George's offensives."

"What was it this year?"

"I don't know," she said, wrinkling her forehead. "I stopped caring about faculty games and interdepartmental warfare about ten years ago, when I found that people appreciated me better as a neutral party and as someone they could trust."

The sheriff cocked one eyebrow and asked, "Did you mean to imply 'someone they could trust, unlike my husband'?"

"I didn't," Dolly sighed, boosting her huge glasses back on to her nose, "but I suppose I could have meant that. Anyway, I know that Brick Wahl was no longer as friendly as he once was, and that Lance Sterling had some burr under his saddle. Mrs. Armbruster? Maybe George had some expansion deal cooking. I tried not to think about it."

"What about Sherwin and Mae Williams?"

"Oh, they were my pick this year. They had never been here, and Mae is so nice. Her husband is a little silly, and can be pompous at times, but he's not as bad as everyone says."

"And what about, uh, Sally Ann Pennwright?" Knutson asked nervously.

"Sally Ann has been at all of our dinners, every year. She knows the faculty, the administration, the townspeople, and representatives from the State University Board. She mixes, matches, and essentially serves as co-host. I couldn't get along without her."

Dolly paused, but Knutson could tell that she still had more to say. Finally she looked away and said, "I could tell from the way you asked about Sally Ann that you had heard something about George and her. I can only assume that you have heard that he and Sally Ann had an affair and that is the reason that she is now in Fergus Falls. I would like to tell you that it is not true. I can't. I regret that I can't deny it, not for the sake of George or even myself, however, but for the sake of Sally Ann. Sure, it is not something that any wife wants to learn. I learned of it long before George ever thought I suspected. But you know that eternal question: 'Are you better off with him or without him?' I thought, at the time, that I was better off with him. The children were still at home. I was still young enough and probably naive enough to enjoy the prestigious nature of being the university 'first lady.' It was a constant humiliation having her around and having, as I imagined, half the university and community sniggering at me. Every time we would open our home to one of those gatherings like we had the other night, there would be Sally Ann—the indispensable personal secretary and unsecret mistress. I hated her. Then, as I later found out, she dumped him. Oh, no, George never confided in me about that, because to do so would have been to admit that he had a mistress in the first place. No, I put two and two together on that all by myself. Curiously, with the affair over, I found that I couldn't keep hating Sally Ann. I started to find her almost as indispensable as George did. I even started to like her. And now, after the way she has been these last two days, I'm just mad at George for exploiting her the way he did everybody else."

"Forgive me for asking this," Knutson said quietly, "but I hope you can appreciate the potential significance of this line of questioning. To your knowledge, did George have any other, er, 'liaisons' with anyone else—anyone who could have been in attendance the other night?"

Dolly sadly shook her head and said, "I don't think so. At least, I hope not. But, you know, odd as it might seem, I've even wondered about him and Dr. Corazon."

"Speaking of her," Knutson asked pointedly, "in which category of guest would she be?"

She tossed back her hair and answered, "As I said, I stopped trying to play that game. But it would be my guess that she and Dr. Winston would either be in the ruffled feathers category or in the honors category. Both deserved honors, I might add, especially Winston, for all the recognition he has brought this university, but, knowing George, there was probably another motive."

"Do you remember the order in which your guests arrived? If we can somehow determine when your husband was killed, it may at least prove who was not capable of killing him."

Mrs. Gherkin seemed relieved that the question was merely one of fact and not of opinion. "I know that Sherwin and Mae came first, and then Sally Ann. I'm pretty sure that the Sterlings were next to arrive. I remember looking at my watch about twenty after six and they were the only people there. Everybody else came within the next ten minutes, though, so I don't think there was much of an opportunity for anybody to attack George at that time.

Besides, he was still singing for at least another half hour after everybody was there."

"Just out of curiosity, did you find this singing embarrassing?"

"I used to find all those little faults embarrassing. Then I discovered that I was actually getting sympathy from other people for George's antics. I finally came to the conclusion that if he wanted to act like a clown . . ." Dolly stopped in mid-sentence. "I just remembered, he was acting like a clown, wasn't he? Roaring out *I Pagliacci*! Anyway, if he wanted to do that it was his business and it didn't reflect on me, and ever since I came to that conclusion I have been a happier woman and, I might add, a much more liberated one."

"At any time, especially after George stopped singing, did you notice anyone acting nervously, or suspiciously, or doing anything out of the ordinary?"

Dolly hesitated and then answered, "No, I don't think so. Of course, I don't know all of them well enough to be able to judge what is out of the ordinary for them."

The sheriff immediately followed up this line of inquiry by asking, "Did you notice anybody who seemed to be absent at any time?"

"Lord, no!" she scoffed. "People moved around a lot. Judging by the number of empty beer bottles, there must have been several trips to the bathroom. Besides, do you know what it's like trying to keep ten guests supplied with food and drink while attempting to show an interest in their lives? Remembering who teaches what or who has done what for the university? I was traipsing in and out of the living room, out to the patio and down to the dock for two solid hours. The guests were getting hungry and everybody was running out of things to say and I was starting to worry about George and frankly, I don't think you could expect me to keep tabs on all the guests."

Palmer Knutson offered her an understanding smile and said, "No, no, of course not. Had George ever kept his guests waiting this long before, at any of the other 'back to school' gatherings?"

"No, never, that's why I was beginning to worry by 7:30. I think he had served the chicken Kiev for the last dozen years, ever since it became famous, but it was always ready before seven. I remember thinking we were going to run out of beer and wondering if Francis Olson had some of that cheap domestic swill that he seems to prefer packed in a cooler in his pickup."

Knutson smiled and asked, "Did you spend most of the day with Dr. Gherkin?"

"Yes, although we really didn't talk too much. There were a couple of trips to town to get last-minute ingredients and beer and wine and things. I went out to the greenhouse on the edge of town to get a centerpiece for the table. For the most part, I suppose, we worked in our separate spheres."

"Had he ever been threatened? Did he seem worried or anxious in any way?"

"No," Dolly answered, and continued in a wistful, thoughtful manner, "in fact, the last time I saw him alive he seemed to be gloating about something. I am sure of one thing. He never expected death."

"And the last time you talked to him was, uh, when?"

"Just as the first guests arrived. He locked the door behind me and I went into my hostess mode."

"What were his last words to you, if this isn't too painful a question?"

"I really don't remember," Dolly said impatiently. "I mean, no one hears someone speak and then thinks, 'Oh, these are going to be his last words so I'd better remember them.' I think it was some comment about the chicken, however undramatic that may sound."

The sheriff looked at his deputy and asked, "Orly, do you have anything you would like to ask Mrs. Gherkin?"

"Yeah, just something I'm curious about. The last time anyone heard from your husband he was singing along with an opera. When that opera was over, according to what we understand, you turned off the tape player and turned the radio on to classical music and switched over to the living room speakers. Did Dr. Gherkin say anything about that? I mean, did he yell 'put on another opera'? Could you hear him humming along with the music on the radio? Any sounds from him at all?"

"I'm sorry, Deputy Peterson," Dolly answered with a sympathy that was almost motherly. "I just don't know. I was in and out and although he may have said something, I just don't remember it. Maybe somebody else heard something, but I just don't think I did. As I recall, though, the music on the radio wasn't the sort of thing anyone sings along with."

Orly appreciated the thoughtful reply to a question that, he hoped, won points from his superior. "Thank you, Mrs. Gherkin. I have no further questions. Sheriff?"

Knutson nodded and Orly turned off the tape recorder. As both men stood up to go, Palmer turned to Dolly, took one of her hands in both of his, and said, "Please let us know if there is anything we can do. And if you think of anything that may help us solve this, please call us. Don't bother Miss Pennwright, we'll find our way out."

It was almost noon. The town was rapidly emptying out as anyone who had a cottage at a lake had already left, and anyone who had friends or relatives with a cottage was planning a nice surprise visit. Palmer knew that Ellie was expecting him for Sunday dinner. There were more investigations to carry out in the afternoon. As they slammed their car doors in a curious unison he looked at Orly, inwardly sighed about the inevitability of the whole thing, and asked, "Look, Orly, why don't you just come home with me for lunch. We have plenty, and Ellie will be delighted to have you. "

The latter statement was not really true, but it wasn't exactly untrue, either. Ellie enjoyed company.

Orly smartly snapped in his seat belt and said, "Hey, that would be great, Palmer, then we can discuss the case."

Knutson reached over and grabbed the steering wheel and tersely said, "No, that is the one thing we cannot do. I don't want to bring murder into my home. It's my Sunday dinner and I just won't have it."

Noting the penitential expression on his deputy's face, however, the sheriff softened and said, "We're not there yet, though, so what do you think about it?"

As they drove off, the deputy appreciated the question and confidently replied, "Well, early days yet, of course, but so far my money is on Williams. If I had a boss like that I might get homicidal myself. Er, sorry, ah, that wasn't a threat. But from what Miss Pennwright indicated there might be something nasty with Sterling or Wahl, or even the mayor if it comes to that."

"The mayor is a woman though, isn't she?" Knutson smiled. "I thought you said it's a man's crime."

"Well, I still think it is. Could you see either Sally Ann Pennwright or Dolly Gherkin swing a meat cleaver?"

The sheriff thought a bit and said, "Yes, come to think of it, I can see either one of them doing it."

FIFTEEN

The pizza was better than Orly had expected. It was just an ordinary Tony's Pizza, the kind you could get on special for three bucks at the supermarket, but Ellie always added a little more cheese and olives and Orly washed it down with more than his share of Cherry Coke. It was a thoroughly enjoyable meal and Orly had been let in on a family tradition. For years either Palmer or Ellie had taught Sunday school, and neither felt in the mood to work on a large Sunday dinner. The kids had been more than happy to accept pizza for Sunday dinner. It gave them a certain status when they bragged about it to the other kids.

Orly gave Ellie his heartfelt thanks and waited for his boss to move. "So, what next, Sheriff?"

"Well, it's a nice day. What say we go out to the lake?"

Knutson had chosen his itinerary for the investigation with a maximum of convenience to himself. The afternoon was scheduled to include an interview with Lance and Ruth Sterling. The Sterlings owned a cabin on the huge Otter Tail Lake. In light of the murder and the resulting publicity, Lance Sterling had requested that, if at all possible, he would like to remain at the lake for the weekend. Of course, the fact that it was the last weekend before Labor Day and Sterling had set aside this time for serious loafing affected this desire. In any event, it suited the sheriff, because he could stop by the park at Phelps Mill on the way out to interview the Sterlings. There was a large gathering of people there for the Farmer's Union county picnic. They were generally dependable voters, and Knutson thought that he would drop by and assure them that they were in no danger of being murdered.

Phelps Mill is one of those well-kept secrets of western Minnesota. It is incredibly picturesque, one of those places that really isn't supposed to exist anymore. Orly had never seen Palmer "campaign" before, and he was quite surprised at what he saw. The sheriff simply spent a half hour ambling about the grounds, talked to three kids fishing by the mill, and generally answered people's questions about the murder. Yet, Orly realized, Knutson really didn't answer them, he just left people satisfied. As they climbed back into the car, Orly could just feel the unspoken "good old Palmer Knutson" in the air. In truth, he realized he felt just that way himself.

By three o'clock they reached the lake home of Lance and Ruth Sterling. Otter Tail Lake is the largest lake in the county, and there was considerable development on it. The most considerable of all, however, was the "summer residence" of the Sterlings. It was larger than the home of Gherkin, but it blended in with its surroundings much more tastefully. It was a low, rambling house, employing neutral browns and greens to meld carefully with the landscape.

The view from the living room overlooking the lake was spectacular. Ruth met them at the door.

At the Gherkin dinner party, Ruth had looked smashing. Now she was merely smashed. She did not look like the well-groomed but edgy woman they had met earlier. Her henna hair no longer looked well constructed—in fact, it was as yet unbuilt. Sundays at the lake did not usually include a rendezvous with the hairdresser, but in Ruth's case, perhaps it should have. Also gone was the elegant dress of fine fabric, replaced by hideous flowered shorts and an obscene halter top. But one thing could not be denied—she was friendly.

"Come in. Come in. Can I fix you a drink? Lance is out in the boat pretending to drown worms, but he's probably just after bottle bass. You can see him from here. I'll just give him a signal to come in."

"Before you do, Mrs. Sterling," said the sheriff, in his soothing manner, "we'd like to talk to you alone for just a few minutes, if you don't mind. "

"Talk to me? Nobody ever wants to talk to me. What can I get you? Gin and tonic? A little Scotch maybe? Or just a beer?"

"I'm sorry, Mrs. Sterling, we're driving and we're on duty. Perhaps if you had a Coke."

"Oh, aren't we being official. Well, suit yourself. I think I'll have just a little G and T, if you don't mind. I'll be right back."

Knutson and Peterson settled into the elegant sofa that was perfectly aligned to provide the best view of the lake. Within a short time Ruth had joined them with her drink and two cans of root beer. The officers looked at the root beer and each other, shrugged, and thanked their host.

"Now then," said Mrs. Sterling. "What can I tell you?"

This was Peterson's usual cue, and he didn't miss it. "As this is an official interview, Mrs. Sterling, would you have any objection if we recorded it?"

"Record my interview? How flattering! No, you go right ahead."

"Very well," began Palmer, "at what time did you get to the Gherkin residence?"

Whether Mrs. Sterling was thinking or just taking her time her glassy eyes did not reveal. Finally she said, "I suppose it was a quarter past six or so. We weren't the first ones there, but we weren't the last either. Lance was so afraid we were going to be late that he waited outside in the car for me. But I tried to tell him nobody ever arrives at the time stated in the invitation. His response was to tell me about the importance of appointments in the real-estate business."

"Had you ever been to President Gherkin's home before?"

"Sure, lots of times."

"So you knew the configuration of the house well?"

"You bet."

"And what was your attitude toward President Gherkin?"

"I hated the son of a—oops, we're on tape aren't we!"

"Why did you dislike him, Mrs. Sterling?" asked Orly Peterson, with inappropriate overeagerness.

Ruth drained half a glass of gin and tonic, smacked her lips appreciatively, and said, "Well, mostly because Lance did, you know, but he was snotty to me too. I asked him to be chairman of the Heart Fund. All he really had to do was have his name on the brochure; I would have done all the work. But no, he couldn't be bothered. No, he had other things to do. No, he wouldn't come to our banquet even if it was free. Know what he said to me? He said I was a busybody do-gooder! I'll tell you who the do-gooder is! He's the one that stuck the cleaver in Gherkin's head!"

Knutson, with his head cocked to one side, asked, "You said you disliked him mostly because Lance did. What was your husband's quarrel with Gherkin?"

"Oh, no. You're not going to get me to talk about my husband's motive for murdering the old fool. I mean, for your thinking he murdered him. Whatever. I'm not saying a word more about that. I'm not going to tell you about the years of work that Lance put in to help that stupid university, the meetings, the fundraisers, the boring, tedious alumni picnics and receptions that I've been dragged to. Lance was supposed to get that building named after him. Well, it would have been named after all of us, the whole family, I suppose. Did you know that our four kids all went to that stupid university? They were smart enough and we had enough money to send them to a decent private college like Concordia or St. Olaf. But nooooooooo, Lance said they should stay home and attend good old FFSU. They had to be Flying Falcons, every one of them. Oh, I suppose they got their basic education, but they hardly made any contacts in society. Look at the people they married! Last night we got a call . . ."

At this point Orly got an inspiration that earned him later praise from his boss. "Speaking of telephone calls, Mrs. Sterling, when you were at the Gherkins that night, did you ever hear the phone ring?"

Although the question had no relevance whatsoever to the investigation, Ruth apparently thought it did and immediately turned whatever concentration she could muster to the question. At last she said, "No, no, I don't think so."

Following up, Palmer asked, "Do you remember at any time any of the guests leaving the party for any length of time?"

"As a matter of fact I do. I was talking to that Corazon woman when all of a sudden she rudely left me on the patio, saying she had to go to the bathroom. I had just asked her what she thought the business building should have been called and she just left me. I waited for an answer but she must have been in that biffy for at least ten or fifteen minutes. What she was doing there, well, you'll just have to ask her, won't you."

"What about you? Did you at any time leave the group?"

"Of course not."

"Did you at any time talk to Dr. Gherkin?"

"Dr. Gherkin! The old fraud? No, of course not!"

"Did you notice whether or not your husband ever left the group?"

"Hah! That's a good one," responded Ruth, with unmistakable bitterness in her voice. "He leaves me the moment we get to a group like that. He's ashamed of me, Lance is. He'd rather follow that broken-down old football hero around, basking in his reflected glory. No, I stopped trying to keep track of Lance at gatherings like that."

The sheriff tried to get the interview back on track. "Can you think of anyone who would have wanted to kill President Gherkin?"

Ruth seemed distracted and distant. Her eyes looked slightly glazed. "Tell you the truth, I've been thinking about that a lot. A lot of people wanted him dead, but I can't see any of us guests actually doing it. I really can't."

Knutson gave a short nod in the direction of the lake. Peterson stood, and shutting off the tape recorder said, "Well, thank you, Mrs. Sterling, now perhaps we can have a word with your husband. I noticed he is just coming in to the dock."

"Sure thing," said Ruth, standing up a little too quickly for her own good. She slid the massive sliding glass door open and said, "Walk this way," and began ambling down to the dock.

Palmer couldn't resist it. He followed immediately behind his host, walking in a perfect exaggerated stagger that mimed her drunken gait. Peterson, who was constantly surprised by the sheriff, unsuccessfully wrestled with his propensity to giggle.

Knutson inwardly sighed when he saw Lance Sterling. This was just the kind of person he and his wife had in mind when they sang along with the old Jacques Brel song, "The Middle Class, They're Just Like Pigs!" Well, that had been the late sixties, but some members of the middle class apparently felt a moral responsibility for retaining its inanities and its conspicuous consumption.

Sterling was hardly dressed for fishing. He was wearing expensive deck shoes, the kind that should never get wet. He had on navy-blue linen trousers and a white shirt festooned with blue and gold epaulettes. The whole effect was crowned by a captain's cap. As they approached him, Sterling completed the effect with a hearty, "Ahoy, there!"

Palmer eyed the boat with a mixture of envy and contempt. In principle he wanted to storm away from such luxury, but he was also curious and readily agreed when Sterling said, "Why don't we just have our little talk aboard my boat. Watch your head, now."

Ruth walked unsteadily back to the house while the three men ignored her and settled into the cabin of the boat. It was clean and unexpectedly spacious. "Roomy, huh? When my kids are home they sometimes sleep six people on this boat. How about this CD system? Hey, what can I give you? Beer? Wine cooler? Or maybe I can fix you something else. This baby has a wet bar too."

Palmer noted how Orly looked longingly at the beer in the cooler. Well, it was a hot day. Who cared? "Yah, maybe we'll have a beer. What do you say, Orly?"

"You bet!"

Orly adroitly spun the cap off a bottle of Corona and handed it to Palmer. Lance, meanwhile, turned his attention back to a massive insulated tumbler with a short straw. After a long pull on the straw he grinned and said, "Strawberry margarita. I make the best in the world."

"We'd like to record this conversation if we may," said Peterson.

"Certainly, certainly, I quite understand," Sterling replied with a wave of magnanimity.

"According to your wife," began Palmer, "you arrived about a quarter after six and the rest of the guests arrived soon afterwards. Did you notice anything different? Was any member of the party acting in an unusual manner?"

Sterling scoffed. "Well, that stuffy history professor is always acting unusual, if you ask me, and then there's that loony artist. But I wouldn't say that they acted any differently than they always did."

"You were a friend of President Gherkin's?"

"Oh, yes, yes. Great friends."

"How did he seem to you on Friday night?"

"Well, I really didn't talk to him. His opera voice was better than ever, I think. But you see, even though we are, or were, great friends, I respected his privacy when he wanted it."

"Did you leave the party at any time?"

"No, of course not. Wait, wait, that's not right. I did leave for just a couple of minutes. When it started to look like rain I went out to see if my car windows were rolled up."

"Were they?"

"Were the windows rolled up?"

"Yes."

"Oh sure. I always roll up my windows."

For a few seconds the sheriff wondered if this line of questioning would result in anything valuable. He decided to drop it and asked, "And what time was this?"

"I don't know, must have been a quarter after seven or so?"

"Don't you usually drive your car with your air conditioner on?" interrupted Orly.

"Oh, you bet! Must have been close to ninety when we came out here that night. I tell you, I wouldn't buy a car without air these days."

"Then why did you think the windows might be rolled down?"

"Well, uh, I suppose I really didn't think they were, but I figured I'd better check."

"Did you see anybody else leave the party?"

"No."

With a rapid change in direction, Knutson came back with, "Can you think of anyone who would want to kill George Gherkin?"

"No, no, of course not. Everyone loved George. He was the greatest man in the history of our college. He will be sorely missed I can tell you. I can't imagine anyone doing such a horrible thing."

"We understand that you were upset with the president concerning the naming of the business education building. According to our sources, it was going to be called the Sterling Center until Gherkin decided it should be named after the governor." Knutson could not see this as a real motive for murder, but concluded a little testing of the waters was in order.

"Now, who told you that? Sure, there was some talk about it being named after me, er, us, but George thought that for the good of the college we needed to attain a higher visibility in St. Paul. All I'm ever interested in is the welfare of the university. Look, I'll tell you something in private. See all those red, white, and blue signs over there along the lake?"

The sheriff followed the direction of Sterling's knobby index finger. "Yah, what about them?"

"They all say 'Sterling Quality Real Estate.' I own all that property. I keep taking offers for that property, but you know what? That property ain't for sale. George and me were going to be partners. I acquired the property, and he was going to head a group of investors to put up a conference center. It was going to be bigger and nicer than that Radisson resort by Alexandria. All we were waiting for was to get a zoning permit from the county. Woulda been a good thing for the university, too. We coulda given 'em special rates for all sorts of retreats and things. Yeah, George thought it was a great idea."

It was this speech that revealed how inebriated Sterling was. There was little point in going on, but Knutson couldn't resist trying one last line of inquiry. "So, as head of the alumni association, what do you see as the future of the university now that Gherkin is gone?"

Sterling settled into a posture that was almost Churchillian. "Well, it will be tough, you know, but we'll muddle through. I expect that the alumni association will have a definite role in the selection of the new president. Already a few names have been suggested to me—in confidence, of course—and I'm sure that under the new administration the alumni association will continue to provide valuable input. Hey, what do you say, boys? Let me give you a speedboat ride. Let's get out on the lake and really open this puppy up!"

Palmer reached over and removed the keys from the ignition. "That is one thing you will not do, Mr. Sterling. There is no more excuse for operating a boat while alcohol impaired than there is for operating an automobile. I'm taking these keys to the house. Furthermore, I don't expect you to drive back into town until you sober up."

Sterling meekly acquiesced and the sheriff added, "It's for your own good, you know. But thank you for the beer and thank you for your cooperation. Don't bother to see us back to our car, you just rest and enjoy the afternoon."

On the way back to town Knutson asked, "So, Deputy of the Law, what do you think?"

"In the first place," Orly replied, "I don't for a minute believe there is any real grief over Gherkin's passing as far as either Sterling is concerned. I don't think they were drinking to drown their sorrows. Those folks were celebrating!"

"Drunk, three sheets to the wind, plowed."

"Not to mention blithered, snockered, stinky, smelly, and stewed to the gills," Orly added. "But could either of them kill anybody?"

"I've tried to tell you, Orly. Anybody could kill anybody. In any event, I'm done for the day. I'm going home and try not to think about it. Tomorrow we get the official BCA report, although I don't expect any surprises in it. That conference center is a new angle. Tomorrow we see the mayor and Brick Wahl. Perhaps they can tell us something about that. Got a date tonight?"

"Nah, I suppose I'll just stay home. I want to look over my notes and do some thinking and some reading. You know, while the BCA will help, I'd like to be able to say we solved this case on our own."

"I'd like that, too," added the sheriff. "And so would the voters of Otter Tail County."

SIXTEEN

ORLY PETERSON TOOK HIS time going to work on Monday. He reasoned, with justification, that he had put in a lot of hours on Sunday and that the county could only expect so much from a man. Nevertheless, as he walked into the office at 9:30, he looked at the sheriff's door with a certain amount of apprehension.

He need not have worried. Sheriff Knutson had wanted to use the same justification as Peterson to go to bed early and to get up late. Just after breakfast, however, Ellie reminded him how handy it would be if he could size the bathroom walls before he went to work so that later in the day she could begin wallpapering. "Why not?" he asked himself. "I certainly don't have any new leads to report to the media, and home is the most pleasant place to be until then." It was with the smell of sizing on his fingers and a sense of reluctance, therefore, that he finally went to the Otter Tail County Law Enforcement Center. He had made an appointment with Mayor Abigail Armbruster for ten o'clock.

Knutson hated empty gestures of respect for authority but, perhaps subconsciously, he had made himself unusually presentable for his interview with the mayor. He allowed himself about ten minutes to spiff up his office and at almost exactly ten o'clock Armbruster burst into the Law Enforcement Center, walked past the receptionist, stuck her head in his inner office, and said, "I'm here, Sheriff."

"She looks better than ever," thought Palmer Knutson, "but why does she feel she has to dress up for an interview with a county sheriff?" As if reading his mind, Abigail continued, "I suppose I look a little overdressed to give testimony in a murder investigation, but we have a meeting at the University to help plan the 'Welcome Back, FFSU Students' week. It was supposed to be with George, of course, but I called Isabel Corazon and told her we just couldn't wait for that kind of planning and she said that she supposed that she could sit in since she is a vice-president and in lieu of anybody else, she assumed the reins of power as acting president and I told her, I said, 'I think that's just grand,' and it is, you know. She'll do a great job and I wouldn't mind seeing that made permanent, although I suppose it never will be because she is a woman, but she would do a good job, don't you think?"

Stunned by this volcanic verbal eruption, Knutson grunted, "Uh, yah, I guess I do."

"Well, I mean, she's trained for it and she's got a lot of good ideas and frankly, well, not to speak ill of the dead or anything, but I've heard that she has really been running the academic end of the college for some time while Sally Ann runs the rest of the place. I mean, maybe now they can get credit and equal pay for doing it. Do you have any idea what a college president gets these days, why it's . . ."

"Mrs. Armbruster, Mrs. Armbruster, please. I'd like to get some of this on tape. Please, sit down. Would you like a cup of coffee? We only made it last week. Just kidding, it's a new pot. Want cream or sugar or anything in it?"

"Sheriff, I didn't get where I am today by turning down free cups of coffee. Just black will do. Now, where are you going?"

"I have to get Orly in on the interview. Orly!" Knutson bellowed across the reception area. "You in yet? Get your tape recorder and get in here. The mayor's here for her interview."

Within seconds Orly arrived at Knutson's office, giving the appearance of having been working since eight in the morning. "Good morning, Mrs. Armbruster. How you doing today?"

The mayor dismissed him like an ant at a picnic. "Fine, fine. But let's get down to business. I've got to be up at the college in an hour."

Outwardly ignoring the curt dismissal, Peterson tried out his charm and continued in his casual manner, "Right, well, I have a tape recorder here and we would like to record this interview. I trust that is all right?"

"No, it is not," Mrs. Armbruster said sharply. "I do not like to have my conversations recorded. I see it as an infringement on my constitutional freedoms. I can't help but feel that I lose control of things once somebody else has my voice on tape. Look what happened to Tricky Dicky Nixon. They can do marvelous things with tape these days. On the other hand, I know you have a job to do and I can't demand any special treatment just because I'm mayor. So record!" she exclaimed dramatically. "And preserve it for a grateful posterity. But if there is something I don't want recorded, I trust you will be able to turn off that thing?"

Orly didn't know what to say and looked to Knutson for approval. The sheriff imperceptibly nodded and the deputy said, "Of course," and turned on the recorder.

The sheriff assumed his air of crack law enforcement authority and began, "Now Mrs. Armbruster, at what time did you get to the dinner party on Friday night?"

The mayor thought for a bit, beating out a rhythm with her fingernails on the arm of the chair. "Must have been about twenty after six. We were invited for six, but I had to go by and pick up Brick and he wasn't ready. I tell you, everybody makes jokes about women primping and being late for an occasion. How many times have we seen Dagwood waiting for Blondie? Well, Brick is worse than Blondie ever was. Anyhow, we were about twenty minutes late, but we didn't seem to have missed anything. One really never does, or did, I suppose, at George's parties."

"Was everyone else there when you came?"

"Everybody but the murderer, unless, that is," she gasped, as though the thought had just occurred to her, "you think it was one of us?"

Knutson ignored the implied question and continued, "Did you ever hear any car outside or any door opening or anything else that might lead you to think someone else might have entered the house?"

"Well, no," Mrs. Armbruster answered thoughtfully, "I can't really say I did."

"Did you notice that there were any unusual absences from the dinner party—that is, did anybody seem to be gone for a while?"

"You mean, with time to sneak in and bump off George? Well, I've tried to think of that," she said, belying her earlier incredulity that the murderer was a guest at the dinner party, "and I really don't have anything to tell you. Nobody even saw him, of course. All we heard was that awful opera. You know, George didn't have that bad a voice. If he sang something decent and a little softer, maybe it would even have been pleasant. In any event, I know that nobody gathered around to hear him sing. At one time I did see that painter go off in the general direction of the kitchen, but then, of course, he may just have gone out the front door. He was gone for at least ten minutes. And I remember Dr. Corazon heading for that area, and she was gone for quite a while. I remember that because Ruth Sterling and I were talking to her when she left rather abruptly, and when she came back she looked a little sick. But the more I think about it, I suppose anybody could have gone there without asking me. What are the chances I'm going to keep track of anybody as dull as that history teacher, for instance? You might ask Brick. I seem to remember he kept pretty close track of wherever Sally Ann Pennwright or that artist's cute little wife went!"

The sheriff looked at his knees, noticed a coffee stain on his trousers, coughed, and replied, "Yes, of course, we will be talking to Mr. Wahl. But tell us, can you think of any reason why anyone would want to kill President Gherkin?"

Mrs. Armbruster smiled and wagged a finger. "The old 'who's got the motive,' eh? Well, I don't know of anyone who would want to actually snuff him out, but I don't know if very many of the tears shed at the funeral will be real ones. I know Brick had even become a little disenchanted with Gherkin over the last few years."

"And why was that?"

"Why Brick didn't like him? Wait a minute, I don't want to give Brick a motive for murder. Tell you what, though, turn that thing off and I'll tell you what I know about Gherkin's business dealings."

Again Knutson nodded and Peterson surged forward to turn off the recorder. "All right," the sheriff said, "what can you tell us?"

"Well, as you probably know," she began conspiratorially, "Brick and his company have built most of the buildings put up at the university over the last twenty years. That didn't happen by accident. Contracts for state buildings of that nature are awarded by competitive bids, of course, and Brick always bid the lowest. Well, I was curious as to why that was. I just assumed that since Brick's company was local he could bid lower because of transportation and labor costs, but I mean, one hundred percent of the large contracts? Could nobody underbid him? Well, Brick rarely drinks, but there was that Norwegian Day celebration, what do they call it? *Syttende Mai*? May 17th, in any event. Anyway, he had gotten into the sauce with a lot of toasting and he said he was going to get the contract for the new business building—at that time everybody was calling it the Sterling Center—and he boasted about how he had made some big investments on new machinery. I said, 'How do you know you'll get the contract?' 'Don't I always?' he says, with this cat-who-swallowed the-canary look on his face. 'How?' I says. Well, he won't come out and tell me, but he keeps this supercilious smirk on his kisser and hints that bids are due one day but opened and read the next day. From what I gathered, Wahl submitted an empty envelope. Gherkin fiddled with the bids, steamed 'em open or something I suppose, phoned Brick with the low figures, Brick filled in lower figures on his bid and sneaked it and a wad of hundred dollar bills up to the President's office. The low figures were slipped into the empty envelope and opened the next morning. Gherkin's own little private retirement account mysteriously grows from a grateful Wahl. Hey, I wonder if Dolly even knows about that little nest egg?

"Well, like I said, that was in May, a couple of years ago now. The bids were opened a couple of weeks later and a Moorhead construction firm had submitted the low bid. Apparently, Brick was shocked and, from a little grumbling that I heard from him, somewhat financially overextended. And he was certainly not palsy-walsy with Gherkin after that."

The sheriff arched his eyebrows suggestively and asked, "Was Mr. Wahl upset enough to contemplate murder?"

The mayor nodded at the possibility. "Maybe at the time, but that was then, this is now, and I think they were happy again. In fact, now this is just rumor, you understand, so I don't want this on tape either—I got it from my secretary whose sister is secretary to an architect—but anyway, Brick was apparently in the process of going into a business arrangement with Gherkin."

"What was that all about?"

"Well, now I don't know all the facts of course, but Lance Sterling was buying up property on Otter Tail Lake for a conference center. Gherkin thought it was a great idea. So great, in fact, that he was in the process of stealing it from him. Brick was buying up land on the other side of the lake, the side closest to the highway and the side with the best beach. They were going to set up a dummy corporation, Brick was going to build it and Gherkin would steer all university business there, as well as much of the state business that would come because of his cozy relationship with the governor." Abigail Armbruster patted down her frosted brown hair, pushed up her silver wire-rimmed glasses and gave a triumphant upraising of her eyebrows. "How do you like them apples, Sheriff?"

"So what you're implying is that whereas Brick may have had his differences with Gherkin over the business building, he now had every reason to keep him alive?"

"You bet! At least that's the way I've got it figured."

The sheriff abruptly changed the direction of the interrogation. "What about your relationship to President Gherkin? As the two most important leaders in the community, surely your swords must have crossed on occasion?" Knutson caught Peterson's eye and indicated that he should start the recorder.

Mrs. Armbruster noticed, looked the deputy directly in the eye, nodded, and continued, "Well, no. Not really. I have always been a supporter of FFSU. It is the heart and soul of our community. It has brought in a lot of business and although the university itself is not a source of tax revenue, a lot of businesses that depend on it are. Besides, I have always had a respect for the students and for higher education in general . . ."

Oh, Lord, thought Knutson, she's going into her set campaign speech to the university community. After all these years she believes it herself.

"And, if there is anything that the city can do to aid the university, we will do it to the best of our ability. Speaking of the city, I mean, while we're on the subject, I hope this business gets cleared up soon. I don't want Fergus Falls to be known as the murder capital of Minnesota. I mean, this is the first murder to occur here that I can remember and it's bad for our image. Still, I have to admit it does provide us with some publicity. Did you see the ABC news on Saturday night? They opened with a nice vista of Lincoln Avenue and then a nice shot of Lake Alice. I mean, we couldn't buy that kind of publicity. It's a shame, of course, but still, well. . . ."

"Yes, um, we're doing our best to clear this matter up," muttered Sheriff Knutson. "But just one more thing. I have also heard rumors about you and Gherkin."

"Me and George? Oh come now, Sheriff," she said with a smile that was positively coquettish. "I am not a home wrecker and am not about to chase after a married man. I suppose I find it flattering that rumors can still connect me with anyone, but really, that is quite ridiculous!"

The sheriff hastened to make himself clear. "That's not exactly what I meant. It seems that when Wal-Mart was first coming to town they had a prime spot near the interstate highway all picked out. Land that you owned, I hear. All they needed was a little strip of land from the university golf course. Now I don't know what happened next, whether Gherkin's asking price was too high or he had other reasons for blocking the deal, but if Wal-Mart goes someplace else, you might lose a very lucrative land sale. Is that right?"

Abigail Armbruster was no longer ebullient. She sneered at Knutson, asking, "Where did you get that information? And what business is that of yours anyway?"

"As to where I got it, that has no relevance. As to what business it is of mine, I think it would be a pretty good motive for murder, don't you?"

"I have nothing more to say on this," replied Mrs. Armbruster hotly. "And you, Deputy, turn that thing off! I have to go to a meeting."

Knutson politely rose to indicate that the interview was at an end. "Mrs. Armbruster, we do thank you for your time. I know that you are extremely busy and we appreciate it. I trust that you accept that I have a job to do same as anybody else. I do want you to realize one more thing. Even though we turned off the recorder, we still treat what you told us as evidence. We accept that it was given to us in confidence and we will not use it unless we have to. Nevertheless, this is a murder case, and we can't promise anything. We appreciate all the cooperation that exists between the city and the county and we appreciate all that you are doing for the community. Just as long as we understand each other. Murder is murder."

A much more subdued Mrs. Armbruster picked up her purse and moved thoughtfully out of the office.

"So, what do you think? Could she have done it?" asked the deputy, as soon as the mayor was out of earshot.

"Orly!"

"Yes, I know. Anybody could have done it. She, like everybody it seems, had a motive. By the way, the BCA just faxed their report on the scene-of-the-crime investigation. I just barely had an opportunity to scan it before the mayor came in," Orly said, handing the fax to his boss. "I couldn't really find anything that does us a lot of good. The only fingerprints they found are the ones you might expect, Gherkin and Dolly, as well as some partial prints by the light switch, which we can probably assume belong to Dr. Winston, since he is the one who is supposed to have turned on the lights. No footprints in the flower bed or anything like that. No tell-tale missing button found at the scene of the crime."

The sheriff sighed and accepted the report. "Yah, well, it's almost time for lunch. Why don't you just leave it with me and I'll read it over the noon hour. Be back here by one o'clock if you can. Brick Wahl is coming in early this afternoon."

———

Palmer Knutson closed the door to his office and purely out of habit switched on Minnesota Public Radio. He made a deliberate ritual of taking out his lunch—an orange, a granola bar, and a cup of coffee from the office machine. He longed for a ham and cheese sandwich, but he looked sorrowfully at the way his shirt bulged over his belt, and unwrapped the granola bar.

He had earlier examined the autopsy report and found nothing of interest. According to the medical examiner, death had been almost instantaneous—certainly no time for the victim to write the name of his murderer in loose vegetables or chicken entrails. And, of course, there was never any doubt as to the cause of death. The time of death, meanwhile, was about the same as estimated by the doctor on the scene, somewhere between 5:30 and 7:30 on Friday.

Well, maybe the scene-of-the-crime experts had something for him, thought Palmer, although he was starting to trust Orly's opinion more all the time. The report from the BCA was sterile of life and humor. No prints that should not have been there had been found in the kitchen. No evidence of forced entry. No evidence of tampering with any of the locks, and, it went without saying, no secret passages or mirrors. Once again the intuition returned to Palmer that if he could solve the "how," he would solve the "who," and find out the "why" later. As he played with an orange peel Knutson finally found a meaningful fact in the BCA report. What did it mean that there were no other fingerprints? Either the murderer wore gloves—possible but not likely in the summertime—or the murderer took pains to wipe off other prints. But there were no areas that had been systematically cleaned of all prints; George's and Dolly's prints were all over the place. Had the killer been extraordinarily neat or had he just not needed to touch anything but the cleaver? And how would he or she have done this? The fact that there were no prints on the cleaver was not significant. Anyone could have held that with a handkerchief or could have used a handkerchief to wipe it off after the blow was struck. But how did one get into and out of a locked room without leaving a trace? Maybe the door was unlocked especially for the murderer, only to be locked somehow after the murder had been committed. If that were the case, Gherkin had apparently trusted his killer enough to turn his back on him.

———

The sheriff was deep in thought when the door burst open, startling him. Orly was back from his lunch. "Hey Palmer, how was your lunch? I just saw Brick Wahl coming up the sidewalk. Should I show him right in?"

With difficulty, the sheriff cleared his mind to the task at hand. "No. Let him report to the desk and let him cool his heels a bit. It has been my experience that when somebody is called in to talk they prepare a little speech. When they don't get to say it right away they get a little nervous and forget it and you can get a few more honest answers. What did you have for lunch?"

"Couple of super burritos and a large Coke. I hope I can do some outside work today, if you know what I mean."

Knutson rolled his eyes and said starchily, "After we get done talking to Wahl I don't care what you do. You're still working on a couple of other cases aren't you?"

"Yeah, there was that break-in last night at that resort by Pelican Rapids, on Lake Lida, so I thought I'd better get up there and look into it."

"Good. Keep busy and show the badge around to let the citizens know they are protected. Murder makes everyone nervous. Make a copy of this BCA report and bring Wahl back with you."

Within a few minutes Orly returned ushering in Brick Wahl. As usual, Wahl had taken care with his appearance. His hair, or at least what remained of it, was carefully brushed back to hide the moles on his lumpy skull. He wore a light gray suit with a white shirt that set off a maroon and charcoal gray tie. His lapel prominently featured his gold "Five F's" pin which displayed the logo of the Fergus Falls Flying Falcons Foundation.

The sheriff rose to greet him, shook his hand, and asked him to be seated. Wahl was used to such attention, and accepted it as though he deserved it, which, considering his position in the city and the county, perhaps he did.

"Coffee, Mr. Wahl?" Knutson asked politely.

"No, no, I just came from a luncheon meeting at Mabel Murphy's. Couldn't have another drop. And don't call me 'Mr. Wahl,' Palmer. Call me Brick."

"Well, sure, Brick, but this is serious business. In fact, Orly here is going to tape our conversation, if that's all right with you."

"Yah, sure, I guess so. I got nothing to hide."

"Now, we've already talked to Mrs. Armbruster, and she said you got there about twenty after six. That right?"

"Yah."

"Notice anything unusual about that dinner party?"

"Nope."

"Notice anybody come or go or act out of the ordinary in any way?"

"Nope. I only heard George singing that opera stuff. Uffda."

"Did you at any time talk to President Gherkin that night?"

"Nope."

The sheriff continued to drone his questions in a monotone voice. "At any time, did you notice anybody absent from the gathering for any length of time?"

"Nope. No, wait. I did. I had listened to that smart-aleck intellectual, that history teacher, say all kinds of nasty things about Mr. Reagan. I thought about that for some time and the more I thought about it the madder I got. I went to tell him a few things because if he's a history teacher, I don't want him teaching that kinda history."

"That reminds me, Brick, weren't you part of a national committee to put Reagan's head on Mount Rushmore? How's that going?"

"Well, not so good. We found out that they wouldn't let us add anything to Mount Rushmore, so we started looking for another mountain in the same general area. We found one that would have been in a good site, but the rock wasn't hard enough for Reagan's head."

Palmer was able to keep a straight face and nod sympathetically. He could hardly wait to get home and tell that one to Ellie. With luck, every Democrat in town would have heard of it by sundown.

"So you went to confront Winston about what he had said about Reagan. Where was he at this time?"

"Well, that's just it, you see. He was supposed to be in the living room all the time. Except when I went there, he was nowhere to be seen."

"Did you ever find him?"

"Of course, later, but for the time being I went out on the patio. When I saw him again he was talking to Dr. Corazon so I never did get to have it out with him."

"Can you think of anyone who may have wanted to murder Dr. Gherkin?"

"Of course not!" Wahl said indignantly. "After what that man has brought to our university and our community? No sireee! We all looked up to him."

"And yet," Palmer began tentatively, "I understand that you were a little upset with him when you didn't get the contract for the business building?"

Like a little boy caught in a big fib, Wahl looked from one to the other and confessed, "Well, sure I was upset. I mean, I had built all of those dorms and classroom buildings, hadn't I? But I got over that. I mean, one can't get too greedy. And that Moorhead company did a fine job and a couple of companies that I own were able to get some of the subcontracted jobs. Besides, I wanted to keep on good terms with Gherkin for future jobs. No use to poison the well, don't you know."

Feigning ignorance, Palmer asked, "And what might these future projects have been?"

Wahl leaned forward. "Now, I don't know how much of this is for public consumption, but George and I talked about the feasibility of a new athletic complex covered with a mini-dome. A place that our Flying Falcons deserve. I would have liked to bid on that. No assurances that I would have gotten the bid, of course, but after talking to George I was pretty sure that my bid would be in the ballpark, so to speak. Er, actually, that was George's little joke."

"Did you ever have any private dealings with Dr. Gherkin?" asked Palmer in an exploratory, tentative manner.

"No, no. It was just professional."

"I was thinking about the possible conference center on Otter Tail Lake?"

"What?" Wahl said anxiously. "How did you find out about that? Anyway, that was just in the speculative stage."

The sheriff decided to press him. "Have you acquired any property?"

"Not that it's any of your business, but yes, I have."

"Did you know that Lance Sterling was also involved in a conference center proposal with Dr. Gherkin?"

Wahl looked petulantly at Knutson before finally saying, "I suppose you've been talking to Sterling. Yah, I found that out Friday night. Sterling started bragging about his big plans."

"And this conference center, the one that Sterling was talking about, was a different project, right?"

"Of course. On the other side of the lake. Sterling's property. You don't think two conference centers, each with an exclusive arrangement with Fergus Falls State University, would be built, do you?"

"I suppose not. And how did you feel about this?"

"Well, I got to admit, not so good. But then I figured, what does Sterling really have to offer? Gherkin is talking about a deal with him just so he doesn't feel left out. Nothing would ever have come of the deal and Sterling might have bought up some property that would have risen in value because of the conference center. Everybody would have been happy."

"Did you let Sterling know about your plans for a conference center?"

"Not in so many words, but maybe I was mad enough to let something slip," the contractor worriedly admitted.

"One last thing, Brick. When you failed to get the contract for the business building, were you overextended? I hear that your company might have fallen on hard times."

Brick straightened up in his chair and squared his shoulders. "I don't know where you got that information. But it's not true. Sure, the loss of that contract didn't help. But I've got enough socked away to lose a lot more contracts if I have to. You don't have to worry about the Brick! Who have you been talking to, anyway?"

"Well, maybe they were wrong," said the sheriff, dismissing the subject. "Look, Brick, I appreciate your coming in. Stay in touch with us, will you?"

"Yah, sure, you bet, Sheriff," Wahl said, all smiles again. "I know you got a job to do and I hope you find out who did it so everything can get back to normal. It's the kind of thing that won't do our university or community any good at all. Still, maybe now I won't have to hire so many of those football players for construction jobs that don't really need to be done."

As Wahl said this he broke into an exaggerated chuckle and rose from his chair. Orly deftly switched off the tape recorder and stood with him. As he guided Wahl to the door, Orly turned back to the sheriff and said, "So I'll go up to Pelican Rapids, then. Call me on my cell phone if you need anything."

"Yah, Orly. Good luck."

As Orly closed the door behind him Knutson could not help wondering if a businessman as successful as Brick Wahl seemed to be could remain successful if he had such a forgiving nature. He doubted it.

SEVENTEEN

On Tuesday morning Orly Peterson was writing a report on his computer when Palmer Knutson peeked in through his open door. "What did you find out about that break-in at that Pelican Rapids resort?"

Without looking up Orly replied, "Ah, it was just some kids stealing beer."

Knutson walked in and sat next to the desk, waiting patiently for his deputy to finish a paragraph. Everybody hates to type while someone else is watching, of course, and after three successive mistakes Orly rolled his chair back and repeated, "Just some kids stealing beer."

"So, how did you handle it?" the sheriff asked with a bland interest.

Peterson smiled and replied, "Ever met old Milo Hansen, that old Dane who runs the place? He thought he had been hit with the biggest crime wave in the history of Minnesota. Actually, somebody had just forced the screen door and gotten into a porch area behind the main building. That's where he keeps the beer. He claims that he likes to have it on hand to treat fishermen who rent his boats. Everybody knows he sells it, but of course he won't apply for a license to do so. Anyway, if you rent a boat with beer it is five dollars more per six-pack. But he's been doing it for almost forty years, and nobody wants to say anything. Well, he figures maybe a couple of cases of beer were swiped. So I listen to him and ask him questions about the time of the theft—somewhere between 9:00 p.m. and 9:00 a.m. was as close as he was prepared to guess—and I ask him if there were any suspicious characters around. They all were, according to Milo. I took a lot of notes and did a lot of 'tsk-tsk-ing'. There are only two ways we'll ever catch who did it, and that's if and when the kids start bragging to their friends or when a patrol car happens to catch them in the act when they do it again and scare them into confessing about this job. Of course, I didn't tell Milo that. I even took out a tape measure and measured the distance from the screen door to the refrigerator. I think that impressed him greatly. He also promised to tell us if anything else concerning the crime occurs to him."

Knutson smiled. "You're learning, Orly. We'll turn you into an ace crime fighter yet. Meanwhile, we have to go to the college today. I have appointments set up with Francis Olson, Harold Winston, and Isabel Corazon. I think I'll drive my car. We don't want to show up on campus in a patrol car. They are starting freshmen orientation today and there is nothing like a sheriff's department car to cause stares and uneasiness. Think about it. Didn't you always wonder who had done what whenever you saw a cop car parked where it ordinarily wasn't? Besides, if we show up in an official sheriff's vehicle anywhere near the football field, Coach Olson would probably lose half of his recruits."

It had been some time since Palmer Knutson had visited the offices of the athletic department at Fergus Falls State University. He had last been there as a senior in college. At that time they had been located under the seating of the field house and boxes of tape and broken football gear were wedged in the lowest part of the room. He remembered an old steel desk, on which someone had scratched "Flying Falcons Forever," an old black dial telephone, and a bulletin board with press clippings and motivational slogans. Therefore, he was not prepared for what he saw as he was ushered into the offices of Francis Olson.

Olson's office was in the new administrative annex to the field house. His office, accessible only through a secretary-receptionist's room, was about fifteen feet square with plush carpeting and Danish modern office furniture. On the desk were three telephones, one of which was part of a fax machine. The walls were covered with sports art (which Palmer considered an oxymoron) and autographed pictures of Olson in his professional uniform posing with senators, movie stars, and two ex-presidents. A trophy case filled with gold and silver footballs and partially deflated game balls graced one side of the room. Olson, dressed casually but at least not wearing a whistle, greeted them, steered them to a pair of leather sofas arranged in a conversational grouping, and blandly agreed to Orly's request to tape the interview.

"Well, what can I tell ya?" he began. "It was an awful thing, just awful. You know, it seems as though I can still smell the blood. Can you imagine? A murdered man's blood dripping into a pan of chicken? I'm no stranger to blood, but usually I caused it on other people. Know what I mean? But jeez, this was something else!"

The sheriff nodded in man-to-man sympathy and asked, "Now, when did you get to Dr. Gherkin's home?"

"Must'a been about a quarter after six. I picked up Harold Winston on my way out. Good guy, Harold. Boy, does he know history!"

"Yah, so I've heard. Listen, what did you do when you got there?"

"Nothing much. Hung around the patio for a while, drank some beer. Gherkin always goes for that foreign stuff. Or, I guess I should say, he used to. I suppose it's not bad once you get used to it. I suppose if you drink enough of it you just don't care what it is. Tell you the truth, that's sort of what I was aiming at. After a while Sterling starts talking sports and me and him went down to the dock and sat there for a while, chewing the fat. What the hay? He doesn't know diddly about sports, but at least it got me far away from Corazon, and away from Gherkin and his long-hair music. That's a good one, huh? Gherkin liked long-hair music and he was almost bald." The coach chuckled at his own wit and abruptly stopped when it became obvious that nobody else was joining in.

After an uncomfortable silence of a few seconds the sheriff asked, "Did you notice anybody arrive or leave or make any kind of unexpected appearance or disappearance during the evening?"

"Huh? What do you mean?"

Orly, noticing the bewildered expression on Olson's face, bluntly asked, "Did anybody seem to be gone long enough to commit a murder?"

With comprehension advancing like sunrise over the desert, Olson looked cagey for a second and replied simply, "Not that I noticed. Of course, I wasn't looking for that kind of thing and I didn't keep track of people. Mostly I just looked out on the lake, wondering if I should sell my fishing boat. If I ever leave FFSU, I probably won't have any use for that."

Knutson's eyebrows went up as his glasses slid down. "Are you planning on leaving the Flying Falcons?"

"Well, you never know," Olson smiled. "If an opportunity arose I think I'd like to give Division One a try. You never know how high you can soar until you try. That's what I tell my players, the Flying Falcons. I've accomplished about all I can here, and there's really nothing holding me back."

Directing the investigation back to the matter at hand, the sheriff asked, "Was there any time when you were away from the group?"

"I get it. Was there any time for me to sneak up and take a whack at Gherkin you mean. Nope, I was there all the time, with everybody else."

Knutson decided it was worth a shot. "That's not what we've heard. We've been told by others that you were gone for a few minutes. About seven o'clock?"

"Oh yeah? Oh yeah. Geez! I didn't think anyone would notice. Sure I took a little break. I'd been down on the dock drinking beer. I had to whiz. I didn't want to walk all the way back up to the house. I noticed a few bushes a little ways down the shoreline and I assumed no one would miss me for a while. So I just took a little walk."

"Anybody see you there?"

"I hope not! That was the whole purpose of going behind the bushes, wasn't it?"

This sounded reasonable to Knutson. "Yah, I suppose. Did you talk to President Gherkin at all that night?"

"Did anybody? No, of course I didn't. I hadn't seen him for a couple of days."

"Can you think of anybody who might have had a motive for killing Gherkin?"

"The old 'Who inherits?' Yeah, I can tell you who inherits right away. Isabel Corazon. You can be sure as soon as she gets her mitts on this university the football budget is going to go right down the tubes. I think that lady would kill for power. I'll tell you someone else who would have liked to kill the Great One. Harold Winston! And I couldn't blame him if he did, the way Gherkin always shafted him and the history department. But I also know that Harold wouldn't hurt a fly. Personally, though, I think there's money behind it. There always is, isn't there?"

Orly, sensing that Olson was on a roll, interjected, "What about Williams?"

"Sherwin Williams? You got to be kidding! He's too full of himself. If he gets introduced to someone wearing sunglasses, he uses the opportunity to admire himself in the reflection."

Knutson took the time to appreciate the image and, looking the coach in the eye, asked, "Just one more thing, Mr. Olson. Was President Gherkin aware of your interest in leaving FFSU?"

For a few moments Olson was silent, as though calculating the best answer. Finally he said, "Yeah, he was. And you may find out anyway so I'll level with you. He said he would never let me go because of the kind of contract I had signed." A sly grin spread across the coach's face. "I guess that, as Gherkin would have said, 'no longer obtains.'"

"I guess that covers it," said the sheriff as he stood up. "I suppose you are a busy man these days. Thanks for your cooperation. Stay close and don't go away without telling us. Meanwhile, have a good season. We'll look forward to it."

"Thanks. And good luck on your investigation."

With handshakes and a kind of artificial bonhomie, Palmer and Orly were shown out of the office. "Who's next?" asked the deputy.

"That most revered scholar, Dr. Harold Winston."

———

Winston's office was in the same location as it had been when Knutson had attended college. It was on the third floor of Old Main, reached by two and a half flights of stairs. The door was half open, but Knutson knocked anyway. Winston flung open the door and soon filled the entire doorway.

"Come in. Come in. I've been expecting you."

"Thank you, Dr. Winston. Remember Orly Peterson, my deputy?"

"Of course," Winston lied. "Too bad we had to meet under such unpleasant circumstances. Uh, I didn't realize there would be two of you. Let me get another chair."

Winston found an unsteady wooden, straight-backed chair behind a folding table in the hall. He brought it in and, by kicking aside a stack of research papers of indeterminate age, found a place for it. He was able to place the chair so that the shortest leg rested on the place where the floor was the most warped. The result was that the chair gave the most security it could ever give. Winston's office was approximately seven feet square, with floor-to-ceiling bookcases. Only one dirty and cracked window, high up in the wall, provided an alternative light source to the long white fluorescent fixture, discolored by years of accumulated fly-specks and giving off an annoying drone. An old Royal manual typewriter and an old black dial telephone graced the messy surface of a dented steel desk, on which was scratched "Flying Falcons Forever."

"Sit down, sit down. I've got some coffee in a thermos here and I can find a couple of cups if you'd like to share it?"

Knutson looked at the badly stained white coffee cups, stolen years earlier from the university food service, and politely declined. "Actually, Dr. Winston, although you gave us a statement on Friday night, we are just interviewing everyone who had any connection with the murder of Dr. Gherkin. As you were on the scene when the murder was probably committed, we'd just like to ask you a few more questions about what you did that night?"

The professor nodded and looked ashamed. "Yes. I regret what I did that night. The poor, unsuspecting old fool. I took advantage of him and just let him have it when I couldn't stand it anymore. He was asking for it, but I've felt badly about it ever since."

Orly's eyes were bulging out. He frantically scrambled for his tape recorder.

The sheriff, also plainly shocked, said, "Are you confessing to the murder of George Gherkin? If so, I must read you your rights."

Winston blinked furiously behind his spectacles. "What? Me murdering Gherkin? Don't be silly. No, I was talking about how I upset that harmless nincompoop Brick Wahl. He was going on

and on about that appallingly ignorant, senile, essentially dishonest, and confused old fool, Ronald Reagan. I couldn't take that
kind of stupidity from anybody while he was president, and I find
it even more offensive from a certain perspective in time. Anyway,
I started to harangue him about Reagan having the brains of a car-
rot and being the worst president in American history, or, at least
until now! Old Wahl almost had a stroke. And I probably overdid
it. I mean, maybe Reagan wasn't any dumber than Andrew Johnson or Warren G. Harding. Wahl took it hard, though."

Knutson acknowledged this. "We just talked to him yesterday.
He is still pretty upset. But that's hardly why we came to see you.
We wanted to know what you saw at Gherkin's house that night."

"And about what I did at Gherkin's house that night, Inspector?" said the professor, leaning back in his dangerously squeaking
chair. "No, seriously, I know you've got a job to do, Sheriff, and I'll
do whatever I can to help. You'll want to tape this, I suppose?"

"Yes, if we may," responded Orly, taking out his omnipresent
recorder.

"Sure, why not? Although, I've got some friends who are strict
civil libertarians who would be shocked at it. What can I tell you?"

Orly, who found that talking about murder was more cheery
than contemplating the depressing nature of the office, replied,
"We have been talking to Francis Olson, and he says you got to the
president's home about a quarter after six. Did you see or talk to
Dr. Gherkin?"

"No. In fact, not only did I not see him or talk to him that
night, I hadn't seen him or talked to him for about two months, at
the time we hired our current chair. Sally Ann Pennwright called
me with the invitation. So when I heard him singing on Friday

night in his dreadful attempt to imitate *I Pagliacci*, it was the first time I had heard his nauseating voice for a long time."

"So you and Dr. Gherkin were not, shall we say, the best of friends?"

"All right, we shall say that. We were not the best of friends. I think the world and especially this university will be a better place without him. I won't deny he did some wonderful things for this university. He had the gall and the chutzpa to go for things I never thought possible and he built up the university to a size I never thought I'd see. He had a way with the legislature and the governor and got a lot for this place. But at what price! In a way, it may all turn out for the best. We now have a chance to get someone with academic integrity who can turn these fine facilities into a real center of learning."

Knutson tried to avoid looking around at the "fine facilities" and decided not to press the issue. "Did you notice anybody from your dinner party who was absent for any amount of time?"

The chair moaned painfully as the professor shifted his weight forward. He waved his hand to dismiss the notion. "You know how it is at a 'do' like that. There were some people on the patio who think they have to talk to somebody in the house and there are people in the house who decide to talk to somebody down by the lake. People move around and drift and you really can't keep track of them. I presume you want to know if there was anybody that I saw who went in the direction of the kitchen door and stayed long enough to play executioner. Well, I've been thinking about that. I was in the living room almost all the time. I don't particularly like fresh air, especially when it's hot fresh air. I decided to sit in air-conditioned comfort. Anyway, from where I was in the living room, if anyone passed me to go to the bathroom or to the kitchen or to go out to where the cars were parked, I probably would have seen them. Over the course of the evening, I probably saw everybody go in the direction of the bathroom at least once. But I recall only three people who were gone a significant amount of time, Sherwin Williams, his wife, and Isabel Corazon."

Orly interrupted the professor to ask, "But you have no idea where they went, just that they could have gone to the kitchen, the bathroom, or outside?"

"Yes, that's right."

Knutson resumed the questioning. "Can you think of anyone who would wish to kill President Gherkin?"

"Only anybody who cared about the university, academic integrity, or the restoration of cosmos to a chaotic universe. Ah, that's probably not fair. I didn't like him, but I certainly didn't go out and kill him. One hears things on a college campus. A falling out between Gherkin and Sally Ann Pennwright, a spat with Dr. Corazon, and broken promises to almost every faculty member. Let's just leave it at this: I don't know who killed him, but it was time for a change."

"Just one more thing before we go. Perhaps you can clear this up. Brick Wahl says that when he came up to the house you were nowhere to be seen. You've just said you spent most of your time in the living room. Care to comment on that?"

Winston made no attempt to hide his distaste. "So that's his way of getting even, is it! Typical of a crowd that can deify a criminal like Ollie North and praise scandal! He's just trying to get back at me, Sheriff. Pay no attention to him."

Knutson eyed Dr. Winston evenly and said, "We give everyone's word equal weight in an investigation of this sort. Yours as well as his. Now, you want to try that question again?"

"Yeah, okay. I just forgot about it, that's all. Yeah, I saw him turn toward the house and come toward me. But the important thing is, I saw him first. I didn't want to hear any of that right-wing loony stuff again so I just ducked out the front door for a little bit. Five minutes, maybe. Ten at the most."

"So during this time, then, anybody could have gone into the kitchen and you would not have seen them?"

"Yeah, I guess that's right," the professor admitted.

Knutson stood up and said, "Well, I do thank you for your time. Orly, shut that thing off. We've got one more stop to make. Dr. Winston? Don't leave town without telling us until this thing is cleared up and don't hesitate to call either of us if you think of anything that might be of use in our investigations."

Dr. Winston aimed to part on a friendly note. "I don't suppose you are any nearer to solving his case, but don't lose heart. I'm reminded of what Ebert, the President of the Weimar Republic said with regard to the financial crisis of 1924. He said he had been in the position of a condemned man who is offered a year of his life if he will teach a horse to fly. 'One does not turn down such an offer,' he said, 'after all, before the year is out, the king, or I, or the horse may die, and anyway, who knows? Perhaps the horse will really learn to fly.' Hang in there, Sheriff."

Knutson said, "Stressemann."

Winston looked at the sheriff doubtfully and said, "Huh?"

"Thank you for your encouragement, Dr. Winston, but it wasn't Ebert, it was the German Foreign Minister Gustav Stressemann. And he was talking about the Dawes Plan."

"You sure about that, Knutson?"

"Yah."

"How, may I ask, do you come by that little pearl of information?"

"I had a good teacher in college. I just liked the quote and remembered it."

"And who was this Socrates who made such an impression on you?"

"You. I had you for Western Civilization my first year in college."

"Amazing! And I said Stressemann? I guess I'd better check that again!"

As Knutson walked down the stairs of Old Main he was overcome by a wave of nostalgia. "Look," he said to Peterson, "we don't have to meet with Dr. Corazon until one o'clock. What say we go down to the student union and have lunch at the Falcon's Nest?"

———

At five minutes to one, as Palmer Knutson popped two Rolaids into his mouth, he remembered why he had so few good memories of the campus food service. As they walked into the new glass and brick and steel administration building, he remembered when the students had occupied the old administration building, which now housed the education department. While he had never broken faith with the student radicals, his actions at the time established his stature in the sheriff's department.

After giving their names to Dr. Corazon's secretary they were shown into her office. This was almost as much of a contrast to Winston's office as Olson's office had been. Corazon's office featured oak furniture with pastel fabric covering, two oil paintings, and a genuine Toulouse-Lautrec poster preserved behind glass. A jungle of green plants surrounded a spacious desk complete with a fax machine and a bright-colored iMac computer with a color monitor playing geometric designs that resembled sort of a high-tech lava lamp.

Dr. Corazon remained seated as they entered. Behind a desk she did not look quite so dumpy, and her tinted glasses gave her a rather exotic aura. Clearly she knew how to make an impression on her own turf.

"Mr. Knutson, Mr. Peterson. So glad you could come to my office. It is our busiest time of the year to begin with, and now with no president and the memorial funeral service set for tomorrow, there are just so many things to attend to. I really appreciate your coming here."

"Our pleasure, Dr. Corazon," the sheriff responded with a gracious smile. "We'll try to take up as little of your valuable time as possible. My deputy here will record our interview, if that's all right with you. It does allow for a smoother, more efficient interview if we don't have to take notes all the time."

"Yes, of course, go ahead," she answered with a hint of impatience. "Now, what do you want to know?"

The sheriff began with the by-now standard question. "When did you arrive at Dr. Gherkin's home?"

"It was about a quarter after six. I pulled in just behind this nasty pickup truck. Turns out it carried two more of the guests."

"So we understand. Did you talk to Dr. Gherkin at all that evening?"

"No, I did not. This was the first 'back to school' party I had ever gone to at his house, but I had heard about them. I was told that George never came out of the kitchen except to announce that dinner was served. I did, of course, hear him singing. He really did have excellent taste in music, you know, even though his opinion of his performances may have been higher than his listener's. I had been warned about that, but I have to admit he was better than I thought he would be."

"Did you have any occasion to observe anyone come to or leave from the party?"

"Certainly. I was already there when the mayor and that construction fellow came, and I already told you that a pickup truck preceded me. Francis Olson and Dr. Winston were in the truck. An odd pair, I must say."

The sheriff nodded in agreement and continued, "Actually, we're more concerned about later on, perhaps about the time George Gherkin stopped singing. Did you see anybody or, perhaps more significantly, fail to see anybody at that time?"

Corazon smiled in a manner that was positively ghoulish. "Somebody who could have sneaked into the kitchen and split poor George's head open, I suppose you mean. No, I noticed nothing."

"Did you yourself leave the dinner party for any length of time?"

"No, I believe I was on the patio most of the evening."

"Dr. Corazon," the sheriff began tentatively, "we have been told that you were seen going in the direction of the kitchen and that you stayed away from the group for some time. Would you care to comment on that?"

"Yes, I believe I did find it necessary to go to the bathroom."

"I hate to be rude and nosy, but it is my job to be. We were told you stayed away for at least ten minutes. That's quite a long time to be in the bathroom, isn't it?"

Dr. Corazon stared at them coldly for at least forty seconds before saying tersely, "If you must know, I had a bad case of diarrhea."

Orly blushed, and Knutson realized it would be pointless to follow up that line of inquiry. He quickly followed with a question of a different nature. "Can you think of anyone who may have had a reason for murdering President Gherkin?"

"In the two years since I came here, I think I have found more people who wanted to murder him than I could ever have believed possible. He was not a well-liked man, Sheriff, as you have probably discovered by now. His business dealings were shady and his personal dealings were manipulative. He had very little academic integrity, he was greedy, and he was unfaithful to his wife. He was one of the most self-centered people on the face of the globe. How this university remains standing after two decades with him at the helm I fail to understand. There is, in fact, only one thing more puzzling, and that is that I agreed to stand up at the funeral tomorrow to laud his accomplishments and his service to the university."

After an awkward silence, Knutson asked, "What about your own relations with Gherkin?"

With a rueful expression on her face, she answered, "You mean, what motive could I have, don't you? I'm afraid I'm going to have to disappoint you there. Gherkin did give me my big break. Without him I'd still be at Jerkwater State. But we did have our differences. He had indicated that we would build a humanities center as the first university priority but had recently begun to renege on that in favor of a stupid domed stadium. I think one domed stadium for a state the size of Minnesota is quite enough. From that point of view his death is timely. We can get away from the pressure of the athletic department and turn the direction back to academics. But would I have killed for that? Don't be absurd!"

It seemed like the end of the interview, and Orly looked expectantly up at Knutson. He nodded and Orly turned off the tape recorder. The two officers stood up together as though they were choreographed. "Thank you for taking some of your valuable time to see us, Dr. Corazon. We wish you the best of luck for the coming year and in getting through the administrative confusion that I'm sure will ensue with the selection of a new president. Incidentally, will you be applying?"

"It's too early to say. I haven't seen a job description and I don't know if I would be considered qualified," she added, with transparently false modesty.

"Yes, well, perhaps we'll see you at the funeral tomorrow."

EIGHTEEN

PALMER KNUTSON EASED THE Acura out of the visitor's parking lot. At this point the investigation seemed to be going nowhere. He needed time to think. "I'm going to just drop you back at the office and go home for the rest of the day," he told his deputy. "What I don't need are media requests, questions, and additional cases. I mean, we have now talked to everyone who was there that night, and I don't feel we are any closer to a solution. What do you think, Orly?"

"First of all, have we eliminated the possibility that someone from the outside entered the house at the time of the dinner party? I would say we have." Knutson nodded his agreement and Peterson continued: "To murder someone and then leave a room locked like that would take incredible planning; we still don't know how it was done. Furthermore, no one would plan to come to a house to do a murder in the middle of a dinner party. The chances of being seen and to have to explain one's presence would be too great. No one saw anybody they didn't expect to see nor did anybody even hear another car. I suppose it is not impossible for a stealthy, trained hit man to creep in and kill Gherkin, but for all practical purposes I think the conclusion has to be that he was murdered by someone who was present in the house."

"And?" the sheriff asked encouragingly.

"Yeah, who and how? I don't know. Ten guests and at your insistence I suppose we have to include Mrs. Gherkin. It still seems a gruesome crime to be committed by a woman. As we interviewed the guests it seemed that virtually every one of 'em had a motive and, if we can figure out how one could commit murder and leave a room locked from the inside, all of 'em had an opportunity. Sterling, Wahl, and Armbruster all had financial motives, and from what we know about Gherkin's business dealings, some pretty good ones. Winston, Corazon, Olson, Williams, and Pennwright all had career motives, in one way or the other. Again, some pretty good ones if what we have unearthed so far is any indication. Finally, although these hardly seem like killing motives, there had been definite personal affronts to Ruth Sterling, Mae Williams, and Dolly Gherkin. We can theorize all we want, but until we get evidence against anyone we are hardly near making an arrest."

Knutson drove up to the sidewalk of the Law Enforcement Center and kept the motor running. As Peterson started to get out, the sheriff said, "Nevertheless, I can't help but feel there is something obvious that is just staring us in the face. Look, if something comes up at the office the rest of the afternoon, try to handle it yourself. I'll see you tomorrow. And dress up. We have a funeral to go to."

"Dress uniform?" asked Orly hopefully.

"No. Wear a suit and tie and be as inconspicuous as possible. We want to watch people, not have people watch us," Knutson politely explained. "I suspect that everyone who was at the dinner party will be at the funeral. Not to go would not look good, and nobody wants to look bad in the course of a murder investigation that is as high profile as this one is. And leave the sunglasses at home for once."

———

Tuesday was Palmer and Ellie's wedding anniversary. They usually went out to dinner to mark the event, but with the publicity surrounding the murder and with reporters gathering to cover the funeral, Palmer and Ellie decided to postpone their night out. They had a pizza delivered instead.

Palmer was preoccupied with the case and was not a congenial supper companion. Ellie tried to divert him with small talk about the events of her day, but eventually gave up and went into the den to watch a syndicated re-run of *Seinfeld*. Palmer puttered around the kitchen, putting plates and glasses into the dishwasher. He spent an inordinate amount of time clearing off the kitchen counter, trying to force the dishrag into the crack where the sink joined the Formica. At last he wrung out the rag, folded it neatly, and hung it to dry on the towel rack. This bit of nocturnal ritual completed, he decided it was time to go home. He informed Ellie, who knew what home meant to Palmer, and climbed into the Acura.

Home now consisted of a grove of trees and an acre of grass four miles from the village of Underwood. Palmer had grown up there, and it remained the place where, for him, life could sort itself out. The driveway consisted of two deep ruts where decades of horse-drawn wagons, tractors, farm machinery, and eventually cars had worn paths that still were impervious to vegetation. In the center of the pair of tracks, however, high grass grew, undisturbed for weeks at a time. Palmer trusted that there was still enough clearance to allow the passage of his low-riding car, even as one wheel or the other sank into the puddles remaining from Friday night's storm.

There really wasn't much to see of the old farmstead. After Palmer's father retired from farming he rented the land on a sharecrop basis to a neighboring farmer who was expanding his operation. When Palmer was a boy, the farm had consisted of 160 acres, an average-sized farm in the 1950s. Now it was farmed by a man who treated it as just a small part of his three-thousand- acre operation. After Palmer's father died, his mother moved into a new elderly housing project in Fergus Falls. On Palmer's advice, his mother sold the property just one year before the dramatic rise in farm prices that occurred in the late 1970s.

To the new owner, it was a piece of property to be treated in the manner best calculated to turn a profit. He was not insensitive toward Palmer's attachment to his "home place," but there was no reason not to farm as much of the land as possible. The barn was the first to go. After salvaging some of the boards for scrap lumber, the new owner simply burned it down and within a year was planting corn in what had been the barnyard for Palmer's bovine childhood companions. The chicken coop and the hog house, never substantial buildings at the best of times, fell victim to a bulldozer called in to remove a line of trees. The chicken coop, the hog house, and a two-holer outhouse (tipped over years before by Halloween vandals trying to recapture the glory days of their fathers' youth) were crunched together in a mangle of box elder trunks and were burned. A year later, only the well, still capped by a tall windmill, and the house remained.

To Palmer, the removal of the house was emotionally painful. For several years it stood in poignant loneliness and had almost looked inhabited. Hollyhocks continued to spring up every summer and crowded around the south-side windows. But storms began to blow away the shingles and vandalizing teenagers, surely from a town other than Underwood, broke out the windows, and empty beer cans soon littered the floor where he had taken his first steps. At last the new owner decided to make an asset out of a liability. The structure was still sound, and it cost surprisingly little to move the house off its foundation to a new resting place a mile away. The house that had given Palmer Knutson life, for he had been born in that home, was now converted into a granary for wheat.

Palmer parked the car by the windmill, the only feature visible from the road that could testify to the fact that this had once been a farm and a home. Amazingly, most of the fans on the wheel were still in place and they turned slowly in the light evening breeze, giving off a squeak that was almost a perfect octave higher than the cricket's song. He walked over and sat on the stone steps, the only remaining vestige of the house. The mosquitoes, aptly called Minnesota State Birds, had been disturbed as he had walked through the tall grass and now began to look for feeding opportunities.

It was a brilliant evening. The sun was near the horizon, earlier now that the beginning of September was near. It was so quiet that the hum of the mosquitoes could compete with the regular music of the old windmill and the chorus of the crickets. Palmer sat heavily on the old steps and stared down at the concrete basement. The new owner was using it as a stone dump and soon it would be filled and covered with earth. He loved that basement. He remembered how a cousin of his had given him a pair of used roller skates. The cousin had gone all around the sidewalks of St. Paul on those skates, but Palmer had used them on a small ten-foot track in his basement, looking forward to taking them to school where he could skate on the school sidewalks.

His mind soon wandered in a nostalgic brown study. He gazed at the place where the big cottonwood tree had been, where his father had fixed up that wonderful tire swing. He gazed at the corner of the crumbling foundation where, in the winter, the wind would form a huge drift and he could tunnel into it and form his own little snow palace. The words of the Blood, Sweat, and Tears song came to him. "Sometimes in Winter." And then he was thinking about that old album that had been practically the only album that he and Ellie had owned during the first year of their marriage. It had that old Billie Holiday song, "God Bless the Child That's Got His Own." And it had "And When I Die" on side one. Palmer Knutson, in his loneliness for times past began to sing: "'And when I die, and when I'm gone, there'll be one child born in the world to carry on, to carry on." He thought he sounded like David Clayton-Thomas, at least a little bit. "Let's see," he mused, "the first cut on that side was 'Variations on a Theme' by Eric Satie. How did that go again?"

And Sheriff Palmer Knutson started to hum, and as he did so the obvious solution to how the murder was committed came to him, and so too, sadly, did the identity of the murderer.

NINETEEN

When Orly Peterson got back to the Law Enforcement Center, he had a telephone message waiting for him. It said simply "Call Allysha—231-7709." With a purr of satisfaction, Orly thanked the receptionist and went into his office to return the call.

"Hello," answered the sweet, youthful female voice.

"Hello. This is Orly. You called?"

"Yes, Orly. How are you? I was just thinking about you this afternoon, and well, I certainly had a nice time Saturday night, and I'm out here at my parents' cottage on Star Lake. You know where that is?"

"Of course," said Orly, trying unsuccessfully to keep the anticipation out of his voice.

"Well, our cottage is just off that tarred road a couple miles west of Dent, almost exactly seven-tenths of a mile off Highway 108. You can't miss it."

"Yes, so?"

"It's just that it's so beautiful out here and I was wondering if maybe, you know, after work, you would like to come out here and we can put some steaks on the grill and go for a swim and things."

The idea certainly appealed to the deputy, especially the "and things." "Allysha, I can't think of anything I'd rather do. When shall I come?"

"What time do you get off duty?"

"In my job, I'm never really off duty," Orly said, with an air of self-importance, "but I suppose I could be out there by, say, five-thirty?"

"That's great! I'll tell my dad to pick up another steak on his way out from town. "

"Did you say, 'your dad'?" Orly asked, totally unable to keep the disappointment out of his voice, his visions of having the lovely Allysha all to himself vanishing in a second.

"Of course. My whole family is always out here any chance we get. I'm eager for you to meet my folks. That's all right, isn't it?"

Orly tried, but was unable to sound enthusiastic when he said, "Absolutely. It will be my pleasure."

So Orly had a date, sort of. He slipped out of the office about 4:30 and went back to his westside apartment. It had been a warm afternoon, and a shower was necessary and welcome. He shaved again, although it really wasn't necessary, and then spent a needlessly long time brushing his teeth. He tried to pick out a shirt—the uniform shirt wouldn't do, even if it were clean. He ruefully picked up a mesh tank top that showed off the effect of his one hundred sit-ups a day. "Nah, not for meeting the folks." He finally settled on a safe, neat, but slightly worn Fergus Falls State University football tee shirt. It had always been a favorite of his and he considered it to be sort of a lucky shirt. He had bought it at the FFSU varsity bookstore and it featured the number 10, Francis Olson's retired number. As he looked at how the pale colors of the jersey showed off his attractive tan, he reflected that, when he bought the shirt, he certainly would never have imagined Olson as a prime suspect in a murder investigation.

Orly drove northward out of Fergus Falls on US Highway 59. It was a road he had traveled many times in his life, for it led to his hometown. Pelican Rapids had a population of just under two thousand people, and was noted for two things. On the north end of town, there was a large turkey plant that provided jobs for workers from miles around the area as well as for a growing Latino population. And then there was the pelican. The pelican was a twenty-foot-high concrete statue that stood at the base of an artificially created waterfall on the Pelican River. The town kept the site clean and the pelican painted and there was not a summer day when at least one set of tourists did not have their picture taken by the avian monument. One could still hear Norwegian spoken on the streets, at least in the summertime, and in the winter one could hear it around the coffee counter in the Rapids Cafe. It was a pleasant town, and Orly realized it, but as Orly had plans for better things, he would tell sympathetic listeners in college that it was "a great town to be 'from.'"

Orly drove a used Camaro Beretta. Knutson had given him a hard time about it, noting that he drove a Beretta and carried a Beretta and it was clearly a case of a gun fetish. Orly had vehemently denied it at the time, but privately admitted to himself that the name of the car was one of the things that appealed to him. It was not in good shape when he had acquired it at a police auction, but he had seen possibilities for the car and decided to spend the money on a "Ming job" that miraculously restored the finish, and it was now rapidly reaching the age where it could be considered a classic. He also added his own stereo equipment and as he sped toward Star Lake at not too much over the limit, he put in his favorite new compact disc, by Velvet Revolver. Singing along to songs on the stereo was something Orly did when no one else was in the car. It was a wise bit of discretion on his part.

He found the Holm home, as Orly was starting to refer to it in his mind, without difficulty and was, in fact, so early that he considered driving around for a while. Reasoning that informality has always ruled lake living, however, he drove up to the cottage. It was far more modest than the last two lake homes he had visited. It was smaller than the Gherkin or the Sterling house, but was probably in better taste than either.

Orly was met at the door by an attractive, middle-aged woman who introduced herself as Allysha's mother. "Come in, come in. You must be Orly Peterson. I was just reading your name in the paper. That's some murder case you've got there." Mrs. Holm continued to talk as she ushered Orly into a sunny room overlooking the lake. "Allysha is down by the lake with her little brother. I yelled for her when I saw you drive up. I don't think she was expecting you so soon. Would you like a Coke?"

Orly, who had been rather hoping for a cold beer, nevertheless gratefully accepted. "Thank you. That would be nice. Lovely cottage you have here."

"Well, it's only a summer home, you know. We don't get out here much during the rest of the year. But we like it, and it's been in the family for years." Abruptly changing the subject and with a note of conspiratorial excitement, she added, "So, do you think you are any closer to solving the case?"

"I'm sorry, Mrs. Holm. I'm really not supposed to discuss it. But we are making some progress, I think. In fact, I was telling the sheriff this afternoon that . . ."

Orly was interrupted by Allysha, who materialized before him wearing an oversized Minnesota Vikings tee shirt. She had managed to slip into the house by another door in time to work on her hair and add just a touch of lipstick that had not been necessary while she played with her brother. "Hi, Orly. I see you've met my mother. Wanna go down to the lake for a swim?"

"Sure, er, that is, your mother was just bringing me a can of pop and . . ."

"That's all right. I'll get one too and we'll take it down with us."

Orly, hoping to impress Allysha's mother, asked, "Did you want to take one down for your little brother?"

"No, I think I'll tell Eddy I left one for him up at the house."

Ooooh, I like the way she thinks, thought Orly. And I like the way she looks. "I'll just change in the bathroom, OK?"

Allysha led the way down to the lake and on to the dock. Eddy was pointedly uninterested in Orly and after a bored "hi" was happy to accept the suggestion of the pop back in the house. "I wonder if he knows I'm a detective," Orly thought. "When I was a kid I would have loved to have met a detective from the sheriff's office. Maybe I should have told him. Nah, let's get him out of the way." As little Eddy ran back to the house, Orly looked around him on the dock. As a boat owner, Allysha's father was not in the same league as Lance Sterling, but a small boat, that could serve as both a fishing boat and a speed boat, rocked against the side of the dock. The boat had a motor that might be able to lift a skier out of the water and Orly entertained the notion that he might be able to impress Allysha with his water-skiing skills.

There was no doubt that Allysha was worth impressing. She was a fifth-year senior at Minnesota State University, Moorhead, majoring in special education. She had grown up in Moorhead and was a perpetual summer visitor to the lake country. Even though her family had recently moved to Fergus Falls, Orly considered her to be a little more urban than the local girls. She was about five-feet-six, with rare natural blonde hair. Palmer Knutson would have called it the kind of hair that Mary Travers, of Peter, Paul, and Mary, used to have. The comparison would have meant nothing to Orly, but it was a good one. She had the deep blue eyes of her Swedish ancestors, a thin nose and full lips. She now peeled off her tee shirt and revealed a tanned body barely covered by a bright purple bikini. Orly took an appreciative glance and decided he should dive in the lake. Allysha executed a graceful dive and joined him and together they swam out to the swimming raft.

The swimming raft had been built by Allysha's father. It was not an artful creation, but it had served all of their swimming relatives for the last twenty years. It consisted of planks laid across a frame that was fastened to four oil drums, the quintessential Minnesota swimming raft. Orly reached the raft first, but waited for Allysha to reach it, partly so he could observe her climb up the ladder.

Orly and Allysha laid down on their stomachs and felt the raft gently waft high on the water. It was indescribably peaceful. The warm sun quickly dried them off and with the gentle breeze off the lake there were no mosquitoes to contend with. Orly could see down into the clear water all the way to the bottom of the lake, at least ten feet below the raft, and felt his usual irritation as he saw another Grain Belt beer can reflecting faint light back to the surface. He could see perch and sunfish darting close to the surface and somewhat deeper he saw a small northern pike. He remembered how he used to go fishing with his father on this lake. Of course, his father had, for reasons best known to himself, preferred ice fishing. Sitting in a dark fish house staring at a hole in the ice had never been Orly's idea of a good time. Now this! This lying on a raft with a beautiful woman while the late summer sun warmed your very soul! This was living! All it lacked was a cold beer.

Allysha leaned over the side of the raft and extricated something from a net. "Here," she said. "I thought you might like a can of beer out here, so I put some in earlier. It's no longer too cold, but the lake has kept it somewhat cool."

"I think I'm going to marry this woman," thought Orly. He sat up and took a sip of his beer and looked out across the lake where a large Glastron boat was pulling two slalom skiers. The sun sparkling off the water was so bright that he could barely keep his eyes open. He thought the closed eyelash bit made him look sexy anyway, and he may have been right, but instead of verbalizing a tender moment,

Allysha asked him, "Orly, tell me about the murder investigation. Who do you think did it?"

The romantic spell was broken, but at least Orly could play the macho deputy. "I'm not supposed to talk about it, you know," he said, and after a significant pause added, "the sheriff wouldn't like it. But you wouldn't say anything to anyone, would you?"

"Of course not!" Allysha said in a shallow whisper. "Just tell me what you've been doing on it, that's all. I've never talked to anyone who's trying to solve a real murder case before. Is it anything like it is on TV?"

"Well, in a way it is," he answered, shading his eyes with his hand to keep out the sun and to keep Allysha from noticing that he was ogling her string bikini. "I mean, we go through and interview people and take their statements and check backgrounds and see if anyone is lying and then we try to figure out why they may be lying and sort of try to find a pattern behind their actions that will fit with the facts of the case. You generally see that in a lot of television shows. But this is my first murder investigation too, and I have to admit it is different than I thought it would be."

"How so?"

"Well, it's exciting, but in a different way. There isn't a feeling of danger or tension. Part of that comes from working with Palmer Knutson. You talk about your laid-back guys! He's droll, he's easygoing, and yet, I don't know, he makes you feel like you don't want to do anything dumb around him. I have to admit, when I saw the body, when I saw Dr. Gherkin sitting there with a meat cleaver in his head and blood all over, I felt a little woozy. Since then, however, we've systematically paid a visit to everyone who was involved and, and, I don't know, but you'd think you'd have the feeling like,

'Here I am, talking to a murderer.' But this case isn't like that at all. I know one of them must have done it, and you wouldn't believe the motives we've turned up. I mean, every one of them could have had a reason to kill him—after hearing them all and how he treated people I was about ready to kill him if it hadn't already been done—but still, it's hard to imagine one of those people as a killer."

"So, what were some of the motives?"

"Now that's something I'd really better not talk about. I can tell you, though, that they are, in many ways, traditional motives—you know, greed, ambition, revenge, or unrequited love."

"So there were no scene-of-the-crime clues, no fingerprints that you can trace to prove who dunnit?"

"No, not really, at least nothing that I can see from the Bureau's report."

"You mean, the FBI is in on this? How exciting!" Allysha said, suppressing a slight shiver in spite of the warm sun.

"No, not yet, at least. I meant the Bureau of Criminal Apprehension," Orly smiled superciliously. "It's a state organization that can be called in to handle some of the technical things that we could probably do, but for which they are better equipped. I worked with them on Saturday." Orly could see that he had Allysha captivated, and he was not about to lose her attention. "I spent the night at the house after the murder and met the Bureau when they came the next day."

"Wasn't it creepy to spend the night in a house where someone had just been murdered?" Orly appreciated how large her blue eyes had become.

"I had old Harvey Holte with me," the deputy replied in what he hoped was a cool manner, "although he spent most of the night sound asleep. But, yeah, it was sort of weird. I spent most of the time trying to figure out how someone could have murdered Gherkin and locked the door afterward. When the Bureau came the next morning, I let them in and observed their methods. It was a thrill just to watch them work."

"So, how did the murderer do it? According to what they said on the news it is a real 'locked room mystery.'"

"I wish I knew," the deputy replied quietly. "Palmer, er, Sheriff Knutson, says that when we figure that out we'll figure out who did it."

"When you were talking to these people, knowing that at least one of them was a murderer, did you, I don't know how to put this, get suspicious? I mean, was there anybody you thought was lying but you just couldn't prove it?"

Orly thought for a while and said, "Looking back, yeah, there were several times I felt that way." Then, abruptly he added, "But wait! What did you say? 'At least one of them was a murderer?'"

"Sure. I mean, that's always a possibility, isn't it? You just said that a lot of people had a motive. Why couldn't more than one of them have been in on the murder?"

"You mean," the deputy sputtered, "like *Murder on the Orient Express*?"

"What's that?"

"That's a famous Agatha Christie mystery where this guy is killed on a train and there are twelve suspects and it turns out that all of them did it."

"Oh yeah. I saw that movie. Albert Finney, wasn't it? No. I don't mean anything that silly. I just mean one person could have swung the cleaver while someone else acted as lookout or something. And as for that locked room business, well, I read about that in the *Star Tribune* and it said that while the windows and outside door were bolted, the inside door was merely locked by a key. And it made me think. I had my dad put on a new lock on my bedroom door at home. Eddy was developing a nasty habit of coming into my room whenever I least wanted him to. So, anyway, I got a new lock and assumed that it would keep him out. One day I left my room and locked the door and when I returned, there was Eddy sitting on my bed. I asked him how he managed that neat little trick and he said that he had just used the key that had been in the lock in his room. The same key fit both. So, even as I was reading about that Gherkin murder, I was thinking, 'Big deal! Anyone could just use a generic key for those cheap interior locks and chances are it would work!' I mean, so you decide to murder somebody, all you need is a few keys and more than likely one of them will work for a simple lock. Have you ever tried those little locks that come on luggage? It's almost a case of one key fits all! Anyway, if you could find a key that would open the door, you could lock it again, and there's your locked room mystery."

Even as she spoke Orly's mind was racing. When had he been suspicious? Who were the suspects most likely to work together? Who were the two worst liars he had come across in the course of his investigation? It was a rocket from the firmament. It was a light bulb turning on in his head. Suddenly it seemed so obvious! How come he hadn't seen it before? How come Knutson hadn't seen it before? Everything now pointed to a well-planned conspiracy and that made it Murder One! Even as he arrived at his conclusion, he was sad. He didn't want it to be them! But still, he somehow felt he had solved it, and the sheriff would now have to give him his due. Maybe he would now apply to the FBI! He looked over at Allysha. The sun danced in her eyes as the raft gently rocked on the water. He grabbed her in his arms and gave her a long commitment-type kiss.

"I hope that's a commitment-type kiss," thought Mr. Holm, as he walked out on the dock to shout to his daughter and her guest that supper was almost ready.

TWENTY

I<small>T WAS AN APPROPRIATE</small> day for a funeral. The bright August sun, which might have injected a measure of happiness, was mercifully hidden by overcast skies. It was humid and still, the kind of day that a hundred years ago would have been called "a day thick with fate." Palmer felt it as well, knowing that before the day was out he would have to confront the murderer of the late George Gherkin.

There were four notable structures in Fergus Falls. The state hospital was a massive structure that dominated a hill on the north edge of the city. The second impressive edifice was the Fergus Falls post office, a building that also contained the federal bankruptcy court. Built in 1903 and doubling in size in the 1930s, it was a fine example of Renaissance Revival architecture and the citizens of Fergus Falls were justly proud of its magnificently ornate molded plaster ceilings. Sheriff Knutson always hoped that he would be able to avoid both of those buildings in the course of his duties.

The other two notable buildings, however, could not be avoided. A career in law enforcement (or in law breaking, for that matter) inexorably led to the Otter Tail County Courthouse, a remarkable structure for such a small city. Built in 1921 of cream brick and Bedford stone, with architecture in the Beaux Arts tradition, it reminded some of Independence Hall in Philadelphia. It was complete with a white clock tower crowned by a shining cupola with a weather vane. Inside, there was attention to detail such as is seldom found in modern buildings, with brass doorknobs that had an otter molded on them. The courtroom on the third floor held the most magnificent feature—a beautiful stained-glass rotunda. What made this feature unique was that there was no dome outside. When the courthouse was constructed, the dome was eliminated to save money, but the decorative interior features were retained to give dignity and beauty to solemn occasions. As Knutson drove past on his way to the church, he hoped that it would be used only for a plea and for sentencing.

The sheriff parked his Acura in an unobtrusive spot behind the First Norwegian Lutheran Church. This was the fourth great structure to define the community. Lutherans do not build cathedrals, at least not in America, and most would have thought that referring to their place of worship in such a manner would smack of papistry. But many an officially designated cathedral lacked this church's size or splendor. It was constructed of a dark-brown brick that rose in the front to a square tower, crowned by an awe-inspiring steeple. The interior featured graceful but powerful wooden beams that took such stress off of the walls that tall, pointed stained-glass windows could be utilized everywhere. The result was that, instead of the gloominess found in many churches of its size, First Norwegian possessed a dazzling lightness that projected the joy of God's creation. A broad aisle down the center of the church separated solid, light-finished oak pews, each with a small brass plate recognizing individual donors. It was an aisle most suitable for advancing brides and retreating coffins. With the university and the state hospital for the mind, the federal building and the courthouse for the law, and this church for the Gospel, Fergus Falls seemed to have all bases covered.

"Lord, have mercy upon us," intoned the Reverend Rolf Knutson as he began the Kyrie, and one of the people in the congregation added silently, "for I have taken a life." Mrs. Gherkin had asked that the service be conducted from the old "Red Hymnal." This was not because Dr. Gherkin had been a faithful member of the congregation; in fact, he seldom entered the church and was not known to have any religious affiliation. But Dolly Gherkin became a member of the church almost as soon as they arrived in Fergus Falls. She served on the church council and made sure all of her children went through confirmation. George Gherkin could not be considered a loyal son of the church, but he was Dolly's husband. Besides, First Norwegian was the largest church in town, and a large crowd was expected.

As Knutson looked around, he noticed that they were all there, including George Gherkin, the center of attention as usual. At least, presumably it was George Gherkin, for it was a closed casket service. No mortician, no matter how talented, could make presentable a head that had suffered such a mortal wound. In the front pew sat Dolly Gherkin, surrounded by all those family members who could, for her sake, conveniently attend. The murder had created a rather strange camaraderie. In another pew, Francis Olson, Sherwin and Mae Williams, Harold Winston, and Sally Ann Pennwright sat together. Two pews back sat Lance and Ruth Sterling. On the other side of the aisle, ready to take an official part in the service, sat Isabel Corazon. Next to her, officially representing the city of Fergus Falls, sat the mayor. Of the people who had attended the unfortunate dinner party only five days before, only Brick Wahl isolated himself from the rest, in a far corner partly behind a pillar. Their proximity was a fortunate development for Palmer Knutson, who had come to watch a murderer. Orly Peterson, seated next to the sheriff, was there for the same reason.

As Knutson looked down from an excellent vantage point in the balcony, he noticed that, in fact, a smaller church would have sufficed. The governor was indeed there, and the usual crowd that assembles whenever the governor appears was also in attendance. There were a few fellow university presidents, and the FFSU administration was there en masse. But for the most part, out of pressing concern for the beginning of the school year or out of total indifference, the faculty had chosen to give a miss to the Gherkin sendoff. The sheriff, however, was occupied with something other than counting people or noting celebrities. He kept his eye and mind not on the victim, but on the killer.

Palmer looked down upon his brother with a measure of love and admiration. They had never been particularly close. There was too great a difference in their ages for that, but Rolf had always been the quintessential big brother and Palmer was always rather awed by him. It would have been hard to imagine him in any other profession than the ministry. He had an impressive head of snow-white hair which, combined with a pure white surplice and pale, almost translucent skin, made him look almost unworldly. His voice, deep and trained over the years, could easily have come from a burning bush. Reverend Knutson led the responsive reading of the 23rd Psalm, and then read the lesson from Romans 8. "Nay, in all these things we are more than conquerors through him that loved us." ("Yeah, but someone conquered the slime ball," thought one of the mourners.) "For I am persuaded that neither death, nor life, nor angels, nor principalities, nor powers, nor things past, nor things to come, nor height, nor depth, nor any other creature, shall be able to separate us from the love of God, which is in Christ Jesus our Lord." ("Perhaps not," thought the Reverend's brother, "but some creature with a meat cleaver could separate parts of a head and could separate a university president from life on earth.")

The Reverend Knutson then led the congregation in a Responsory. Next came a few well-chosen words on the transitory nature of man's existence and the saving grace of God. As he listened to the Reverend Knutson's words, the sheriff was reminded again of his brother's skill. "Rolf knows exactly what kind of man Gherkin was," thought Palmer, "and yet, without actually lying, he's made it sound as though he will be deeply missed. Moreover, he's made the congregation also feel that he will be missed. That takes some doing!" Knutson was especially amazed to see the murderer nod in total agreement to everything the pastor said. In fact, as he watched, he saw the start of a tear in the murderer's eye. At this point, Orly leaned forward and, whispering in Knutson's ear, excused himself and left the church. Palmer was puzzled, but turned his attention back to the service.

Isabel Corazon was called upon to eulogize the fallen leader on behalf of the university. She slowly made her way to the front of the church. "Friends, family of Fergus Falls State University, and citizens of Fergus Falls, allow me to speak to you today about Dr. George Gherkin. I come not to praise President Gherkin, his career speaks for itself, but simply to eulogize him as we lay him to rest. Too often, however, the good that people do is forgotten when they are with us no more. Dr. Gherkin was an ambitious person, and his ambition served Fergus Falls State University and the city of Fergus Falls. He brought thousands of people, either as students or as employees, to our community in the two decades that he was our president. This has made a marvelous social and economic impact on our community. He was a caring man, for when the poor cried, President Gherkin wept."

There was something about the last phrase that caused Palmer Knutson to say to himself, "I've heard that before. In fact, the whole speech seems familiar."

Corazon continued. "Dr. Gherkin became a beloved president, and not without cause. Bear with me, members of the university community, for I think I speak for all of us when I say our hearts are in the coffin there with George Gherkin."

That did it. At once Palmer knew where he had heard the words before. Dr. Corazon was paraphrasing *Julius Caesar*. It was a delicious bit of irony and yet was one last bit of viciousness. Palmer was almost shocked when he noted how pleased Isabel was with herself and her triumphant revenge. He looked down on the congregation to see if others had noticed the parody. He observed Dr. Winston poke Francis Olson and give him a hurried explanation in an amused whisper. Olson grinned in appreciation and in a short time Olson had poked Williams and so on down the line until the message reached Sally Ann Pennwright, who looked outraged. Knutson looked to Mrs. Armbruster and saw that she merely gazed on the eulogist with a studied indifference. He saw Lance Sterling slip a business card to the poor sap who was unlucky enough to sit next to him. Brick Wahl leaned back to hide his face behind a pillar. As Knutson gazed upon the murderer, he could not help but remember one of the last lines of Antony's speech, "They that have done this deed are honorable."

He hoped that the murderer would confess and plead guilty and avoid a sensational trial that would do no one proud. The question was, would the murderer come to him, or did he have to make the regrettable move with handcuffs and Miranda rights? When he realized last night who had killed Gherkin and how it was done, he assumed that the killer would come to him. He was still convinced that this would be the case.

Dr. Corazon finished her eulogy with a mean smile and made her way back to her seat. Orly Peterson resumed his seat next to the sheriff and looked extremely pleased with himself. The white-maned pastor droned on with "Lord, now lettest thou Thy servant depart in peace, according to Thy word." ("Nothing became his life like the leaving it," one mourner added mentally.) Reverend Knutson led the congregation in the Lord's Prayer and after Collects and Responses, said: "God of all Grace, who didst send Thy Son, our Savior Jesus Christ, to bring life and immortality to light, most humbly and heartily we give Thee thanks, that by His death He hath destroyed the power of death, and by His glorious resurrection hath opened the kingdom of heaven to all believers." ("That, in itself, should exclude George," thought the murderer.) "Grant us assuredly to know that because He lives we shall live also, and that neither death nor life, nor things present nor things to come, shall be able to separate us from Thy love, which is in Christ Jesus our Lord, who liveth and reigneth with Thee and the Holy Ghost, ever one God, world without end. Amen." ("God, forgive me, but

I'd probably do it again," thought the murderer in the depressing moment of silence that followed.)

The funeral director materialized almost magically and soon the coffin was being wheeled down the center aisle, followed by Dolly Gherkin and her grieving family. Pallbearers unceremoniously whisked the coffin into the black hearse and mourners began making their way to their cars for the graveside service. Some mildly sincere mourners, who felt that they had already done their duty and did not want to make the effort to visit the cemetery, comforted the family.

Shortly before the funeral procession was to leave, the murderer sought out Sheriff Knutson, who was standing unobtrusively near the entrance to the church.

"You know, don't you?"

"Yes, I realized it last night," said Knutson. Incongruously, he couldn't help feeling embarrassed by the conversation. "Will you come in to my office?"

"I'll be there this afternoon."

TWENTY-ONE

IT WAS FOUR O'CLOCK and Palmer Knutson was waiting in his office. He found little joy in the fact that he had solved his first murder case. The murderer would have confessed sooner or later and there would be no press clippings to save about his brilliant detection. Perhaps, therefore, he could be forgiven for savoring the moment when he told Orly Peterson how he figured it out. He had kept his knowledge to himself, and only after the funeral was over and they were back at the Law Enforcement Center did Knutson finally call his deputy in to tell him the news.

"So, Orly," he coyly began, "if you had to lay down money on who the murderer of George Gherkin was, who would you pick?"

Orly didn't hesitate a minute. This was the moment he had been waiting for, the acme of his professional career. "In fact, Sheriff, it was more than one murderer. What we have here is a clever, well thought-out plot concocted by Sherwin Williams and his wife, Mae."

Palmer Knutson stared at his deputy in an expression that showed neither appreciation nor contempt. Finally he said, "And why do you believe that?"

The deputy put on what he intended to be a modest smile. "In truth, I have to give part of the credit to Allysha Holm. She said something last night that implied that more than one person could have been involved. I had never really considered that before. But the more I thought of it, the more it made sense. It would have been extremely risky for any one person to murder Gherkin at the dinner party. I mean, people were walking around all the time. But, if you had one person ensuring that you could kill him in safety and one person to either act as a lookout or as a diversion, you could take your time and clean up after yourself. Which this murderer obviously did."

Palmer nodded appreciatively. "Go on."

The polite manner in which the sheriff accepted his revelations gave Orly supreme confidence. "Now, at this point, I started asking myself, who would be the best pair of murderers? Actually, that in itself did not make things that much clearer. The mayor and Brick Wahl could have conspired. So could Corazon and Pennwright, one for ambition and the other for love. So could Winston and Olson—they are actually quite chummy you know. But then I thought, 'No, who are the best partners? Of course,' I thought, 'married people.' Now I could see Lance Sterling taking somebody out, but I couldn't see Ruth doing anything forceful. But the Williams couple? Perfect. They both had motives and I even think it could be in the character of both of them. Then last night I went back over the tapes. When we interviewed Sherwin Williams, I just knew he was lying. I don't know, maybe he did smoke a cigarette, but big deal, nobody is going to care about that so much that he would have to hide from his wife. No, he had seen something or done something that he wasn't telling us about. And then there was that bit when he denied being there before, but he sure had a feeling for the schedule, you know, when drinks would be served and when Gherkin would be all alone in the kitchen. The more I thought about it, the more he sounded like he had a timetable. He also went to great lengths to blame other people.

"I watched him during the funeral. At first he was ill at ease, then, when I came back in just as Dr. Corazon was finishing her eulogy, he started to snicker. I thought he was going to giggle. It was disgraceful! It was arrogant, but you know, I think you have to be a little arrogant to commit a murder. You have to arrogantly assume that you have the power to decide whether a person lives or dies.

"Then I went over Mae Williams' interview. At first she admitted to seeing him that night, then, she backtracked and said she had only seen him in the role of a corpse. Furthermore, she lied to us. I think both of us realized it at the time and we just assumed it was a little white lie to make her husband seem less like a jerk. She was lying when we asked her if she had seen Sherwin leave the room. We could see it in her face. Of course she had, because she had been his lookout."

"All right then," Knutson acknowledged. "So far, so good. But how was it done?"

"I'd like to take credit for this myself, but again, Palmer, it was something Allysha said last night. What's the best way to enter and leave a locked room? A key. Nothing more complicated than that. Allysha pointed out that interior locks are terribly simple and that almost anybody who had a key for one door could use it in another. Now, everyone admitted that Sherwin and Mae were the first to arrive. Why come so early? To case the joint, as they used to say! Sherwin had brought, we can assume, more than one key with him. At the earliest opportunity, he tried his keys in the kitchen door until he found one that fit. With all the opera singing going on he could do it quietly. He unlocks the door without disturbing Gherkin, gives Mae the nod at an appropriate time, say around seven o'clock, the time they both admit to being away from the gathering, and he slips in, kills Gherkin, goes back out, and locks the door behind him."

Knutson leaned forward and said, "Well, I have to admire your deductive reasoning, but do you have any proof of this?"

Orly had been waiting for this. With a broad grin he whipped out a typed-up request for a search warrant. "You remember, at the funeral, how I slipped out for a few minutes?"

"Yah, I meant to ask you about that. What were you doing?"

The deputy's face wore a look of triumph. "I was searching for evidence and I found it. I decided to look in Sherwin Williams' Volvo. I thought that if I found anything I could always get a search warrant and, you know, look again to make it legal. I looked in the obvious place first, the glove compartment. There was a pair of white gloves. I fully expect that when we examine them we will find particles that have come from Gherkin's kitchen."

The sheriff sighed and leaned back in his chair. "It's not bad, Orly. Not bad. Motive, means, opportunity, and at least the possibility of evidence. Good job." Orly was so clearly pleased with himself that Palmer let him enjoy the moment for a few seconds before he said. "Too bad it's all wrong."

"What do you mean, 'wrong'?" Orly exploded. "Do you know who did it? And how?"

"Yah. I figured it out last night."

"Well thanks for telling me!" the deputy said sarcastically.

"I'm sorry, but I just wanted to make sure the funeral could proceed in peace, and I didn't want you to stare at the murderer. By so obviously looking at someone else, you deflected attention from the real murderer and it means that we can now make our arrest in quiet and confidence."

For Orly, the hurt and resentment rapidly turned to pugnacity. "So what makes you think you're right? What kind of proof do you have?"

"The best. A confession. And we're going to hear a full confession for your little tape recorder in a few minutes."

Orly leaned forward in his chair. "So, who did it? No, wait. Don't tell me. Tell me how you figured it out and how it was done. If I know this, will I know the murderer?"

"Undoubtedly." The sheriff leaned back. "We really should be doing this with brandy and cigars, you know, but I'm not really happy with my discovery. In part, I suppose, because it took me so long to see what was in front of me all along. You know, Orly, you really ought to listen to public radio a little more."

"Huh?"

"Well in a way, you see, that was the key. On Saturday morning, just after you left, I spent a little time snooping around the Gherkin house. I was just checking over that elaborate stereo system they have and I thought about how George had been singing along to *I Pagliacci*. So I looked for a tape of that opera. I finally found it, but only after a search. It had been carefully put away among about a hundred other tapes. More than one person mentioned how Dolly had taken the time to fool around with the stereo system. I thought at the time, 'She sure is tidy. Most people would have just left the tape on the shelf.' The tape deck is a double one, that is, you have one deck for playback only and one for both playback and record, you know, so you can record things off of another tape. On that type of unit, you can also play something back from the record deck. There was a tape in the record deck that had no label on it. I turned it over and played it back. It was a tune that was familiar yet not famous, but one that I knew I had heard recently. Nice tune, and I started humming it myself for a while and then forgot about it.

"Then last night I went back to my old farm home and sat there thinking about the case. I had sort of let my mind wander and started thinking about Blood, Sweat, and Tears, the old big band rock group. On their first album they had an instrumental version of a theme by a French composer who lived around the turn of the century, Erik Satie. Again I started humming that—it is a lovely piece. Then I remembered why it had seemed so fresh on Saturday. I had heard it only the night before on Minnesota Public Radio as I sat in my office. Had I heard, I asked myself, a recording of an MPR broadcast on that tape in Gherkin's machine?

"But if so, why so? Why would Dolly have taken the time to record a radio broadcast when she had company? Maybe she just liked Satie. That was a possible explanation. But then it came to me. What might have been on that tape before? Had she taped over something? See where I'm going with this?"

"No, but keep going. I think I'm getting an idea."

"Okay. Remember! Where were the remote speakers? In the kitchen, of course. It was Gherkin's favorite room, so what could be more natural than to have his opera music piped in. Everybody heard the opera music coming from the kitchen with Gherkin singing along. But if the opera was on tape, why not Gherkin? Get it? It's the old 'Is it live or is it Memorex?' question. In other words, no guest ever heard Gherkin live, er, so to speak."

"So he was dead before anyone came to the house. That means," Peterson sputtered, as comprehension dawned on his face, "Oh my God! Dolly!" The deputy's face assumed the expression of one who had just been told that cows can really speak English but that they merely prefer not to.

"Absolutely!"

"But how? How could she have killed him with the doors and windows all locked?"

"But that really isn't a problem anymore, is it, not if she killed him before anyone else came?"

"Of course it is! She still couldn't float through the walls!"

"Orly, Orly, Orly! Think about it! What did you just tell me was the most common means to open a locked door? A key. As you said, only the outside door and the windows were actually bolted, but the inner door was simply locked. Sure we found a key in the victim's possession, but think about it. You don't have to trust to luck to find a key that fits. What do you get when you go to the hardware store and buy an ordinary interior door lock? You get two keys. Now most people have no idea where one key is unless they use it a lot, let alone both keys. But this was a relatively new house and Gherkin was an organized man. It's extremely likely every key was kept in its proper place. All Dolly would have had

231

to do was to kill her husband, lock the kitchen door with her key, turn on a previously recorded tape of Gherkin doing his opera, and get rid of the key at a later time. I would guess, in fact, that if we needed to we could find the key in the lake at a distance appropriate to a sixty-year-old woman's throwing arm."

"But getting his voice on tape. And, and, you know, staging the whole thing. That's premeditation! That's Murder One!"

Sheriff Knutson nodded sadly. "I know," he said, "and that's what bothers me. Mrs. Gherkin just does not seem the type to plan a murder in detail. And even if she was, why plan it on a night when there would be a house full of people?"

Orly brightened. "Alibi! Of course! She had ten people who could swear that she never went near the kitchen!"

"Very good, Orly, you may be right. In fact, I had thought about that myself. And yet, I just can't associate Dolly with that kind of crime."

"Who's getting soft now? You made fun of me when I insisted it couldn't have been a woman's crime. Why couldn't she have planned it for a long time?"

"Well, we'll soon know for sure. She said she would turn herself in right after the graveside service. Just looking out the window, I've noticed that several cars that were in the funeral procession have already returned."

"So that was what that little scene in front of the church was all about. I thought you were just giving her more comfort. Weren't you taking a little bit of a chance in letting her go? What if she had decided to run for it?"

"Where would she have gone? I suppose it is theoretically possible that she has been salting money away in a Swiss bank account and is even now running off to meet a secret lover, but I think that's highly unlikely, don't you?"

"Like you say, we'll soon know. Here she comes. I'll go get my tape recorder."

———

Dolly Gherkin entered the sheriff's office unescorted. Palmer Knutson ushered her into his office where she took a chair across from his desk. Orly Peterson sat to the side with his tape recorder.

"I knew I could count on you to come in, Dolly. Would you like a cup of coffee?"

"You bet! It's been a tough day."

At a nod from the sheriff, Orly scurried off to bring back three cups of coffee from the outer office. Palmer and Dolly remained silent until Orly had returned.

"Before you begin to get all official and counsel me on my rights and before you have to turn on that tape recorder, I would like to tell you something. I've never hurt a living soul in my life before this, and I have never approved of the taking of a human life for any reason. I'm sorry you had to go to all the trouble interviewing everybody and I'm sorry for all the time and energy and false suspicions that I may have caused. But I had always intended to turn myself in. I only wanted to delay it until after the funeral. I'll always be grateful to you, Palmer, for letting our family have this last function together. The funeral could be devoted to George without the press giving all of its attention to his murdering wife. For one last time our children could think about their father without thinking about how their mother murdered him. You had the authority to arrest me and prevent all that. In fact, you were probably derelict in your duties for not doing so. Thank you, Palmer."

Palmer, like most Scandinavians, was never very good at accepting praise and gratitude. He blushed and stared at the floor and mumbled something that sounded like, "that's all right." He nodded to Peterson to turn on the tape recorder and when he spoke again it was a return to business. "Right, now, uh, Mrs. Gherkin. We would like to take an official statement from you concerning the death of your husband, George Gherkin. My deputy here, Orly Knutson, will be recording your statement. The time is 4:25 p.m. and the date is the thirty-first day of August, 2005. Before we begin, Mrs. Gherkin, I wish to caution you that anything you say can and will be used against you in a court proceeding. You are entitled to have an attorney present at any time. Do you wish to waive this right at this time?"

Dolly looked up into his eyes and gave him a smile of resignation. "Yes I do."

"Mrs. Dolly Gherkin, did you, on the afternoon or evening of August 26th willfully kill your husband, George Gherkin?"

"No."

"Excuse me, Mrs. Gherkin. What did you say?"

"I said 'no.' I did not really willfully kill him. I mean, it wasn't an accident. I did bury that meat cleaver in his head. But I hadn't planned to do it. Looking back on it, I'm still not sure how I feel. I'm sorry I did it, if for no other reason than how it will affect the kids. But last night I was trying to feel a deep remorse and I just couldn't. I asked myself why, after years of marriage, did I pick last Friday night to murder my husband. The answer finally came to me. 'It was just one of those days!' After years of aggravation he finally pushed me too far. The meat cleaver was right there and before I even knew what I was doing I used it with a strength I never knew I had."

"What did you do then?"

"It's funny, you know. My first thought came from all the teasing that our kids had to endure from having a name like 'Gherkin'. I didn't really think about if George had suffered or if he was still alive—as you saw, there could never have been any real doubt about that—I just thought about what I should do. The thought came to me: 'For thirty-five years I've been married to a pickle, and now I'm in one.' I started to laugh at the thought and I knew I needed some time to try to think straight. But our guests were expected to arrive in five minutes or so. It was here George's incredible vanity came in.

"You see, when he sang along to the opera music while he was cooking the dinner, he actually thought he was entertaining the guests. In fact, over the last ten years he has, er had, been saying that he really wished he would have pursued a career in vocal music. Seriously! Well, he started feeling sorry for himself that he couldn't hear himself sing and so he made a tape recording of himself singing *I Pagliacci*. He played the tape of a live performance and got a second recorder set up, microphone and all. He sang and waved his arms through the whole thing. It was only that one opera, thank heavens, but he did listen to it and critique himself. Mostly rave notices, by the way. 'Vanity, vanity, all is vanity' huh? Well, anyway, after I hit him with that cleaver I needed time to think. I wanted to lock the kitchen door but I couldn't find the key. I didn't know George had it in his pocket. George, though, had made a little rack for all the spare keys in the house so I just got the extra key and locked it up. Then I thought it would be strange if people didn't hear George singing, so I put on the tape that George had made of himself singing *I Pagliacci*.

"For the next hour I walked around trying not to think about it. I had to be a hostess, you see, and that always takes a lot of concentration. I didn't know what I was going to do when the tape ran out, and when it did, I practiced my only real bit of deception. Everyone was so convinced that they had heard George singing that I thought I could keep them thinking that a little longer. I simply announced that we could listen to something else so I turned the speaker switch from remote to main and turned on the evening concert on Minnesota Public Radio. At the same time, I simply pushed the record button on the tape deck and recorded over George and his singing. The machine has automatic reverse, as it happens, so I could record over the entire tape."

"I was actually relieved when someone finally became concerned enough to break the door down and find poor George. By this time I had decided to see if I could get through the funeral before I was arrested for murder. You see, George was not a well-liked man. But we had been together a long time. We shared our lives. We went to Little League games and dance recitals together. No one knows better than I that George could be vain and insufferable. George could be dishonest and vindictive and mean. But I had put up with him all these years and I had planned to do so indefinitely."

Palmer Knutson asked gently, "One question, if I may, Mrs. Gherkin. Just what was it that pushed you over the edge this time?"

"I had taught George how to make chicken Kiev. In fact, he never could roll the chicken breasts well enough to keep in the butter, so I always had to do the hard part. Yet, over the years, people began to refer to it as 'George's chicken Kiev.' In truth, I didn't mind even that. It was when George himself began to call it 'My chicken Kiev' that I couldn't stand it. As he sat there fooling around with the olives while I did all the hard work, well, I guess I just lost it. I suppose I'm going to have to get used to being a widow."

It was then that Sheriff Palmer Knutson remembered the first clue he had seen but had forgotten. He cast his mind back to the dead man and his parted skull. There, right on the table, in plain sight of everyone, was the recipe card that would forever serve in Knutson's mind as the epitaph for George Gherkin. It read: "Dolly's Recipe for the Best Chicken Kiev Ever."

ABOUT THE AUTHOR

Gerald Anderson is a history professor at North Dakota State University, teaching Modern European and British history for the past twenty-one years, and in 2005 received the Robert Odney Excellence in Education Award from NDSU. He has studied extensively in Europe, holds an MA from NDSU and à PhD from the University of Iowa (1973).

He is the author of *Fascists, Communists, and the National Government*, a two-volume *Study Guide for the Western Perspective*, and articles and reviews concerning British, European, and Scandinavian-American history in various periodicals. In addition to works in his academic field, Anderson published his first novel, *The Uffda Trial*, in 1994. A native of Hitterdal, Minnesota, he captures in *Death Before Dinner* the cadence and mindset unique to the ethnic heritage of the area.

If you enjoyed *Death Before Dinner*, read on for an excerpt from
Gerald Anderson's next book

Murder Under the Loon

COMING SOON FROM MIDNIGHT INK

PROLOGUE

IT WAS TWENTY-ONE degrees below zero. A quarter-moon hung in the southern sky, but did not cast sufficient light to dull the effects of the aurora borealis in the northern sky. The northern lights shimmered and danced, first forming a curtain, then a halo, then a dazzling curtain again. They were green, then they were blue, then they were a greenish blue. On some nights, they acquired a certain pinkish hue, but not tonight, which was just as well, for there were few eyes that were turned to the heavens.

The only other light quivered across the clear ice of a Minnesota lake, and the only sound that disturbed the total silence of the night came from the same source. It was a snowmobile, emitting a steady whine as it served an appointment with death. On this noisy motorized sled, a rider momentarily thought, "I love to ride my snowmobile; this is one of the most pleasant dreams I've ever had. But the sound is different from my own sled, maybe if I think real hard I can tell the model. But, ooooh, it hurts to think, and I'm so tired." And he stopped dreaming for a while.

Eventually, the snowmobile came to the edge of the lake and went on to a bank that was covered in pure, white snow. The rider felt a tremendous thump on the top of his helmet and it seemed as though the soft snow rose up to welcome him into fluffy, downy arms. An hour passed, during which he would approach the edge of consciousness only to hear the drone of a snowmobile engine.

Then, with a sudden shock, his mind came back from a black oblivion into a state of semi-consciousness. His brain was a collage of confusing sensations. "My God our help in ages past!" he thought. "My head hurts something fierce. I can't bear to move it." It was only then that he became aware of the intense cold that actually hurt his teeth as he breathed in the night air. He could still hear the roar of a small engine and thought, "There's a snowmobile in my bedroom!" Then, "No, that must be coming from a snowmobile outside, but if that is so . . . ?" For several minutes he lay motionless, listening to the machine and trying to will himself into consciousness. Finally, with tremendous assertion, he opened his eyes. Without the strength to scream, he gazed in horror as he saw, illuminated by a billion stars floating in a black sky, a twenty-foot loon staring down at him.

ONE

JOHN HOFSTEAD WAS A pink man. His face had a uniform pinkness that extended from his closely shaved chin to his round pink nose to his glowing pink hairless scalp. The vast expanse of pink was interrupted only by two drifts of snow white hair above his light blue eyes. The only other feature that relieved this ocean of pinkness was a uniform and carefully trimmed fringe of feathery white hair that created a shimmering curtain between the pink pate and the pink neck. From the rear, Hofstead's head looked like a maraschino cherry comfortably nestling in a mound of whipped cream. The overall effect of his pinkness extended even to his hands. The nails, clean and clipped short, had such a translucent quality that the slightly whiter cuticles served to define what looked like ten little buttons.

Perhaps it was something about this color, perhaps it was only the inner peace of the man showing through, but, in any event, Hofstead gave off the aura of a man at peace with himself and at peace with the world. He always wore a suit and tie, and in the winter he usually wore a vest as well. It was hard for anyone to see such a well-scrubbed man and not form an instant liking for him. His pale eyes were the epitome of openness and it seemed impossible that they could hide any deceit. His soft laugh, which verged on a giggle, was disarming to the most hostile of potential foes. Somehow, and without contrivance, he even managed to smell clean. There was no odor of French cologne about him, just the consistent perfume of Ivory Soap.

This was of great benefit to Hofstead in his chosen position. Hofstead was an insurance man. His ingenuous likability proved to be such a tremendous asset for sales that he founded, at the age of twenty-seven, his own insurance company. That was four decades ago, and Hofstead Hail Insurance was now one of the most prosperous firms in Fergus Falls, Minnesota. Hofstead Hail was successful, in part, because the owner and president genuinely believed in his product. He took pride in the fact that he refused to sell more insurance to a client than he really needed, and claimed that he got a great deal of personal satisfaction in handing over a claims check to a deserving farmer who had had the foresight to insure his crops with Hofstead Hail. To be sure, there were those who might have pointed out that Hofstead's idea of what people really needed in the way of insurance was somewhat grander than commonly accepted levels, but nobody could accuse him of not practicing what he preached. His car, his boat, his house, his business, and his teeth were all insured against any untoward event. His life was insured with policies that benefited his three loves. His wife, Martha, would be taken care of in the time of his being "called home," but so would his alma mater, Concordia College, the Lutheran college in Moorhead, Minnesota, to which he attributed every good thing that had happened in his life. His third and most recent love, and the beneficiary of his third major life insurance policy, was the student scholarship program, the "Hofstead Award," at the local Fergus Falls State University. The late president of FFSU, George Gherkin, had been extremely persuasive and when he made the continuation of the college insurance contract contingent upon a meaningful contribution, Hofstead agreed to set up a scholarship fund that would be presented to graduates of Fergus Falls High School, the home of the Otters. He and Martha had never had children, and the intellectual progress of the Hofstead Scholars gave them special enjoyment.

It was a life that reflected accomplishment and personal fulfillment, and this was perhaps part of the reason that the giggles could gush forth so easily from his short and portly body. But it had also been a life of hard work, and the death of a close friend, the unfortunate George Gherkin, had brought home to Hofstead the fleeting nature of life on earth. Hofstead was now sixty-eight years old, and although he didn't really need it, he figured he should be collecting social security. It was time to stop and smell the roses, time to retire and spend all his days at the lake cottage, and time to go back to the old country and see where the Hofsteads had come from in Norway. And it was also time to spend the winters in Fort Myers, Florida, and then watch the Minnesota Twins during spring training.

"The last winter in Minnesota," mused John Hofstead, as he gazed out the frosted windows of his office in the old Hotel Kaddatz. "Boy-oh-boy-oh-boy! I don't think I'm going to miss it at all.

I'm going to give up ice fishing and snowmobiling for golfing in January. What a trade! What a glorious trade!" A smile of anticipation added dental whiteness to the expanses of pink. "And tonight, when I tell Martha the news, I'm going to start by telling her that I don't think she should go out and buy a new coat. Hee-hee. She'll say, 'But I need to replace my old one.' And then I'll say, 'No you don't! No you don't! Hee-hee." He proceeded to write "Florida" in the frosty rime and with a warm pudgy finger melted the ice to form the dot over the i. He caught a reflection of his face in an unfrosted part of the window. "I'm going to spend my time in the sun and get a nice deep tan," he promised himself.

Still, he knew he would miss his office in the old hotel. It was once the grandest hotel in western Minnesota, but when the interstate highway was built, newer hotels with swimming pools and plenty of parking spaces had been built on the edge of town. Only the locals, it seemed, came to downtown Fergus Falls anymore, and they usually didn't need a place to stay. For years the building stood empty, suffering the indignities of abandonment, the ravages of a leaking roof, expanding ice, pigeons, bats, and assorted vermin. Everyone in town wistfully waited for some white knight to open up the grand hotel once more. Finally, and inevitably, it appeared that it would have to be torn down. But John Hofstead, who had spent his wedding night with Martha in room 306, could not bear to see it go. He took the lead in investigating historic preservation grants. He persuaded a local architectural firm to examine the building and prepare projections for alternative uses. Finally, it was he who made the first commitment to relocate his business there. It had taken a lot of volunteer work for the pains-taking restoration, and the top floor was still a long way from completion. The heating was inefficient and the windows would all have to be replaced eventually, but it was Hofstead's pride and joy and when he overheard younger people refer to it as the "Hofstead building" he did not bother to correct them.

Hofstead Hail held a perpetual lease on the front half of the third floor, and it was no coincidence that his own office had once been room 306. All of the other employees of Hofstead Hail, with the exception of seasonal adjusters (usually high school teachers who could not get a job as a driver's education instructor) were located in adjoining rooms. His faithful secretary, Mrs. Borghild Kvamme, could be found in an open area that had once been Room 302. Clarence Sandberg was in old Room 304, Gary Swenson was in Room 305, and Myron Pekanen was in Room 303. That left Room 301 vacant for Hofstead's special professional indulgence, an infrequently used conference room containing a large banquet table from the hotel's Western Empire Room.

The first thing Hofstead did when he decided to retire was to call a company meeting. It was a mark of his dedication to the firm that his employees would know about his plans even before his beloved Martha. He approached the meeting with undisguised glee, keeping all details secret from even the ever-curious Borghild. He wanted everything to be just right for this little swan song and, to his secretary's amazement, he was observed personally cleaning up the conference room, misting the surface of the large table with a can of Pledge. Carefully, the dapper pink man aligned chairs before the ubiquitous note pads and pencils, both of which were embossed with "Season's Greetings from Hofstead Hail." He even considered brewing a fresh pot of coffee for the meeting, but considered that Borghild could just as well maintain her most important office function.

His preparations complete, Hofstead instructed Mrs. Kvamme to hold all calls and proceeded to hole up in his office with the door closed, an occurrence remarkable in itself. For the next half hour, while Borghild used every last bit of her will power to avoid picking up the phone and listening, he was speaking on the telephone in a muffled voice.

At three o'clock, the permanent employees of the company found their way to the meeting room to take their positions at the table. They assumed, correctly, that the chair at the head of the table was reserved for the owner and president of Hofstead Hail. They also assumed that the chair immediately to the right was reserved for Mrs. Kvamme. What occurred next, however, could be seen as a portent of the struggle to come. Sandberg and Swenson entered the room at exactly the same time, a good ten minutes before the meeting was scheduled to begin. "Got any idea what this meeting is all about?" asked Sandberg, desperately trying to suppress the cheerfulness from his voice. He had heard Hofstead make one too many references about Florida not to suspect what was coming. He stretched in front of Swenson and dropped an empty folder at the place immediately to the left of Hofstead's presumed seat, and with measured nonchalance proceeded to the coffee maker.

Swenson blinked at the table for a few seconds and announced, "You know, I think I've already had too much coffee today." He proceeded to slide Sandberg's empty folder down the table, replace it with his own folder, bulging with computer printouts, and sat down with his empty "Hofstead Hail" coffee mug. He continued pleasantly, "I don't expect the meeting to last too long. You see, I've been providing him with material about how we can make our office more efficient and our growth rate stronger through the extensive use of computers. I'm sure he just wants to speak to all of us together about these plans."

Returning with his coffee, Sandberg lugubriously eyed the table. He realized he had no choice but to sit down, pretend he didn't notice, and remember the tactic. The next eight and a half minutes were taken up with staid, frosty, and fatuous communications about the weather while Swenson wondered if he dared to get up for that cup of coffee for which he was ready to kill.

Thirty seconds before the meeting was to begin, Mrs. Kvamme came in with a steno pad and several manila folders containing sales and actuarial figures. Both men were delighted to see her as a welcome relief from seeing each other.

"What's this all about, Borghild?" inquired Clarence Sandberg. "The last time we met in here was when John gave us his United Way pep talk. Has he volunteered us to clean up the litter along a mile of highway or something?"

Borghild scowled and replied, "There's nothing I can tell you, I'm afraid. He's been hiding in his office for a long time making phone calls. When I asked him the purpose of the meeting he just said 'Wait and see!'"

"Maybe it has something to do with the profits from last year," ventured Gary Swenson. "We had a good year. We sold a lot of insurance and Mother Nature was on our side. I know I sold more insurance than I ever have and, Clarence, you even sold more than usual, didn't you? Maybe he's going to announce a bonus or something. He enjoys pleasant little surprises."

Sandberg was trying to come up with a response to the snide use of the word "even" in Swenson's reference, when he heard Hofstead's door opening. Hofstead glanced in to see that Pekanen was not yet seated and walked over to retrieve the late-comer. It was with a degree of repressed joy that Swenson and Sandberg could hear the annoyance in Hofstead's voice as he said, "Come on, Pek. You're late!" This was followed by a somewhat addled, "Huh? Is it three o'clock already? Yah, I'll get my cup and be right there." Hofstead proceeded Pekanen into the room and pulled out the chair at the head of the table. "Sit right down here, Pek. I don't intend to keep anyone too long." Sandberg and Swenson tried to avoid looking at each other and failed.

With that, Hofstead sat down on the other side of Borghild, folded his hands in front of him, and, enjoying every minute of the suspense he had created, said, "I suppose you are wondering why I called you all together." To John Hofstead, it was the perfect cliche.

Nobody spoke, and Hofstead continued to beam at them in all his radiant pinkness. After ten seconds of bewildered silence, Myron Pekanen said, "Yeah, so, what's up?"

"Ha!" said Hofstead with undisguised glee, "thought you'd never ask! I'm quitting!"

"Er, ah, quitting what?" asked the deliberate but hopeful Clarence Sandberg.

"Quitting business. Quitting work. Quitting the rat race. Quitting getting up at six-thirty every morning. Quitting spending my winters in Minnesota. In short, I quit!"

Four minds immediately turned to their own futures. "But," protested Swenson, "you can't just quit!"

"Why not?" said the grinning eminence pink.

"Well, I mean, ah, well, what's to become of the company?" Swenson cautiously inquired.

"Yes, well, you see, that's where you come in."

A stunned but elated expression spread across Swenson's face. "Me?"

"Yah, you. And Clarence. And Pek. And maybe even Borghild if she would consider it."

"What, er, just what is it you mean?" spluttered Clarence Sandberg.

Hofstead leaned back in his chair and beamed. "You see, I've been running this business a long time, and as I see it, if I'm gonna quit, I got two choices. I can sell the business to whoever wants it at the best price I can get and go away and never think about it again. And maybe that's what I should do. But, you know, when you spend your whole life doing something, it isn't so easy just to walk away from it. So I don't want to do that. Instead, I'm gonna own the company, but I'm just not gonna run the company. I'm still gonna own the company, but instead of being president, I'm going to be your Chief Executive Officer." Hofstead paused and smirked, "Your C.E.O.! And I don't intend to do a lick of work. That's where you come in. I intend to hire one of you to be my president."

Hofstead let those words hang in the air like a bountiful pinata, ready to pour blessings down upon a chosen one. Clarence Sandberg looked at his co-workers, and noted with dread the smug expression on the face of Swenson. Borghild Kvamme also looked at her co-workers, and dreaded the thought that one of them would probably be her future boss. Gary Swenson looked confidently at John Hofstead, attempting to convey a message that said, "I'm ready for this, and you know that I'm your man!" Myron Pekanen looked at the rubber band he had unconsciously wrapped around his little finger to the point where it had cut off all circulation.

"Yes, it will be one of you, all right," the new self-appointed C.E.O. continued, "but I haven't made up my mind which one. I presume you would all like the job. I didn't hire you and keep you on all these years if I thought you were the kind of people who would shrink from a challenge or an opportunity. Now, Clarence, you've been with me longer than anyone else. You know the business and would make a good president. Pek? When you joined the company, business just took off and we haven't looked back since. You brought in a lot of policies from territories that we had never even considered. Gary? What can I say? You've been the leading salesman for the last five years. And Borghild? Well, everybody knows who really runs Hofstead Hail, huh?" Everyone patronizingly chuckled as Borghild smiled in the manner she was expected to and blushed appropriately.

"So. It won't be an easy choice. Since I own the business and I still want to make enough money to pay my Florida green fees." He paused to grin from one to the other. "I want to hire the right person. I don't want to go outside the company because I'm sure that

I've got the right person right here right now. You all bring special strengths to the company, and maybe each one of you would make a good president. As owner, I know what each of you can do for the company now. But I don't know what you can do in the future. If the new president is not Sandberg, for instance, I want the new president to make use of his talents. ("What talents?" thought one person at the table.) If the new president of the company is not Pekanen, I want the new president to realize what an asset he is to the company and treat him well. ("Treat him to severance pay," thought two people at the table.) If the new president is not Swenson, I would hope that he would have enough sense to do everything he could to retain a terrific insurance man. ("Fat chance!" thought three people at the table.) Finally, if the new president is not Mrs. Kvamme ("How nice of him to be so inclusive, and isn't that just like John," thought everybody at the table), anyone who would not retain her would have to have rocks in his head.

"I've taken pride in the fact that I put together a darn good insurance team here. In running this outfit, I've seen what each of you can bring to the company and since I still intend to make my living off of the profits of Hofstead Hail—yes, the name will not change—whoever I select will have to demonstrate that he—or she, of course—can work with the remaining members."

Four pairs of eyes looked at the speaker and each pair peeked surreptitiously at the other three. Each member of the firm was concerned with one major question.

"Now, you're probably asking yourself, 'How's he going to decide this?' Well, I'll tell you. I don't know. But I'm going to find out. For the last hour I have been making arrangements for all of us to go to the Otter Slide Resort for one of their Winter Wonderland specials. You know the place. It's on Long Lake just outside of Vergas. Your wives are specifically requested to come along and Borghild, I want to make sure you get Harry to come along with you. Martha and I will look forward to spending more time with you in a relaxed setting where we can just unwind and have fun. I mean, they've got cross-country skiing, snowmobiling, ice fishing, tobogganing, sleigh rides with real horses if you give 'em enough warning—the whole nine yards. And, just for you, Pek, they've even got a sauna. Now maybe you're not the active type, well, that's okay, too. Just bring a good book and sit and relax. All meals are included and it's all on me.

"Now, I didn't have a whole lot of choice when it came to dates, so I just picked January twenty-eighth through January thirtieth. I realize that doesn't leave you will much time to plan. But you don't need to plan for anything. Just show up. I expect you to cancel any other plans you may have and be there. I asked them to send us some brochures on the place that will tell you everything you will need to know.

Hofstead stood up and folded his hands at the point where his vest met his trousers, and in the process made his tummy look like a bowling trophy.

"So. That's about it! Meeting adjourned! Gosh, this was fun! I can hardly wait to get home and break the news to Martha."

WWW.MIDNIGHTINKBOOKS.COM

From the gritty streets of New York City to sacred tombs in the Middle East, it's always midnight somewhere. Join us online at any hour for fresh new voices in mystery fiction, book club questions, author information, mystery resources, and more.

Midnight Ink promises a wild ride filled with cunning villains, conflicted heroes, hilarious hazards, mind-bending puzzles, and enough twists and turns to keep readers on the edge of their seats.

MIDNIGHT INK ORDERING INFORMATION

Order by Phone:
- Call toll-free within the U.S. and Canada at
  1-888-NITEINK (1-888-648-3465)
- We accept VISA, MasterCard, and American Express

Order by Mail:

Send the full price of your order (MN residents add 6.5% sales tax) in U.S. funds, plus postage & handling to:

Midnight Ink
2143 Wooddale Drive
Woodbury, MN 55125-2989

Postage & Handling:

Standard (U.S., Mexico, & Canada). If your order is:
$24.99 and under, add $3.00
$25.00 and over, FREE STANDARD SHIPPING

AK, HI, PR: $15.00 for one book plus $1.00 for each additional book.

International Orders (airmail only):
$16.00 for one book plus $3.00 for each additional book

Orders are processed within 2 business days. Please allow for normal shipping time. Postage and handling rates subject to change.